"She's awake, then," Rafe said, coming into the room

Mary did not turn around, nor was she surprised by his presence. It was uncanny how she had sensed him standing there in the doorway. "Her sleep is restless. She's cried out a few times. Nights seem to be the worst when there is fever."

"I brought you something to eat. I'll sit with her now."

A flash of resentment flared in Mary's mind. It stemmed from the quiet command in his husky voice, that absolute expectation of being obeyed. What right did she have to deny the father's desire to care for his child?

None.

That one word scored deep, as deep as the emptiness of old longings that she tried so hard to remove from her life. Mary turned to face him.

That truant lock of hair had fallen across his forehead. Her arm ached to lift it and put it back to join the rest of his thick hair.

Foolish thought.

You have nothing to give to this man, nothing to give any man.

Dear Reader,

This month we are delighted with the chance to introduce our readers to a new Western series from award-winning author Theresa Michaels. The trilogy begins with *The Merry Widows—Mary*, the tender story of a marriage-shy widow who opens her heart to a lonely widower and his little girl. Don't miss this wonderful story, the first of three tales set in New Mexico.

In the third book of her medieval BRIDE TRILOGY, *The Bride Thief*, Susan Paul, writing as Susan Spencer Paul, tells the story of the youngest Baldwin brother, Justin, a delightful rogue who is being forced by his brothers to marry or lose all he possesses. And *Wildwood*, an exciting new Western from author Lynna Banning, is about a young woman who puts herself smack in the middle of the investigation of her father's murder, despite opposition from the local sheriff, who would rather she butt out.

In our fourth title for the month, *Tempting Kate*, longtime Harlequin Historicals author Deborah Simmons returns to the Regency era for her heartwarming tale of a haughty marquis who falls in love with the penniless daughter of a local earl, after she shoots him by mistake.

Whatever your tastes in reading, we hope you'll keep a lookout for all four books, wherever Harlequin Historicals are sold.

Sincerely,

Tracy Farrell
Senior Editor

Please address questions and book requests to:
Harlequin Reader Service
U.S.: 3010 Walden Ave., P.O. Box 1325, Buffalo, NY 14269
Canadian: P.O. Box 609, Fort Erie, Ont. L2A 5X3

THE MERRY WIDOWS
Mary

THERESA MICHAELS

Harlequin Books

TORONTO • NEW YORK • LONDON
AMSTERDAM • PARIS • SYDNEY • HAMBURG
STOCKHOLM • ATHENS • TOKYO • MILAN
MADRID • WARSAW • BUDAPEST • AUCKLAND

ISBN 0-373-28972-3

THE MERRY WIDOWS—MARY

Copyright © 1997 by Theresa DiBenedetto

Books by Theresa Michaels

Harlequin Historicals

A Corner of Heaven #104
Gifts of Love #145
Fire and Sword #243
Once a Maverick #276
Once an Outlaw #296
Once a Lawman #316
†*The Merry Widows—Mary* #372

Harlequin Books

Renegades 1996
"Apache Fire"

*The Kincaid Trilogy
†The Merry Widows

THERESA MICHAELS

is a former New Yorker who resides in south Florida with her husband and daughter—the last of eight children—and three "rescued" cats. Her avid interest in history and her belief in the power of love are combined in her writing. She has received the *Romantic Times* Reviewers' Choice Award for Best Civil War Romance, the National Readers' Choice Award for Best Series Historical and the B. Dalton Bookseller Award for Bestselling Series Historical. When not writing, she enjoys traveling, adding to her collection of Victorian perfume bottles and searching for the elf to master her computer.

For all my readers

Chapter One

Rafe McCade chafed at the plodding pace set by the army captain leading the detail. Overcast sky and air too heavy to breathe were not unusual for a late-September morning in 1881 on this barren stretch of New Mexico Territory. His hide vest and woven linen shirt were damp against his skin.

"Papa, will I like your home?"

Six-year-old Elizabeth Mary—Beth to him from the moment she was born—squirmed in her place on the saddle in front of him. He didn't blame her for feeling restless. He felt the same.

"When will we get there? Soon, Papa?"

"Soon enough." Her questions had been asked often these past few months. Rafe had not seen his daughter in five years.

Rafe shifted the reins to one hand, wiping his damp palm on a denim-clad thigh. What did he know about raising a little girl? A child who had been pampered by wealth and nursemaids? Damn little, he answered himself.

The sudden change in the air forced his head up. An undefined stillness fraught with tension came with his indrawn breath. Without thought, Rafe curved his arm around his daughter.

The attack was abrupt. Hitting the small group, and the two civilians riding with it, like lightning.

Arrows and bullets rained down from the Apache warriors hidden on the steep-sided rock slopes that had forced the detail to ride single file into the narrow canyon.

Rafe cursed the upstart captain who had overridden his objection to their planned route this morning. The officer swore that it was safe, that they had had no trouble with renegade bands. For that reason, Rafe had chosen to travel home with an army escort. Small bands of Apache, enraged by their treatment on ever-shrinking reservation lands, were prone to escape and attack lone travelers.

Now his little girl might die.

Soldiers forged ahead, only to be met by a thundering avalanche of boulders. Death swiftly took its toll on men, pack mules and horses.

Rafe wasted no time. There was no room to turn and escape back the way they had entered the canyon. He bent low, his only thought to protect his child by pressing her small body forward, against his horse's neck.

He couldn't fire his gun with accuracy from his hunched position, not even with the .44 Russian, a Smith & Wesson gun manufactured on order for the Russian army and among the most accurate shooting pistols on the market. His Winchester rifle was useless in its saddle scabbard. To fire the rifle, he would need to sit back and leave Beth's body exposed to fire.

Dust clouds rose from the churning hooves of the horses and made his vision poor. Hearing the screams of dying men fractured any hope that his weapons would help them win free.

A few of the Apache left the protection of the upper slopes. Their war cries rang loud as they fell on the milling soldiers.

Rafe couldn't see the captain or hear his voice issuing orders. He no longer cursed the man. He prayed for all of them to survive.

At a touch of his spurs, his mountain-bred horse scrambled up the rocky slope. Rafe had his eye on a nest of boulders that offered cover.

He was no stranger to this land. He had done his share of riding its mountains and flats, engaged in fighting the Apaches as an army officer.

He knew the land's yield of treasures, and knew too well its terrors, but he had never made a decision with his daughter's life at stake.

As he fired his gun, his rapid assessment offered the possibility of making a break for the canyon's mouth on foot. The din was unbearable. Every soldier still standing was fighting hand to hand with an Apache.

He was truly between a rock and a hard place, and not for the first time. Time ticked by at an alarming rate.

Traveling on foot carried the risk of being trapped.

He risked his child's capture and his own death if he stayed.

"Beth, we're going to play hide-an'-seek. Just obey me. I swear I'll see you safely away from here."

With no more warning, Rafe kicked free of the stirrups. He grabbed Beth's trembling body with one arm around her waist, plucked the Winchester free, slid from the saddle and yanked her small body tight against his.

"Hold Rebel's reins. Hold them tight, Beth."

The close whine of a bullet smashing into the ground sent him into a crouching run. He murmured assurances to his daughter, uncertain if she heard him above the cries of battle as he picked his way around the fighting by keeping to slightly higher rocky ground.

"Close your eyes, baby," Rafe whispered. The wetness on his hands came from her tears. Rafe didn't want her to see the bodies of soldiers and warriors in the throes of death. He didn't want to view it himself.

"That's my brave girl. Keep your eyes closed. We've just a little farther to go."

A honed sixth sense made him look over his shoulder.

In a smooth motion, Rafe half turned and fired at an Apache poised to knife him.

He scooped Beth up into his arm and started to run.

"Muffy! Papa, get her. I can't leave Muffy." Beth struggled against her father's hold, screaming for her doll.

Rafe hugged the earth as close as he could. A heap of brush and rocks was a little bit farther. He heard rifle fire behind him. He pushed up suddenly and went forward in a charging run. He came in behind the shelter of rocks with bullets snapping about his ears.

And Beth's cries for her doll.

Rafe hesitated. The cloth doll was the only toy Beth had taken with her, the only thing that seemed to soothe her when she had the nightmare. He spied the bright cloth skirt of the doll a few feet behind, close to the dead warrior.

Rafe remained still, gathering his strength. The rocks behind which they were hidden concealed all movement. He quickly slid cartridges from his belt, filling the empty chambers of both hand gun and rifle.

Sweat and dust streaked his face. The air was too heavy to breathe. There was a lull in the firing, but that was the Apache way—retreat, then sudden attack.

He slid his rifle forward and searched the brush and rocks for a target. There was no cover beyond the dead Apache near where the doll had fallen.

It would only take a quick dash....

A bullet smashed the rock in front of him, and he slid back hurriedly, his face stinging from the granite fragments.

Beth's repeated panicked pleas left him no choice.

He pivoted on his bootheels, taking Beth with him. A flat slab behind them rested on two boulders, creating a shallow cave. It was in there that he tucked his daughter. Rebel stood, ears pricked forward, snorting at the smell of death, a few feet to his left. Rafe grabbed the canteen from his saddle and gave it to his daughter.

"Hang on to this, honey. Only a tiny sip when you really need it. No matter what happens, stay here, Beth. And keep your head down."

Her wide, solemn eyes watched him. Her small head bobbed as she clutched the canteen to her body.

"That's my girl."

When the detail failed to return to the camp at Ojo Caliente, the soldiers would come searching their back trail. The camp had been an advance picket post for Fort Craig, built two years before the War between the States broke out to help control the Navaho. It had been abandoned during the war, then in the late '60s became headquarters for the Warm Spring Apache Reservation. Four years ago, after white men ambushed and killed Victorio's son-in-law in Alma, troops had once more been stationed there.

Rafe knew they would find Beth if anything happened to him. He knew, too, that they would care for her until his lawyer came. They knew who she was, what she stood to inherit from him.

But as Rafe studied his chance of running from

shelter and returning, he wondered who would hold his daughter in the dark of the night when she cried out.

To ease her fear, he smiled at her, then plunked his flat-crowned black hat on her head.

"You take care of that for me until I get back with Muffy."

He turned, but Beth caught hold of his vest.

"You'll come back? You won't go away like Mama?"

"I'll be back, Beth."

"I told her I loved her. That last day. I didn't want her to go." She looked into his eyes. "Papa, I...I love you, too."

Rafe caught her close, hugging her. He had to fight back the sting of tears. A well of fury rose inside him. He should not have heard these words for the first time with death facing them. If the rough sea off Long Island Sound hadn't killed his wife, he could at this moment have gone back and done the deed himself for the hell she had put him through. Him and their only child.

The lull in the firing warned him he had little time to make good his promise to get her doll.

"I love you, Beth. More than you know."

The words left a bittersweet tinge on his dry lips.

Firing from cover, Rafe ran from shelter. The sudden burning sting of a bullet grazing his arm made him stumble. Cursing the minor wound, Rafe dropped to his belly and crawled forward until his fingertips touched the edge of the doll's skirt.

Two shots hit the dirt at his side. He jerked the doll to him. Those shots had not been fired from across the canyon. They had come from behind him. He began snaking his way back.

Beth was there. His child, alone.

A thud landing too close to him warned Rafe, as did the kick of sand that nearly blinded him. One of the warriors had lain in wait for him.

Rafe rolled quickly to his side, bringing his gun up with him. A blow to his left shoulder sent him sprawling. The doll flew from his hand, but he managed to hang on to his gun.

He squirmed to the side, then rolled over twice to get a look at his attacker.

Two black eyes burned in a broad face slashed with paint.

"McCade."

The guttural intonation of his name sounded like a death cry. Rafe, with a chill riding his soul, heard the Apache repeat it.

Rafe stared at the rifle rising to the warrior's shoulder. He didn't take his eyes off the barrel aiming at his heart. Twisting, Rafe threw a handful of sand up at the Apache's face. The shot missed Rafe. He raised his own gun to fire. The chamber clicked on empty.

The Apache came at him, swinging the rifle like a club. Rafe moved like a rattler, twisting and rolling till he had the room to rise. He charged the warrior, battering him with his fists, using the butt of his gun.

Even knowing the target his back presented to the other Apaches, Rafe drove the warrior away from the rocks where Beth was hidden.

Drove him with lightning-fast fists, down the rocky slope, forcing him to move with the disadvantage of being unable to see his footing.

Rafe didn't even see the knife until the blade slashed across his forearm. He pulled free his own. Sweat spilled into his eyes.

The Apache closed in for the kill.

Rafe's arms spread wide from his body. He grabbed the Apache's wrist, bearing down and twisting the blade away from his body. With his own knife, he drove the blade home, yanked it free and turned to dodge back to shelter.

"Over here, McCade," the young captain called.

Rafe dropped to his knee and recovered his gun. He fed bullets until the chambers were filled, then looked over at the captain and another soldier behind a man-size boulder.

Rafe stifled the urge to call out and ask how many men were left from the detail. A quick scan of the area said too few. He didn't want the Apaches to have their own guess confirmed.

He started back to his daughter, wiping blood that dropped from his lip. First Beth's safety, and then he would worry about his own wounds.

In a crouching run, he went. Suddenly time froze for Rafe. Terror struck in seconds.

Beth ran out. Ran toward him and her fallen doll.

Her new boots were dusty. The ankle-length navy blue riding skirt was torn. The front of her gray shirt hung over her waistband. She still wore his hat.

"No, Beth! Beth, go back!"

A spray of bullets kicked up rock and dirt in front of Rafe from someone firing down at him. He kept running.

"Go back!"

"Papa, it's Muffy!"

Rocks shattered from rifle fire. Rafe didn't care. His eyes were locked on his daughter's small running figure.

He suddenly looked up as if he had been jerked by a rawhide.

The arrow's flight was too swift to see, far too accurate to stop.

"Beth! Lord, no!"

"Papa!" she cried, tumbling to the earth.

Chapter Two

Twenty-five miles to the south, in the growing town of Hillsboro, Mary Elizabeth Inlow woke with a cry on her lips.

Covered in cold sweat, badly shaken, Mary knew the dream had come again.

A child cried out to her. No matter how she struggled against unseen bonds, she couldn't reach the child, she could not stop the cries.

Mary willed the nausea to subside, willed her limbs to stop shaking as she pressed her hands to her lips. She was strong now, strong enough to beat back the feeling of helplessness and the heartache brought by the dream.

A year of widowhood added to ten years of marriage had taught her the depth of her strength.

But the dream brought back all the doubts that had plagued her year of supposed mourning.

She lay alone in the double-size bed, wondering, as she often had this past year, what she would do.

How would she cope with the days stretching into years before her? Who would she be?

This was the most consuming question she asked

of herself, for she was not the same woman who had married Harry Inlow eleven years ago.

Sixteen. A woman grown. One with five years of keeping house for her father behind her. What had she believed she knew at sixteen?

She had thought she knew how to judge a man. Into her father's blacksmith's shop they had come, the cowhands, the gamblers, the miners and the gunmen. And Harry, handsome Harry, with his rich claim and laughing eyes, had swept her into his arms at a dance and told her she would marry him and no other. He had courted her, flirting and buying her foolish presents, and he had gained her father's approval. Foolish little girl. She had married him and learned she knew nothing of men at all.

Mary briefly closed her eyes. She did not want to remember. After the dream was the worst time, for she felt a stranger to herself. But she would cope. She only had to remind herself that she was strong.

She stared up at the ceiling, and listened to the chirping of birds in the giant cottonwoods that shaded the house. The silence within its walls confirmed that her cry had not disturbed the sleep of her cousin Sarah, or their newly widowed friend Catherine.

Unable to lie still, Mary slipped from the tangled bedding. She smoothed down the wrinkles of the cotton nightgown as she padded barefoot across the wooden floor.

A look out the second-floor window revealed an overcast sky. Not a breath of air stirred the lace curtains. It was on a morning such as this that she most missed her mountainside home, where the wind blew wild and free.

It was the only thing she missed.

Hillsboro lay in a pocket between low hills. From the first cabin, built four years before by the two miners who found gold in the Black Range, the tent camp had grown into a town. This despite its isolated location and the Indian raids. Its name had been chosen from those written on slips of paper and shuffled in a hat.

It was a good place to live.

A good place for Mary to begin anew.

Percha Creek bordered the town, and north were the San Mateo Mountains and the Black Range. There, in hidden pockets were mining camps, outlaw hideouts and places known only to the renegade Chiricahua Apache who had escaped the San Carlos Reservation. A little to the northwest were the Gila wilderness, and the Mogollon Mountains, with its mining camps along Cooper and Mineral creeks. The high mountains made travel between camps difficult, and some said it was a nest of outlaws and claim jumpers.

In the quiet peace of morning, Mary sometimes wondered if men ever thought they might be wrong. They had come into this area and taken away the lands where the Apache lived and hunted. They told those who had roamed free that they could do so no longer.

This was not, to her way of thinking, the path to peace. She could not condone the raiding and killing by white men and by the Apaches. But she could sympathize with people who had been dispossessed of all they held dear.

Sage-covered hummocks blended with thickets of walnut, pine and cedar. Mary loved the quiet walks to gather the abundance of nuts, for the peace of the forest paths were a balm to her wounded spirit.

A hard land, but one filled with beauty. Toward the south lay the railroad and clusters of mining camps, some of them growing into towns.

Far to the east, the Rio Grande curved like a massive scythe to cut the territory in half. Her father claimed the old mountain men had called it the River of Ghosts. He had taken her to a gorge where volcanic flows covered with ancient layers of gray, black, salmon pink, brown and orange lichen reached nearly eight hundred feet down. An early lava flow had crystallized into black basalt, but it was surrounded by sagebrush-carpeted benchlands broken by fields and pastures.

Beautiful and wild lands, which led beyond the river to the Jornada del Muerto—a day's journey of death. Men who had lived to cross the desert land claimed it was aptly named.

Closer to the outskirt of town was the hill where the church foundation of stone and adobe had been laid last week. They had collected fifteen hundred dollars from a hat passed around the saloons for donations. The lot next to the church was staked out for a school.

Children....

The reminder brought back the dream. Its frequency these past weeks unsettled her. Mary rubbed her arms against the someone's-walking-on-your-grave chill.

Turning aside, Mary resisted the temptation to return to bed, aware the choice was hers. She had to remember that. Sometimes it frightened her to once again have the freedom to choose what she would do with every waking moment.

But it was a heady draft, too.

She concentrated on that to help dispel the faint unease lingering from the dream.

After all, she reminded herself, it was not her child that she dreamed about. It couldn't be.

Straightening the bed, she gently smoothed the wrinkles from the newly finished quilt. She had taken little more than her clothes and her horse when she was ordered to leave her home after Harry died.

Each bright square of calico and gingham, every soft velvet piece, was decorated with every fancy embroidery stitch she knew. Her cousin Sarah had offered to help in the evenings, when chores were done and they sat in the warmth of the kitchen, and later Catherine, but Mary had sewn every stitch herself. The quilt was entirely hers.

The thought came not so much from possessiveness or from pride as the desperate need to reassure herself of her worth. By such small things she was going to rebuild her life.

Mentally she jerked back from the direction of her thoughts.

"Stop it." But it was too late for the whispered warning.

The old Mary, the one who had survived as Harry's wife, tried to fill her mind with dreadful memories. All the ones she kept hidden.

The new Mary—for she thought of herself as that—the one who was supported by Sarah's strength and Catherine's determination, refused to give way.

She stripped off the cotton nightgown, crushing the soft cloth between her hands. Head bent, shoulders bowed, she fought the insidious pull of memories so painful they made her tremble.

You can't give in. He'll win. Even from the grave, he'll win.

She *was* strong, and brave, and had fought this fight with demons from the past too many times to count in the past year.

Logic said she could not wipe out ten years of her life in one.

But she yearned with all the recovering spirit within her to do just that.

Mary poured tepid water from the pitcher into the washbowl. She sponged her sweat-dampened body. Her thoughts focused on the last trimming needed to complete a topsy-turvy doll for Nita Mullin's granddaughter. The child's birthday was two days away and Nita was going to visit her in Lake Valley. They were lucky to have a stage line operating from Hillsboro south of the town.

Nita had proved a good friend to Mary. She owned the dress goods shop and gave her the scraps of material and bits of trimming she was unable to use.

Like the quilt, the making of the dolls had helped Mary return to a time when she felt secure in who she was.

She thought of her grandmother's patience as she had taught her to make the cloth-bodied dolls, whose flaring skirts could be flipped over to reveal another doll's body and head.

Little girls loved the dolls, few though they were, and Mary soaked up their pleasure the way the desert soaked up rain.

Thanks again to Nita, P. J. Crabtree had bought a few dolls to sell in his dry goods emporium. Miners with money to spend might buy them for the children they left behind. She hoped they did sell. The only money she earned was from orders to add delicate embroidery to the dressmaker's frocks. Most women hereabouts made their own clothing, so the orders were few and far between. Every penny earned, even the little given by a grateful miner for her limited medical skill, was contributed to the household.

When her father died and she learned that his blacksmith shop, the house and the land had been sold, with the money going to Harry, there had been no stilling her anger.

By the time Harry died and she discovered that his

will left all his worldly possessions to his cousin, Mary could not summon anger, only relief that that chapter of her life was over.

She refused to dwell on how narrow her choices would have been if Sarah, already widowed, had not insisted that she come here to live.

It was a reminder that she was lingering overlong this morning. From the bureau drawer Mary removed a pressed pair of cotton drawers, a camisole and two petticoats. She dressed quickly, foregoing the half corset, as thoughts of comfort won over proper lady's dress.

The rocking chair squeaked when she sat down to pull on neatly darned stockings.

Strange, she mused, how life's paths twisted and turned.

Despite the difference in their ages, she, Sarah and Catherine had been childhood friends. They had shared all the important first happenings that marked their growing-up years.

The progression had run from doll's tea parties to shared giggles over a special look given by a boy after church services. She had lost her parents first, then offered comfort to the others when they were orphaned. She had thought they were lovely, innocent times, as they confided dreams, first kisses, courtships and marriage.

Married first, Mary went to Harry's home in the eastern territory. Mary had missed the women's special closeness. Attending weddings with Harry had ensured there was no time alone with her cousin or her friend.

They had seen little of each other during the years of their marriages.

Now, they had come together again, to share their first year of widowhood.

Guilt sometimes nagged her. Mary had skimmed over the details of her marriage.

She was twenty-seven years old, and shame still played a part in her silence.

Retrieving the only pair of shoes she owned, Mary took the buttonhook off the small floral china tray on the bureau to close the buttons on her shoes. She slipped on a faded violet-and-cream gingham day dress and fluffed out the ruffle around the yoke. She had deliberately made the fit loose, for she was uncomfortable calling attention to her body.

She tugged free her waist-length braid. One of these days she would find the courage to cut it again. The first time had been an act of defiance. Harry, with his possessive love of its red shades and thigh-long length, had forbidden her to ever cut it.

"But Harry's dead," she reminded her reflection in the mirror.

Afraid of finding telltale ghosts in her eyes, Mary looked away as she brushed out the tangles.

Minutes later she placed the last hair pin in a neat cornet of braids. Tying on a fresh apron, she smiled as she left her room.

The old wood floor in the hall gleamed from the waxing she had given it last week. The aroma of coffee drifted up the stairs and told her that Sarah was awake.

Mary hummed on her way to the kitchen. She had a new day to look forward to, ordered and peaceful, as the past days had been.

If the secret sorrow of her heart never left, she still had so much to be thankful for.

She would continue to break the chains of the past. Somehow, some way, she would finally be free.

And when she was, perhaps the terrible haunting dream would not come again.

Chapter Three

Rafe knew every minute of travel stole a moment of his daughter's life. With the dust-brown warriors riding a grudge against every white man, there was no ridge that he could cross without a careful study of the country around it. Much as it galled him, he had to take time to cover his own trail when it was possible. Already he had doubled back, and changed directions twice.

It nagged at him that the Apache knew his name. Rafe had had little trouble with the Indians. But that Apache wanted him dead.

A slow man to rile, Rafe barely contained his fury. Beth was the one who had paid. He rode on to the town of Hillsboro, for he had heard of a doctor there. He made a wide swing around the town to avoid crossing Percha Creek.

Any stranger riding into town in his condition was sure to draw attention. A man dragging a travois behind his horse drew the curious out to the boardwalks lining the main street of Hillsboro.

Almost every stone-and-adobe building was shaded by giant cottonwood trees. He searched the shadows as he rode, especially the alleys between the bank and hotel, cafe and saddlery, each one between the stores and saloons.

It was nothing he had not done before, but now he was doubly wary.

He filed away the fact that the lone man sitting in a chair tipped back against the outer wall of the saloon paid more than passing attention to his arrival. News could not have traveled this fast of the attack on the army detail, or of the fact that out of the forty men he rode into that canyon with, only five had ridden out.

It set in his mind that he was not to be one of the survivors. There was nothing he could do about it now. His child's life was what mattered, not learning who wanted him dead.

He drew rein before the hitching rail of J. P. Crabtree's Dry Goods Emporium.

"Where can I find the doctor?" Rafe demanded as he stepped inside.

P. J. Crabtree, standing behind the counter, eyed the savage-looking stranger striding toward him. The man's bloodstained clothing told a tale, and P.J. had never been one to pass up an opportunity to have the who, what and wherefore on a stranger.

"You've ridden a piece."

"Gavilan Canyon," Rafe returned. "Army detail I was with came under attack."

"Apaches. Damn that Victorio. He's plumb hell."

"Ain't my worry. I need the doctor."

"Last I know, Doc Sieber's drinking his lunch over at the Paradise."

"Drunk?"

"Usually is these days. Lost his wife two months ago. She caught someone stealing his supplies and was shot. Doc, he was up in the hills patching up some miners. Had a cave-in. But say, fella, your wounds don't look like they need doctorin'. I get a real fine liniment here that'll cure most of what ails you. Make it myself.''

Rafe shot the balding man a cold, forbidding look. "I don't need him for myself." He rapidly sorted his options, glancing back toward the open door. "Where is the nearest sober doctor?"

"Tall order. Mighty tall order. Sober, now? Might be one southwest, at Silver City. Or over east, at Caballo. Hear they had some trouble there. Both a far piece to ride."

P.J. leaned out over the counter, but couldn't see more than a fine-looking horse hitched at his rail.

"What the devil do you folks do when the doctor's drunk and you need help? My little girl was wounded during the fighting."

"Hell now! Why didn't you say that right off? You go on up to the merry widows. They'll fix her up, if she ain't dying."

"She's not going to die." Rafe stared at the paunchy man, whose faded red shirt was littered with food stains, and met his pale blue eyes with the force of his own. He knew saying the words did not make them true. But he had to believe them. Yet the thought of taking his daughter to a brothel—for what else could it be?—set ill with him.

"You sure these *widows* have some medical skill? She's hurt bad."

"You ask for Mary. She'll know what to do. She nursed men after the mine cave-in at Kingston. Helped more than a few since she come to town. Nursed her husband, too, I hear. 'Course, he died, but folks said she took mighty good care of him while he lived. That was near to a year—''

"Where?" Rafe heard the edge of desperation in his voice. He didn't like the sound of this, but what choice did he have? Beth couldn't travel another ten miles, much less thirty or more miles, until he found a competent doctor. If he was not terror-stricken at the thought of losing his child, he might have found some humor in a brothel filled with merry widows.

"Ride out south of Main Street. Take the road to Lake Valley. Can't miss the place. Sets back a way from the road. Farmhouse got a fresh coat of white-wash this summer. If you reach the Orchards' stage corral, you've gone too far." But this last was said to the man's back.

"Don't blame you none, fella. Ain't too many men walk away from Apaches and live to tell about it. But a girl..." P.J. shook his head. He slipped his thumbs under his suspenders. Folks would be coming by any minute. He would save his opinions until then.

Rafe hurried outside to his daughter. He crouched near the hitching rail, brushing aside the hair clinging to Beth's forehead. Her hair was as dark as his, and just as curly.

She lay as he had placed her on the quickly rigged travois. It was the best transport he could manage for her. Their packhorses had disappeared along with the Apaches. Even the shavetail captain had remarked about the Indians' disappearance once Beth fell.

Rafe didn't care what had made them leave. He was thankful they had gone.

Beth's eyes remained closed. Her breathing ragged. It tore at his heart to see her so lifeless. He wiped at the streaks left by dirt and her tears. One hand he closed into a fist, the other trembled, touching his child's cheek.

He lifted the blanket. Pain twisted inside him.

Why? Dear God, why?

Beth lay on her side, the thin legs beneath her torn skirt drawn tight to her belly. Her small hands gripped the edge of the blanket, slung and tied between tent poles, that formed the bed of the travois.

Blood seeped from the bandage he had wrapped around her shoulder. The broken arrow shaft protruding from her small body was an obscene sight.

If the arrow had pierced his own flesh, Rafe wouldn't have thought twice about yanking it free. He had done so a time or two.

But this was his Beth…too precious, too small, and too newly reclaimed for him to cause her more pain.

"It's a wild land. Savage. Not fit for a decent woman to live in. I'll not raise my child here. She'll die. We will all die for your stubborn, arrogant insistence we make our home in these forbidding mountains."

Rafe swallowed bile and guilt along with the haunting words. He slowly eased the blanket up to cover Beth.

"You won't die, baby. I won't lose you a second time."

With a graceful movement, he rose and mounted. Despite the driving need to hurry, he kept Rebel to a walk so that Beth wouldn't suffer any more jostling.

He rode with the thong off his gun, his hat pulled low, always aware of the curious gazes of the silent townspeople who watched his slow progression south.

If this widow saved his daughter's life, he'd stake her to a dowry that would make an eastern banker take notice and forget her past. He would never miss the money. Hell, he thought, he would give it all away to see Beth a pink-cheeked, laughing child again.

Stranger things had happened in the territory than finding help at a brothel.

Strange things happened in big cities, too. Like a man believing that a lady's declarations of love and marriage vows meant more than whispered lies.

Valerie....

Rafe bolted the door shut on his past.

Beth was his future. She was all that mattered. All he would ever allow himself to care about.

The gray skies of morning had not delivered their promise of rain, but kept the day steeped in twilight.

Mary sat in a wing chair in the front parlor. She leaned closer to the side table scattered with sewing notions, where the lamp's glow aided her in snipping the thread above the knot.

Setting aside her embroidery scissors, she held up the completed doll. Dark brown satin stitched eyes framed by a feathering of lashes stared back at her. Red berry juice stained the muslin cheeks, and the wide smile invited one in return.

Flipping over the tiny pink-checked calico skirt, Mary touched the lace collar below a face meant to convey tiredness, with half-moon stitches to indicate closed eyes. The mouth drooped a bit. Did she look sad?

Pounding on the front door startled her. She darted a look around the room, touching on the sparse furnishings of the formal parlor suite.

Sarah and Catherine were away from the house, repairing the back pasture fence. They would never hear her if she called out.

Mary did not understand where the sudden fear came from.

The repeated battering on the door held an urgent summons she could not continue to ignore. Unaware she still held the doll, Mary went out into the hall.

Standing off to the side of the door, beneath the front porch's overhang, Rafe cradled Beth's too-warm body against his shoulder. His shirt and vest were stiff with caked sweat, blood and dust. He caught himself swaying.

The house beneath the giant cottonwoods was solidly built and freshly whitewashed, with Apache plume and columbine planted on either side of the steps. Off to the side, behind the house, stood a barn and corral. Four horses moved restively within the pole enclosure. A steel-dust Appaloosa nickered to his horse. It was a fine-looking animal, but something about it nagged at him.

When the door finally opened, his fist, holding his rifle, froze in midair.

Rafe, momentarily taken aback, wondered if he did have the right place.

His first thought was that the lovely woman looked more like a schoolmarm than a fancy woman. His second, that she had the saddest eyes he had ever seen. Eyes the color of new spring grass should sparkle.

Hers held a wealth of sorrow and shadows.

Rafe swept a quick look that raked her from head to toe. The faded gown, the patched apron, the neatly braided hair, added up to cleanliness and pride that glowed like a beacon from her wary stance.

He knew the exact moment she spotted the wound on his arm. The wariness remained, but now was tempered with compassion.

"They say in town I'd find help for my daughter with the widows."

Mary looked from the upraised rifle to the hand gun. She clung to the slightly opened door when she looked at his face. Beneath the brim of his hat, the dark slash of his brows was a warning, like the guarded look in his eyes.

"Help? What kind of help?"

He stepped to the side, revealing the blanket-clad bundle he held.

Mary's gaze shifted from the strong, clean-cut features of his bronzed face to the edge of the blanket, where the child's head was exposed.

"Bring her in," Mary ordered. She pressed against the door to allow space for the tall, gun-toting stranger to pass inside.

Broad shoulders tapered to a narrow waist and lean hips beneath a sun-faded blue shirt and a hide vest. Dusty black denim clung to his legs. The boots had seen use. The gun he wore was no more obvious than the guns of other men, but it seemed to her that it belonged where it was.

He would, Mary decided, look undressed without it. She stared at the knife sheath at the small of his back. Both he and the child had the weary, dust-laden look of heavy travel. His ripped, bloodstained clothing told of fighting.

Mary wasted no time asking foolish questions.

There were men who lived by violence, and those who had no choice. But where was his wife, that he had come seeking help for his child?

"Take her upstairs. First door on your left," she directed. Mary closed the door, with the strangest feeling that she had made some irrevocable decision by letting him inside.

Not him. The child.

Shaken to find that he had turned around and was keeping a bold stare upon her, Mary did not look at him, but only on the child.

"Bullet or knife, or is she ill?"

Rafe hit the first stair. Beth stirred and moaned. The blanket fell back, exposing the broken arrow shaft.

"Dear God." Mary lifted her hands to her mouth. She suddenly realized that she still held the doll.

Beth could not lift her head, but her eyes were open. For a moment, she stared at the woman. Her gaze lowered to the doll.

"Muffy." The word was a ragged murmur, as if it had sapped all her strength to speak.

"Ah, Beth, that's—" Rafe's husky voice broke. He relived those horror-filled moments when he had been helpless to save his child. His gaze found that of the woman's over his daughter's head. "She lost her doll in the fighting."

Rafe had told Beth the same, unwilling to explain his reluctance to touch the blood-soaked cloth, no matter how much the doll meant to her. He never wanted violence to touch his child. He couldn't stop the thought that Valerie had cursed him with her last, water-filled breath.

"Name your price. I'll buy it."

Mary had to look at him then. Pulled forward by an irrepressible need to be near the little girl, she listened to him repeat his blunt offer.

"I'll buy the doll, you, and anything I want or need." They were not the words he spoke, but the ones Mary heard in her mind, and saw the truth of it in his eyes.

"The doll is not for sale."

His mouth tightened, disturbing the full, sensuous line of his lips.

"I said to name your price. Don't let appearances fool you."

"I never have." *A lie, Mary, such a lie. You did once.* "I shall make a gift of the doll to your daughter. That is, if your wife won't object."

"She's dead."

Cold. Flat, hard words holding hidden meanings. Mary shivered. A winter's storm would be warmer than this man's eyes.

"Poor sweeting," she whispered to the child. "If you want her to be your Muffy, that is who she'll be."

"Won't your daughter object?" Rafe asked.

A blunt question that demanded a blunt answer.

"I have no daughter. I have no child." Mary's admission was made in the same flat, cold voice that he had used.

She stood on tiptoe to tuck the soft-bodied doll between the child's arm and the man's back. Her fingers trailed marks in the dust on his leather vest. Mary stepped back. She was uncomfortable with his position, towering over her. But she took with her the scents of sage and cedar, leather, sweat, horse and blood.

"Hurry," she whispered, alarmed by the child's glazed eyes, flushed cheeks.

But she didn't turn away. Two matching pairs of gray eyes stared at her. Stared and pinned her in place.

One pair, beneath dark, slashing brows, held a hunter's wariness. The other pair, even fever-glazed with pain, held a calm far too deep for the child's years.

Yet it was a calm that steadied her.

"Go on," Mary urged. "I'll be there soon."

"Those four horses in the corral. Who do they belong to?"

"To us. The widows." Later she would wonder what possessed her to add, "The merry widows of Sierra County."

Chapter Four

While Mary rushed to the kitchen to boil water before she gathered the dry herbs she needed from the pantry, Rafe McCade faced another surprise, when he stepped inside the bedroom.

He knew the room belonged to the woman with the sad green eyes. The same faint scent he had noted when she stepped close to him lingered in the air.

It was something clean and fresh that put him in mind of a dew-swept meadow on a spring morning.

The scent was nothing like the cloying perfume worn by the ladies on the line working every hole-in-the-wall brothel in the territory.

He had not forgotten her sassy voice claiming ownership of the four horses. He had never heard of the merry widows of Sierra County. But then, if a tent town could spring up overnight, a brothel could do it, too.

Seating himself in the rocking chair—that, in itself, was an oddity in a fancy woman's room—he held tight to Beth, unwilling and unable to release her.

If he could give his daughter his strength, give her his very lifeblood, he would.

As Rafe sat there and waited for the woman to

come, a prayer hovered in his mind. At the same time, a strange feeling came with it. No man had darkened the door of this room, no man had sported on that bed.

He studied the room, as he had often studied the lay of strange land. Carefully. Methodically. He picked up every detail, for upon such care a man rested his life and that of his daughter.

And you failed the first test to protect her.

It was a guilt he would have to live with. There was no way to go back and change what had happened. If what he suspected was true, the attack would have come even if he had ridden off alone with his child. Any man with enough gold or guns could buy a renegade band to attack a rival. And the blame was placed on the Apache. It was something to think about when Beth was out of danger.

There was nothing threatening in the room, but he simply could not put a name to the unease he felt. Something simply was not right.

He wanted to know who he was putting his trust in. He needed to know more about the woman he was entrusting with his daughter's life.

Judging a man was a straightforward call. How a man rode, treated his horse, wore his gun, spoke to others, his dress and even his walk, gave clues to his character if you looked for them.

Women hid things. Bodies bundled under layers of clothes, feelings behind proper manners. They hid good deeds, and those they wished kept secret. It was expected that they hid intelligence from men, though he had never seen the reason for it. Women were born with mystery shrouding them.

But this room could be tracked the same way a man's trail told much of what he was.

Orphaned at twelve, Rafe had had eighteen years

to make the kind of judgments that meant the difference between life and death. He had lied about his age to join the Union army and fight in the last year of the War between the States. He had stayed on, losing his rank of corporal, and come to the western lands to fight Indians.

Rafe closed his eyes. Memories crowded him.

He had worked cattle ranches in Texas, helped drive herds up to the railheads. He had fought Comanche, and renegade bands of men who still lusted for killing after the war. He had survived weather that cost the lives of men and cattle and horses.

He had ridden shotgun for both stage and freight lines through the Arizona and New Mexico territories, gambled his way from New Orleans up the coast to New York, in the best and worst the big cities had to offer, and in more mining camps than he could name.

He had followed the wild mustang herds, broken broncs in Montana, and scouted for the army. He had prospected his way over the southeastern area of the territory.

In not one of these places from his memory did he know of a crib or brothel that allowed a working girl a separate room from the one where she took her customers.

There had been two doors on each side of the upstairs hall, and a window at the far end. No sounds issued forth from the other rooms.

He had noticed the house held an air of emptiness, the sort that comes from the absence of other people, not from abandonment.

Like the woman who had opened the door, the room was neat and clean.

But strangely bare of a fancy woman's fripperies. No boxes of paint, no jar of powder, no array of perfume bottles used to mask the last man's scent, littering the china tray on the bureau.

A small china dish held a few hairpins and a faded, rolled ribbon resting next to a brush and comb. They were not silver-backed, but appeared to be bone. Nor was the buttonhook of any good quality. Even the mirror above the bureau top had a plain wood frame.

A fresh towel was folded over the bar on the side of the washstand. A few more clean, folded towels rested on the shelf below. On a wall peg beside the washstand hung a plain white nightgown.

Nothing there to entice a man's lusty thoughts, unless he had a hankering to play slap and tickle with a schoolmarm.

A tall, narrow wood wardrobe stood against the far wall, the single door closed to conceal its contents.

Rafe had a feeling he would no more find a red satin dress behind the door than he would if he unpacked his own saddlebags.

The bed was as pristine as the woman who slept in it. The wood headboard and lower footboard gleamed with polish, as did the small side table, but there was a roughness to them that suggested they were locally made.

Rafe cast an admiring look at the quilt. The cheerful colors and fine stitching sent an invitation to a weary man to wrap himself in its soft warmth and sleep.

His unease lessened in one respect. His daughter was not about to be cared for in a filthy place. He had seen men die of minor wounds that had festered and poisoned their bodies from the use of whatever dirty rag was at hand.

But his annoyance grew that he found so few clues about the woman.

Perhaps that was the telling clue in itself.

His pondering came to an end when she entered the room. He opened his eyes to watch her. She carried a full bucket of water in one hand, and a steaming kettle with a cloth-wrapped handle in the other.

"How is she?" Mary asked softly, avoiding his gaze as she set the bucket down by the washstand.

"Quiet. Fever's climbing." Rafe saw her remove the big china pitcher from the washbowl and place it on the floor. She filled the bowl with the boiling water. From her pocket she took a small square of cloth.

"I'll put the dry bark and leaves of the quinine bush to soak. By the time I fetch my tray, the water will have cooled a bit."

Rafe wanted to stop her, wanted to say something, but she was gone before the words formed. His head felt heavy, but he heard the whisper of sound she made and realized that she moved quietly, almost too quietly for a woman safe in her own place.

Where had she learned to walk softly?

More important, why?

He knew men who had learned the quiet ways of walking from Indians. He had learned from them, too.

Beth stirred with a sob. Rafe turned his thoughts to his child. Her moan caught at his heart. He murmured promises against her hair, promises he had no right to make, for they were not ones he could keep. They were as empty as a water hole in high summer.

But he whispered them anyway, praying the Lord was listening, praying there was mercy for an innocent child.

A slight rattle alerted him that the woman was returning.

All his attention should have focused on his daughter, but a tiny corner of his mind wrung the admission from him that this woman intrigued him.

Puzzles irritated Rafe. There was an answer to most

puzzles, if a man added things up right. The trouble was, a man had to have all the pieces, and in this case, he had too few to make a decision.

And he never could forget that betrayal was a hard lesson learned.

Rafe McCade lived his life by few laws. First, last and always, he never learned a lesson twice.

When Mary stepped into her room the second time, she judged that no more than twenty minutes had passed since she opened the door to admit this man and his child.

Every minute had mentally ticked away as she worked to gather the items she needed. Did he feel as she did? That every minute had dragged an hour long?

Carefully carrying the loaded tray, Mary rested it on the edge of the bureau. She held it with one hand while she pushed her few belongings to the far corner. There was just enough room for the large tray.

"I brought you coffee," she said, indicating the pot and cup. "And there's food in the kitchen."

"It will keep."

"You've traveled far, and—"

"And I will keep, too."

Warmth spread inside her. This man truly loved his child. What a lucky woman his wife must have been to have shared in such a love.

Mary stood there, willing her hands to stop trembling. She knew the man was watching her. From the first, she had remained aware of his guarded eyes, his studying sweeps. But now his gaze burned like a brand on her back.

Mary began talking as she moved, perhaps to reassure him, but she thought it would help settle her nerves, too.

She tested the heat of the water in the bowl. "Some call the quinine a cliff rose, but whatever the name used, I believe soaking the bark and leaves makes the best wash for wounds."

She left one of the clean towels soaking in the bowl and stepped back in front of the bureau. "I have crushed dried spectacle pod into a powder. I've learned that any injury where the skin is broken does not seem to fester when this is used."

She skimmed her gaze over the remaining few items on the tray. Too few. Why didn't he speak? Didn't he care what she had to treat his daughter's wound?

"This bowl holds a paste I made of pine sap mixed with gunpowder to help stop the bleeding. I've not the faith of some that cobwebs work as well. There's charcoal, saltpeter and sulfur in gunpowder. An old Navajo woman said that one or all help some wounds to heal faster."

The growing tension made her pause. But at the moment, she could not have said which one of them sent tension prowling into the room toward the other.

"I boiled the knife, and the linen is freshly washed."

Mary could not halt the slight quaver in her voice as she finished listing what tools she had to save a child.

She knew she had delayed long enough. But she had to first summon courage to turn around and face him.

His tall, lean as any ironwood tree body, seemed to overwhelm the rocking chair. He had placed his flat-crowned black hat on the floor beside him, but he still wore his gun. Beneath the window, and within his easy reach, rested his rifle.

An armed, dangerous-looking, wary man.

Mary had never known any man who could sit so still, or hold her gaze as steadily and as directly, as this man.

She found herself the first to look away. But her gaze went only as far as his long-fingered hand, stroking his daughter's back. The other curved beneath her bottom to hold her against him.

A lock of dark brown hair fell over his forehead. Mary had to fight the strange urge to brush his hair aside, then confront the stranger feeling that she knew it would slip back into place. It was neatly clipped to collar length.

Her hands twisted the sides of her apron. She steeled herself for what she was about to ask him.

"Have you the courage to hold her?"

A faint line of color flushed Rafe's high-set cheekbones. When he answered, his voice was low, husky from thirst, and filled with a measured calm.

"Have you?"

"No."

Mary did not know if she or he was more surprised by her truthful admission. "If she were my child, I could not watch while someone caused her more pain."

"But you have no intent to hurt her out of a need to do violence to someone smaller, and infinitely more innocent, than yourself."

"You would kill me if I did."

Rafe didn't waste a breath to hesitate. "That's right. I would."

Chapter Five

Mary barely swallowed a cry. It was one thing to suspect what someone would do in a given situation, but quite another to hear his bald admission. It was the lack of hesitation, rather than the words, that struck her with fear.

Harry had loved to see her afraid. She had promised herself that no other man ever would.

"I could ask you to leave."

"You could, but you won't."

"No," she said, "I won't. I have no desire to hurt your daughter. But you know there'll be pain."

"I know." Her spunk in facing him down made the corner of his lips notch into a wry smile. "I wouldn't still be sitting here if I thought otherwise."

"Just so we understand each other. I'll do whatever I can."

"Then get on with it. But first, you'd better get more light in here."

Mary darted a look at the fat tallow candle sitting in a saucer on the side table. She left to gather the lamps from Sarah's and Catherine's rooms. She had started to write them a note, but it would have taken too long to explain what had happened. She had taken a moment to lead his horse to the water trough by the corral. A strange horse would be warning enough that they had company.

He was no stranger to this land, and his horse was as valuable as his gun. A man on foot in this country was a man left to die. Her father had told her as much many times.

It was one reason why a horse thief was hanged. If he was caught.

Mary thought of the wounded men who had come seeking aid. Despite their exhaustion, if they could speak, they first asked care for their horse.

But this man cared for nothing but his child.

Mary set the two kerosene lamps on the bedside table. She lifted the glass chimney from each one, turned up the wicks before she lit them, then replaced the glass. The light threw wavering shadows on the walls.

"Don't you have a lamp?"

"I like the soft glow cast by the candle."

Rafe believed her. She was no taller than his shoulder, slight in build, with a fragile air that suggested a strong wind would blow her along. There was a softness to her voice, to her eyes when she glanced at his daughter, and to the lips she bit as she drew closer.

Rafe lifted his hand to hold the back of Beth's head. His other arm lifted to rest across Beth's lower back.

Mary pushed aside the child's torn shirt. She worked quickly now to soak off the makeshift bandage.

"Talk to me," she whispered, needing the sound of a voice to drown out the child's moans of pain.

"How many *widows* are there living here?"

"Three." Mary winced as she drew a louder cry from Beth, but she got the last bit of cloth free. Nor did she miss the emphasis he placed when calling them widows.

"No matter what you may have heard in town, we really are widows. My cousin Sarah was the first. This is her house. Catherine is our friend, and the most recent of us to lose her husband."

Mary looked over at him. "They will be coming up here when they finish their outside chores."

Her gaze drifted down to his gun. She wanted nothing to startle this man.

"Warning me?"

"If you like."

Mary washed the dirt and dried blood from the girl's pale flesh as she talked, thankful that he anticipated her need and moved his daughter's body to help Mary free her of the shirt and the smaller version of her own camisole. She could not but notice the fine lawn, the delicate embroidery and the lace that trimmed the child's undergarment. No expense had been spared.

"You cut the arrow?"

"Had to. I had a far piece to travel. Brought her in from Gavilan Canyon on a travois. I was afraid any movement would work the point back into her flesh. She'd lost enough blood."

Mary lifted his arm so that he held Beth's body just below where the arrow penetrated her back. She washed the shaft, then wrapped it with a clean dry cloth.

"Hold her tight."

"You're not going to cut it out?"

"I could try, but I've no knowledge of what else I might cut. I could injure your daughter far worse. But this way is more painful."

Their gazes met above Beth's head. To Mary, his silently conveyed their need to do this quickly.

She placed herself in the notch between his legs.

Rafe leaned back to steady the rocking chair, and watched her delicately boned hands grab hold of the arrow shaft.

Sweat soaked his hair and slid down his cheeks. He saw that the woman's forehead was beaded with moisture. Her gaze locked on the arrow.

Mary prayed for the strength to make a clean, quick pull, for the flesh had had time to draw close around the wound, holding the arrow in place.

Her lips moved silently.

Rafe prayed as he never had.

He prayed she had the strength to do this, for he could not rip it free from his daughter's flesh.

He felt sweat dampening his clothes, and saw that for her it was the same. He wanted to urge her to hurry. He kept silent. The woman had to make good with the first try, or Beth would bleed too much and make the way difficult.

He needed to see that obscene arrow gone, his child whole.

He stared at her fingers. The nails were neatly pared. A stupid thing to notice. He measured the woman's fragile appearance. He held Beth tighter.

And Rafe braced himself for the scream that was to come.

In that moment, Beth's scream of agony rang in his ears.

Mary stumbled back, and threw aside the broken arrow shaft.

Seconds passed while she watched the blood well and flow. Then she moved, working quietly but efficiently. She covered his shoulder and arms with clean cloths, and when he protested, she explained. "I'm not protecting your clothes. You're filthy, and I want to keep any dirt from her wound."

"You're not going to cauterize it?"

She didn't like the testing quality of his question, but kept her annoyance from her reply.

"No. And I'm not sewing it closed. I can't say for certain that the Apaches don't poison their arrows, but I wouldn't bet your daughter's life that the arrow was clean. I know she's already weak from loss of blood. Letting it bleed now will clean out the wound."

Mary dragged the bucket of clean water closer. While dressing the wound, she listened to the murmur of the man's voice, its deep tone as soothing to her as to the child.

First she sprinkled the crushed spectacle pod on both chest and back, then, gently as she could, she spread the pine sap paste. From the tray, she took the clean linen strips she had cut into bandages, and wrapped them around the little girl's shoulder.

She stripped off the child's boots, and he helped her remove her torn skirt. Like the camisole, her petticoats and drawers were of the finest materials.

Mary said nothing to him of the fever that threw off enough heat to nearly dry the washcloth. She washed the child twice. The high fever alarmed her. Not even the thought of the tea she had steeping downstairs, which would help eliminate the fever, could calm her.

She worried, too, that the child appeared so pale and thin.

"Has your daughter been ill recently?"

His silence forced Mary to look at his face.

"Has she?" she repeated.

"I don't know."

The words sounded as if they had been dragged from him.

"You don't—" Mary stopped herself from saying

more. The savage look in his eyes did not offer a welcome for her questions.

Mary took one of Beth's hands and washed it, feeling him watch her every move. When she reached over to take the other hand, she couldn't free the child's grip from the doll.

For a moment, Mary's face softened, and a naked yearning appeared in her eyes. She found herself brushing back Beth's hair. One tendril curled around her finger.

"What is it? What's wrong?" Rafe demanded in a low voice.

Mary snatched her hand back. "Nothing."

She turned to the bed, stripping the quilt, then folding it over the footboard. Once she had the top sheet folded back, she motioned to him to put his daughter in bed.

"I'll hold her."

And I dare you to try to take her away from me.

Once again, Mary heard the words in her mind, saw the truth of them in his eyes.

"No, you won't. You have wounds that require tending, too. You're dirty, mister. Your daughter needs frequent bathing to keep her fever down. The best way you can help her and help me is to take yourself down those stairs."

"I'm not leaving her."

"Suit yourself," Mary snapped. "But put her in this bed."

It had been a very long time since anyone issued an order to Rafe with every expectation of being obeyed.

He eyed the slender woman glaring at him. She knew nothing of the devils driving him. She could not know of his need to hold Beth close, protecting her, even when he knew it was not within his power to heal her.

She had not asked for, nor had he volunteered, any details about the attack. His suspicions were corralled for now, but he would need to find out who wanted to kill him.

Rafe glanced at the soft curve of her chin, the firm set of her features. The memory of the naked yearning in her eyes when she looked at his daughter rushed forth.

I have no daughter. I have no child. He had not realized it when she spoke, but the wealth of emptiness behind the words was tucked into his memory.

He could not deny the competent care she had given his child.

He made his decision.

He rose from the chair in a smooth, powerful move to place Beth on the bed. She looked so pale, so helpless, lying there, still clutching the doll.

Mary nudged him aside to draw up the sheet. She bent and lifted Beth's head to spread the tangled dark brown hair on the pillow. Her hair was the exact shade of her father's.

"She is a beautiful little girl."

"Beth? Yes, she is. Especially inside, where it counts." He sounded distracted, and knew he was. The lamp's glow had caught and held in the reddish shades of her hair.

Copper and gold strands mixed with darker spice colors. Where the brighter light touched upon it, Rafe thought of cinnabar, the reddish ore of mercury that he had mined in Mexico.

From the thickness of the neatly wrapped braids around her head, he started to imagine its length. The way her hair would slide down to hide her bare nape, the delicately boned shoulders and back.

Mentally Rafe leaped away from the direction his thoughts were taking him, just as if he had touched a rock baked by summer sun.

Unaware, Mary kept turning over his remark. She was pleased to know he was a man who looked beyond the surface.

But he had said as much when he entered the house. *Don't let appearances fool you.*

Mary could not afford to allow anything or anyone to fool her.

Looking down at the child, she saw that Beth had his dark brown hair and eyes. Her mouth was bow-shaped, her nose tipped up at the end. Her brows arched, where her father's were dark slashes. Mary was curious about the woman who had borne her, and thought became words.

"Does Beth look like her mother?"

"No. And I thank the Lord she doesn't."

Mary shivered to hear that cold, hard voice again. Her envy for the woman had been misplaced. If he had ever loved Beth's mother, that love had not lasted until her death.

She bathed the child's face with cool water, then dipped and wrung out the cloth again. She folded the linen and placed it on Beth's forehead.

"Keep this wet until I return."

Mary straightened, then turned around.

Rafe moved without thought. He caught hold of her upper arm and dragged her closer to his body.

"You're not leaving her."

Mary immediately realized that his fingers held her in a firm grip meant to stop her, not to hurt her. But she knew how easily her flesh bruised.

She was alone in the house with him. Was he a man who would use his strength against a woman?

She didn't know this man. She didn't—and the sudden realization hit her hard—even know his name.

She refused to cower.

The feel of his naked hand pressing against the side of her breast made her feel light-headed. The warmth of his flesh seeped through the thin cloth of her gown and camisole.

Mary dragged at a breath. An odd, shimmering sensation went through her. She was held motionless by his lean fingers curling around her arm. Her heart was hammering so fiercely she was afraid that he could hear it. Her nipples tightened and pushed against the soft cotton in twin hard peaks.

She barely heard the swift, ripping sound of his breath over her own.

Her gaze lifted from his hand and the heat he imparted to her skin. Her eyes tracked the dark curling hair in the vee of his shirt, moving up the strong column of his throat.

There were dust streaks over the shadow of beard stubble on his cheeks. She stared at the full, sensuous line of his mouth, the straight, proud angle of his nose.

The firm jut of his chin spoke to her more eloquently than words of a man who had things his own way more often than not.

By the time she looked directly into his eyes, she was trembling. But not from fear. It was the glittering intensity of his gray-eyed gaze that sent a strange wave of weakness through her.

Mary drew a deep, steadying breath, ready to demand her freedom.

She never formed the words.

"What I said before wasn't true. I've never raised a hand to a woman, and what's more, never will." Rafe had had no choice but to speak. She trembled against him like a willow caught in a wind. "You don't have to be afraid of me."

"I'm..."

The cocking of a gun hammer was as loud as a shot in the tension-filled room.

"Nice an' easy now, let her go."

From the sound of Sarah's voice, Mary guessed she was angry. A look showed her cousin holding a rifle. Slightly behind and to Sarah's left, Catherine stood aiming a pistol at the man's back. Mary knew he had no idea that Sarah was an excellent shot with the Spencer repeater.

Mary wasn't sure why she didn't speak. Was she hoping he would pass some sort of test?

"I ordered you to let her go," came Sarah's husky-voiced demand.

Rafe was tired. His wounds ached, his muscles burned with exhaustion. He had been distracted by the needs of his daughter. For the past few minutes he had struggled with his sudden, fierce arousal, drawn forth by a woman who had done nothing to incite it.

He was in no position to argue with a cocked gun.

Especially one held by a woman who sounded as if she not only meant business, but knew how to close the deal in her favor.

"I'm friendly," Rafe said, and wondered as he did why he did not let the woman go. He had told her the truth. He had never once raised his hand to any woman, and the Lord knew Valerie had provoked him.

"Mister, I'm saying this once. I've seen friendly, and you're not it. My daddy said I shouldn't aim a gun at a man unless I was prepared to shoot. Listen up, stranger. I'm aiming it. Aiming it right at you."

Chapter Six

"Sarah, there is no call for holding a rifle on him."

"I beg to differ, Mary. I find a strange horse with a bloodstained saddle and a travois standing by my corral and think of you alone in the house—"

"Sarah, please. He didn't want me to leave his child. She was wounded by an Apache arrow." Mary eased her arm from his grasp.

Rafe, with his acute sense of hearing, listened to the gun hammer sliding back in place. Tension seeped from him.

He looked at the woman beside him. He stood a hair over six feet. The top of her head reached his shoulder.

When he spoke, it was softly, and only to her. "If I hurt you, I'm sorry. Beth means everything to me... Why, I don't even know your name."

"Mary. Mary Inlow. The woman with the rifle at your back is my cousin Sarah Westfall. And our friend with the pistol is Catherine Hill."

"Westfall? Judd Westfall's widow?"

Mary glanced from the man to her cousin. What did he know about Judd? She saw Sarah's black eyes grow chillingly cold at the mention of her husband's name. And Mary wondered if Sarah hadn't kept a few secrets of her own.

"What do you want with Judd's widow?" The question came from Catherine. "And just who are you, mister?"

Rafe still had not turned around, nor was he feeling encouraged to do so by the silence of Judd's widow. Her voice was husky, the other had a lilt to it.

He stared at Mary, once again noting the many shades of her hair. His gaze slid down the soft line of her flushed cheek, and then to her mouth. Soft full lips. It was a mouth a man looked at twice and speculated about ten times over.

"Who are you?" Mary asked.

"Rafe McCade."

"McCade? I've heard that name." Catherine shared a knowing look with Sarah.

Mary grew puzzled. What did they know about this man that she did not?

Rafe eased his arms up and out from his sides, then slowly turned around.

"From the sound of your voice, whatever you've heard wasn't good."

"I never said that," Catherine protested.

Rafe studied the two women framed in the doorway. The husky-voiced one, Judd's widow, stood tall, lissome, her skin a beautiful olive that owed nothing to the sun. He glimpsed hair as black as her eyes beneath the floppy brim of a man's felt hat. There was an annoyingly self-possessed air to the way she held the rifle. He supposed the buckskin jacket, work pants and boots added to his impression.

The other woman, Catherine, had a bright, fresh face framed by blond hair pulled back at the sides. Dressed much like Sarah, she stood a few inches shorter than her companion. Despite her dainty appearance, Rafe gazed into blue eyes that silently conveyed a competence with the gun she held.

Merry widows? Hell, he thought. Black widows, more likely. But not the woman called Mary.

He eyed the guns. "Like I said, I'm friendly."

"That remains to be seen," Sarah said.

"I need to get the tea I left steeping. The child has a high fever."

"Wait," Rafe said as Mary stepped away from him. "I haven't thanked you for all you've done. But I will. I'm good for—"

Mary did not move, but he felt her withdrawal.

"What is it? What did I say that upset you?"

"Mr. McCade," Mary began, summoning every ounce of dignity she possessed. "This is not the time nor the place to speak of money. Pray, if you can. We have a long way to go before your child is well."

Mary followed his gaze to the bed where Beth tossed restlessly. She touched her hand to his arm. "Come down to the kitchen with me and let me tend your wounds. My cousin or Catherine will stay with her."

Rake felt outflanked, outmaneuvered and outnumbered. Mary, he was fast learning, was a soft-looking woman with quiet ways that cloaked a steely determination. He looked back to see Catherine already replacing the cloth on Beth's forehead.

Sarah stood aside as Mary and Rafe went down the hall. She stepped into the room and whispered to Catherine. "I've never seen Mary look at any man like that. She's never one to take to strangers, not even for the sake of a child."

"If you're worried, Sarah, don't leave him alone with her. I've seen wolves hunt before. But would a man like Rafe McCade have any dealings with Judd?"

"What do you mean?"

Catherine stepped away from the bed, then faced her friend. "I love you and Mary as if you truly were my sisters. You've said more than once that Judd was a drunken, no-account opportunist."

"And more," Sarah added.

"And more," Catherine agreed. "A man like McCade wouldn't have anything to do with him, Sarah. Not unless he was hunting him. Until the day he died my husband loved ranching. But my father-in-law was obsessed with any mining going on in the territory. Rafe McCade is a wealthy man, Sarah. He has a stake in the Sierra Grande mining company. Before I left Santa Fe, they had taken almost a million dollars in silver out of one mine in less than a year. From only one claim, one piece of ore weighed over six hundred pounds. The assayer placed a value of seven thousand dollars on it.

"There's rumors he owns a piece of the Pinos Altos mining company, too. Something to the tune of three million in gold just last year. He's made money in mining, but with cattle and railroads, too. But a curious thing about McCade. He's a lone wolf. No one knows for sure where his home is. Just that it is north in the Black Range. There was also a rumor that he had gone east to marry some years ago. If the child is his, I guess that is true."

Catherine glanced at the child in the bed, and saw that Sarah was watching her, too. Strange, she thought, that the three of them remained childless.

"Sarah, I could tell the moment you heard his name that you knew who he was."

Sarah gripped the rifle. She looked at her younger friend. Within Catherine's once innocent blue eyes now resided a cynical gleam. The three of them had come away from their marriages with scars. But she doubted that either Mary or Catherine was as guilt-ridden as she was.

"Sarah, what's wrong? Is it more than McCade being here?"

"No. And you were right. I know who he is. About four years ago, when Judd went to a big-stakes poker game in Lordsburg, I saw..." She closed her eyes briefly, drew and released a deep shuddering breath. "It was there I saw Rafe McCade kill a man."

Mary had to dilute the tea, for it was much too strong. She glanced at where Rafe McCade sat with the coffee she had poured for him, at the round oak table.

She had loved the farm-size kitchen from the first, but tonight, even with the coal-oil lamp fixture lit above the table chasing the evening shadows from the corners, she felt as if the room had shrunk around her.

The blame rested squarely on Rafe's presence. In the year that she had lived here, no man had sat at the table.

"Have you another shirt?" she asked.

"A shirt? What for?"

"Yours is quite ruined." She poured heated water into a basin and brought it to the table, where she had placed soap and a towel.

"Can you remove your shirt without help?" Even as she asked, Mary did not want him to. Half of her thoughts had remained behind in her bedroom with a child who needed care. The other half was far too aware of the masculine presence of Rafe McCade.

And she was annoyed with herself for thinking about him as a man, for noticing the breadth of his shoulders, the bronze of his skin.

Mary's innate honesty forced her to admit that she was a little frightened of the special awareness in his eyes that she was an attractive woman. Each time, it had lasted only a few moments, a trembly warmth shimmering inside her, but long enough to warn her to step with care around this man.

She would never have another man ordering her life. Never.

"Finish your coffee, Mr. McCade. I'll be right back. Sarah may have a spare shirt of her husband's you could wear."

"I've got one in my saddlebags. I'll fetch it. All of Beth's things were lost with the packhorses."

Rafe looked up at her. "It bothered you when I mentioned money." And because he was watching for it, he didn't miss the slight tightening of her mouth, the small movement she made to square her shoulders.

"Yes, it did."

An honest woman? He hid his surprise. And the reason he pushed her.

"Tell me why?"

"I won't put a price on helping someone in need." Mary found it difficult to keep her gaze steady and direct on his. *Because I still have pride, Mr. McCade.* Listen to yourself. *You need money, you all need money. Pride, indeed?*

"Go fetch your shirt. I'm sure Sarah left your saddlebags in the barn. I'll bring the tea upstairs and see how Beth is doing. Then I'll come back."

She held the cup with both hands to still a growing anger.

At the doorway, Mary paused. She bit her lip, then impulsively gave way to the anger. "Mr. McCade, don't get your water hot about money. It can be replaced. That little girl upstairs can't be."

Rafe didn't move. He should be furious over her

snapped reminder about Beth. As if he could forget. As if he ever would.

But she didn't know that.

He had added a few pieces to the puzzle of Mary Inlow, but instead of feeling satisfied, he found himself strangely restless. And curious.

Man-to-woman curious.

And Rafe didn't like that feeling at all.

Climbing the stairs, Mary unknowingly shared his feeling.

The murmur of voices in her bedroom made her pause.

"It was there I saw Rafe McCade kill a man."

Sarah's voice. Sarah knew him?

Mary was never more thankful that she had learned to walk softly so as not to draw Harry's attention. She flattened herself against the wall. She was ashamed of eavesdropping, but couldn't make herself step into the room until she heard the rest.

"McCade's known to be handy with a gun, Sarah. The fact that he got himself and his child out of a fight with Apaches proves that."

"Handy, Catherine? You've never seen anyone move like him. There were a few men hanging around the livery when Judd and I pulled in. With the railroad there, Lordsburg drew men from all over. A big brute of a man stood there in that hot sun, beating his horse. When his wife tried to stop him, he turned on her.

"Like I said, he was big, and he wore a gun. He silenced a few protests with the challenge that he'd kill any man who interfered between him and his wife. Judd wasn't about to, and he wouldn't let me move from the buckboard. One man even remarked that a few slaps kept a woman in line.

"Then McCade showed up. He went sailing at that

bully with his fists. And McCade whipped that brute and left him lying in the dust.

"But when McCade turned his back to retrieve his hat and gun, that coward grabbed his rifle. He was going to shoot McCade in the back. I don't know what or who warned McCade, the man even got off the first shot, but McCade moved, Catherine. And I'll never forget how fast.

"Lightning hangs fire by comparison. McCade drew his gun and shot him. I swear to this day that I only heard one sound, but when Judd asked about it later, he was told the man died with two bullet holes in the heart. Two holes so close together, they could be covered with a silver dollar."

"Did he meet Judd then? Or was it later, at the poker game?"

"I don't know, Catherine. I stayed in the hotel room the whole three days."

"You had a hard life with Judd. Do you suspect that McCade came here deliberately? I mean, would he have reason to? Did Judd owe him money or something?"

"I don't know. What's more, I don't want to know. If he came here looking for money, McCade's out of luck. I don't have any to give him."

"Sarah, wait. Will you let him stay?"

"It's not my decision alone to make. It's ours. Do we have a choice? Look at that child, Catherine. Could you demand that he leave with her? I couldn't. And there's Mary. My cousin would likely leave with him. Mary hungers to hold a child, even if that child belongs to someone else, and even if it lasts only a little while."

In the hallway, Mary leaned her head back against the wall and fought the burning sting of tears. Dear God! Her insides felt as if they had congealed into a huge knot, tightening and then twisting with unbearable pain.

Her secret hunger for a child was not a secret at all. She had thought herself clever to fend off Sarah's questions about why there were no children with the excuse that she and Harry had made a mutual decision not to have any.

She had said those words, lying to Sarah, lying to herself. As if she would not want a child, had not tried, had never once cried at the monthly flow she had come to hate. And with her hate had come Harry's.

Dear Lord, give me strength, she pleaded. *I need to face them.*

The pain was a raw, livid wound inside her. Not a secret sorrow. Not hidden now, not ever hidden again.

You're worthless, Mary. I can hire a woman to cook and clean for me and entertain my friends. But I bought you to give me a son. A man needs sons, Mary. He is nothing without them. You shame me with every month that passes. Shame me! Do you hear? Do you? Do...

No! The scream was a silent one. But it brought Mary back from the brink of a hellish nightmare.

There was a child in that room who needed her.

And Harry was dead. She had to keep him and his haunting taunts buried.

Mary stepped into the room before Sarah reached the doorway.

"You heard us?"

"Yes. But you were wrong about one thing. This is your home. I'll abide by your wishes." Mary had to set the cup of tea on the tray. She didn't trust herself not to spill it.

"Mary, I hurt you, and I'm sorry." Sarah came to

stand beside her. "Say you'll forgive me." She hugged her cousin, her eyes suspiciously moist.

"And it's not my decision. This is our home. We three stick together."

Sarah pulled back and looked at Mary. "Whatever McCade brought to us, we'll find a way to handle it."

"Agreed." Mary spread her arm to include Catherine in their embrace.

"All right," Catherine said after a few moments. "We agree to remain bosom friends. Share and share alike. Heroes all."

"Heroines," Mary corrected.

Laughing, Catherine shook her head, then stepped away. "No, heroes. There's little men can do that we can't do, too."

"Someday," Mary warned, "talk like that will get you in trouble."

"Perhaps. But if McCade gives us the wrong kind of trouble, we'll deal with him."

"Honestly, Catherine, this is not the time—"

"Mary, I'm teasing you. I can't stand to see you sad." Catherine looked at Sarah.

"Of course she's teasing."

"Try to sound as if you both believe that."

"I do." Mary placed her hand on Sarah's arm. "He's gone to fetch his saddlebags from the barn. Why don't you go down and talk to him? Both of you. You need to eat, and the stew is hot. I left what you'll need to tend his wounds on the table. And take the tray with you. I won't change the child's bandage until tomorrow."

Mary rinsed the cloth and began to sponge Beth's face.

She then decided to tell them. "He offered me money for helping him, for his daughter. As if any man could pay for what I give with my heart. She is a needy child. I feel it, and in some strange way know it is true.''

Mary looked at her cousin, then Catherine. "If that man demands anything, any kind of payment from you, you tell him whatever debt he thinks to collect is paid.''

Chapter Seven

Sarah went into her room. Catherine went downstairs and found the kitchen empty of the disturbing Mr. McCade's presence. She hung her hat and jacket on the wall pegs near the back door. She assumed McCade had the missing lantern.

She removed her father's pistol from her waistband.

Lightning hangs fire by comparison. Sarah's description of McCade's speed stuck in her mind. She placed her weapon in the inside pocket of her jacket.

She glanced out the window, but with the barn doors closed, she couldn't tell if McCade was inside.

The tantalizing aroma of Mary's hunter's stew came from the cast-iron pot on the stove. When they first decided to divide the chores, each had cooked a week's worth of meals. Mary had won the place as cook because of her baking, and her knowledge of using herbs, not only for healing, but to add a variety of tastes and flavors to their food.

She reached into the stove's warming oven and took out a towel-wrapped loaf of fresh bread. One sniff told her that Mary had made one of her favorites. Catherine quickly sliced off the end. It was crusty on the outside and dotted with thyme, onions, coriander, parsley and lots of pepper inside. She munched on it as she set the table.

The tablecloth was patched and darned, but each time Mary made a repair she had added some embroidery. The colorful flowers and leaves covered its shabby state. From the upper shelf of the corner cupboard she took plates, then silverware from the round basket on the shelf below, along with three linen napkins rolled in wooden holders carved to resemble birds.

The back door opened, and Catherine turned at the sound.

"I was wondering where you had gone."

"Seeing to my horse," Rafe answered. He hung his hat on the empty peg, but held on to his saddlebags.

Catherine boldly ran an appreciative eye over the tall man.

"Oh, I'd say you did a sight more, McCade. You clean up real nice."

Her impish grin invited his in return. But Rafe didn't mistake the message in her eyes. It wasn't sexual. He easily imagined himself looking at a dozen women the same way. *You're easy on the eyes, and that's as far as it goes.*

Now, if it had been Mary looking at him like that... He forced the thought to die.

Catherine glanced at the raw scrape on his cheek. His dark, curly hair held a few random drops of water. His gray linen shirt, hand tailored to fit the masculine wedge of chest and shoulders, still retained the sheen of newness. The color made his eyes appear a silver-gray. Most of the dust had been beaten from his pants and wiped from his boots. He no longer wore the leather vest, but his gunbelt rode low on his lean hips.

She stared at the weapon, then gestured toward it.

"You won't need that in here." She looked at his face. "Don't you trust us?"

"Funny question from a woman who greeted me with gun in hand."

"But this is our home. We are three women alone. If we don't protect each other, who would?"

"A valid point."

Catherine knew then that he was not about to remove his gunbelt. "Suit yourself," she said, then shrugged.

"I usually do, Mrs. Hill."

Catherine added a fresh napkin for the fourth place setting. "Please call me Catherine. I have a feeling we'll all be in each other's pockets before you leave."

"Catherine, then. I'd like to thank whoever saw to Rebel. He deserved that bait of corn."

"Sarah. She's best with horses."

While she sliced the bread, Rafe glanced around the kitchen. Earlier, he had poked through the pantry. Their food supplies were as low as the feed and hay in the barn. He was wary of pricking another widow's pride as he had Mary's, but he had never been a man to shy from what needed to be done.

"Which one of you is going to talk sense to me about money? And don't put me off like Mary by saying you don't need it. I can see for myself that you all do."

"Then talk to me, Mr. McCade," Sarah said from the doorway. "Mary needs more water. Would you fetch it, Catherine?" She closed the distance to hand over the bucket.

"I should go up to my daughter."

"There's no need. Mary's with her. You can't do more than she can. And you couldn't ask for a better nurse."

Catherine agreed and went outside.

"Sit down, Mr. McCade. I'll get your supper."

Restless and helpless, Rafe stared at the doorway. He had seen the care Mary gave his daughter. It just didn't feel right not to be there, too.

He watched as Sarah ladled one scoop of stew on each of the three plates, but heaped two on his. He shot a look at the back door, wondering why Catherine seemed to be taking so long to fill the bucket. The well was ten feet from the door.

"Before we discuss money, Mrs. Westfall, I'm sure you are curious about my knowing that you're Judd's widow."

"Am I?" Sarah didn't look at him. She checked the level in the coffeepot, then lined up cups on the edge of the stove.

"I know in your place I would be."

Sarah willed her hand to remain steady as she poured coffee. "Better sit and eat before the stew cools. I'll take this up to Mary."

Catherine, having delayed as long as she could, came inside and heard the last. She caught the quick shake of Sarah's head and suggested she take up the coffee.

Rafe reached her in two strides. "Let me carry the bucket. It's too heavy for you to lug up the stairs."

"Mr. McCade—"

"Rafe. First names, remember?"

"Rafe, then. I've carried water up those stairs before you came, and I'll be carrying it up when you're gone. Sit down and eat," she said in a firm voice. "I don't want to be tripping over you or arguing at every turn."

"As the lady wishes."

"That's right. This lady does for herself."

Rafe caught the quick smile that came and went on

Sarah's mouth. By silent agreement, they waited until they heard Catherine's steps on the stairs. Rafe pulled out a chair for Sarah. He didn't understand her hesitation.

"You will keep me company, won't you? You three are of the opinion I should be banished from my child's side. It would be easier to bear with company."

Rafe saw that, once seated, she made no move to eat. There wasn't any reason to wait to talk to her.

"I had hoped to find Judd's widow before this," he began in a soft voice. "I won't speak ill of your husband, for a dead man can't defend himself, but you know that your husband was a gambler."

It was not a question. Sarah, with her parched throat and too-dry lips, couldn't have answered if she wanted to.

"I first met Judd in a poker game in Lordsburg a few years back. But the first time I saw him was at the livery, the day before the game was slated to begin."

He remembered. Dear Lord, what was he going to tell her? Sarah began to crumble her bread.

Rafe covered her slender hand with his own larger one.

"If I bring bad memories with my story, I apologize. But I need to tell this in my own way."

His pause forced her to look at him. There was sympathy in his cool gray gaze, but there was something akin to admiration, too.

"All right. I'll hear you out."

"Thank you. I don't think you'll be sorry. I had other business in town, and was about to leave when a friend mentioned a high-stakes poker game and asked me to sit in. I had gone back to the livery to

make arrangements to board my horse for a few days
more.

"I saw a woman try to grab a buggy whip from
the man seated beside her. She wanted to stop the
cowardly attack on another woman and a horse. I've
always admired courage, and learned at an early age
that it comes in many forms. A woman who tried to
go against her man—"

"I did nothing." Sarah stared at her plate. She
didn't see the stew. She saw that woman's face. The
bruises... "Judd refused to help her. He wouldn't let
me do anything. It was you who put a stop to that
senseless beating. And when you killed him, you
ended that woman's misery."

"I didn't want to kill him. But I'm a man who'll
live by laws when there is law. And when there are
none, I make my own."

"I never forgot that day," she murmured.
"Never."

"It eases my mind to hear you say that I put that
woman out of her misery. I gave her money to see
her and her children on their way, but it's the Lord's
truth, she didn't thank me for killing her man."

"Then she was a foolish woman."

"Perhaps. But I never did stay for the poker game.
It was a few months later than I ran into Judd again.
He stepped in for another player in a game up north
in Socorro.

"A good poker player studies the men he plays
with more than the hands he is dealt. I was winning,
and Judd had been steadily losing. The last raise was
mine, and his to call or fold. He threw in a deed to a
mining claim to cover my raise.

"Now, mining circles are small, no matter how
vast an area they cover. I knew that claim. I had tried

to buy it a year before, from Old Pony Temple, who first filed the claim.

"You may not understand how a miner finds what he's looking for on a claim. I won't bore you with details, but Old Pony's eyesight had been failing for a time. I assume that Judd won the claim from him, but he didn't know what he had, either. He thought it was a worthless deed because there was no sign of color. Gold," he added when she glanced at him.

"I let the bet stand, because I had seen reddish sand at the digging. When I had the claim filed in my name, I had the sand assayed. I had figured it was worth more than Judd dreamed. That reddish color sand is carbonate of lead, with a silver content so high, no one around there had seen its like.

"I made a great deal of money from that mine before I sold off a few shares."

"What has this to do with me? Judd lost a poker hand, and you got rich. Nothing new for me. You were smarter and saw other possibilities than what other men viewed."

"There is a debt between us."

"No. Not a one, Mr. McCade."

"I beg to differ. I didn't know about Judd's death until a few months ago. Unfortunately, I had to go east. And it seemed no one knew what had happened to his widow."

"Why were you looking for me? Judd was the one—"

"Judd would have lost anything I gave him. And any woman who managed to buy land and a house and hold them against a gambler like Judd deserves to profit from his mistake."

Rafe waited for more denials, and when none were forthcoming, he heaved a sigh of relief.

"I don't have much cash with me, but I'll wire my lawyer to release the funds to you."

"I still don't understand why you want to do this."

"Haven't you heard the expression about not looking a gift horse in the mouth?"

"Mr. McCade, you're not a horse." Sarah fought a smile and lost. "If I remember the story, the horse brought more trouble than gifts."

And her words brought back to Rafe the whisper of his name from the Apache's lips. He had enemies. But which had the money and the knowledge to set up a raid to kill him?

"Let's hope that I'll bring no more trouble to your home, Sarah." He rose. "If you will excuse me, I'll bring my supper and Mary's upstairs. And you might think about what you'll do with five thousand dollars."

"Five thousand—"

"That was the amount of my raise that Judd covered with the claim. A fair exchange, don't you agree?"

But Sarah didn't answer. Nor did she watch him leave. She sat straight in her chair, eyes unseeing. It was not the amount he named that held her still. Judd had won and lost more in a matter of days. But this money would be hers, all hers.

"Sarah? Sarah, what did he say to you?"

Sarah started. "Sit down, Catherine. But first, tell me how the child is?"

"The fever's high. I helped Mary bathe her body again. But please, what did he say?"

"I shouldn't look a gift horse in the mouth."

"He bought you a horse?"

"No, silly. He made me a gift. A most welcome one."

"What?"

"Freedom, Catherine. Rafe McCade has given me the kind of freedom I've dreamed of having. Sit down. I'll tell you while we eat."

Chapter Eight

The lamps were gone from the room. Rafe saw the lone candle cast a feeble, wavering light over the upper corner of the bed. Mary knelt on the floor, the bucket close by, her voice so soft it took him a few moments to understand that she was murmuring reassurances to Beth.

"She's awake, then," Rafe said, coming into the room.

Mary did not turn around, nor was she surprised by his presence. It was uncanny how she had sensed him standing there in the doorway.

"Her sleep is restless. She's cried out a few times. Nights seem to be the worst when there is fever. The tea I made for her is of chamomile and a bit of mint. It should help the fever and wound, as well as help her to sleep. Beth's almost finished her second cup."

"I brought you something to eat. I'll sit with her now."

A flash of resentment flared in Mary's mind. The feeling was uncalled-for, and she rarely lied to herself. It stemmed from the quiet command in his husky voice, that absolute expectation of being obeyed.

What right did she have to refuse him?

None.

That one word scored deep, as deep as the emptiness of the old longings that she had tried so hard to remove from her life.

Mary rose without complaint. She tilted her head from side to side to release the aching knot at the base of her neck. Then she turned to face him.

The dust-ridden stranger was gone. He had not shaved, and the dark shadows on his lower face created the look of a lean, dangerous wolf. She could barely make out the slight thickness indicating a bandage on his upper arm.

She had the strange feeling that he would resent her asking about his wound, and so she kept silent.

That truant lock of hair had fallen across his forehead. Her arm ached to lift and put it back to join the rest of his thick hair.

Foolish thought.

You have nothing to give this man, nothing to give any man.

Rafe held out the plate to her. He noted her pointed look at his own supper.

"I had a feeling you wouldn't leave Beth, so I came to keep you company while you ate."

"Do you often read someone's thoughts?"

Mary started for the end of the bed, only to find him blocking the way.

"Sit in the chair. You'll be more comfortable there. I'll sit on the floor. And no, now that you mention it, Mary, I've never noticed any ability to read someone's thoughts."

It wasn't exactly a lie. He had never consciously acknowledged any ability. It had come to him, the same way his handling of a gun had come, the same way he found worth where other men found nothing.

Mary sat in the rocking chair. She watched the

graceful flow of his body dropping into an Indian-style seat on the floor. So had men sat around camp-fires for as long as she could remember.

He reached up and drew Beth's small hand to his lips, then held the child's palm against his cheek before he put it to rest on the bed.

Mary's breath caught. The act was as natural as his breathing. She thought of his strong-looking hand stroking his daughter, the husky murmur of his voice that soothed.

More than the food Rafe had brought to her, Mary feasted on the nourishment of Rafe's expressing his love for his child.

There had been no artifice in the kiss he gave Beth. Mary felt certain he had not done it to impress her. Rafe had no reason to. Beth, resting more quietly now, was likely unaware of it.

Mary thought of her own father. She knew he had loved her in his own way. He did not speak the words or use signs of affection. His love was simply there. Whenever she looked, there had been a quiet pride in his eyes.

Harry had not been an affectionate man. She often thought of the first few years of her marriage to him as a banquet she had believed would never end.

The more she needed Harry's affection, his every expression of love, the more bitter Harry had grown. And so her love had died, and she had withered, the way her small herb garden would turn to dust without care, water and sun.

She looked up to find Rafe's intent gaze upon her.

"Something's made you sad again."

"Thoughts that have no place here," she answered, and wished those dark thoughts away.

"I wanted to tell you—" Rafe abruptly stopped. The candlelight bathed her lower face with slight shadow, but highlighted her beautiful eyes. *Tell her what?*

He couldn't remember. Whatever he had thought to say was simply gone from his mind. He couldn't remember a time when that had happened. She was watching him expectantly, waiting for him to say something.

"How long before Beth can travel?"

"Travel?"

"Be moved?"

Mary looked everywhere but at him. Leave? He was already talking of leaving?

But he had started to tell her something, not ask a question. What had he seen looking at her that made him change his mind?

"I can't answer you. Not now. It's simply too soon to tell."

"You're a cautious woman."

"Yes. Yes, I am."

"I didn't mean only about Beth's—"

"I know." Uncomfortable with the personal direction of their talk, Mary asked him to tell her about the attack.

"I'll tell if you'll eat. You haven't touched a bite."

Without embellishment, Rafe spoke, and Mary listened to the stark words that created the images of the attack. She forced herself to eat. She would need her strength to nurse Beth.

She realized Rafe had come to the end of his tale.

"I understand a little more why Beth wouldn't let me take the doll. Twice while I was bathing her I tried, but she clung that much tighter." Mary hesitated, then could not seem to stop herself. "You're a brave man to risk your life for a child's toy. Your daughter is a lucky little girl to have so much love."

"My insistence on bringing her to my home nearly

got her killed. I don't know how much love that shows.''

"Don't feel guilty. Perhaps I shouldn't say this, but when you admitted that you didn't know if she had been ill, I had a feeling that you hadn't seen Beth in a while.''

Mary wished she could recall the words. His silence was answer enough that she had overstepped herself. She rose and placed her plate on the bureau.

"I made a mistake about you when I first came here.''

"Mistake? I'm sorry if I poked into your personal business, Mr. McCade—''

"Rafe. And I meant it somewhat differently than you've taken my words. The fella over at the emporium directed me to the merry widows. I thought I was bringing my daughter to a brothel.''

"And still you came?''

Rafe barely made out the hint of a curve to her lips, but he heard a smile in her voice.

"Yes, I came. With the doctor drunk, there wasn't much choice.''

"Not here or in a hundred small towns like Hillsboro.''

"I didn't insult you?''

This time there was no doubt about her smile. Her soft laughter washed over him. "You weren't the first to make that assumption. I admit I was angry the first time I heard what Sarah's neighbors were calling us, a few months ago. It was right after Catherine came to live with us.''

"Well, you must admit it's strange to find three lovely young women living together.''

"Thank you for the compliment, but what has that to do with anything?''

"Women, widowed or single white women who

are ladies, are rare in the territory," Rafe explained, with a patience he did not feel. "Surely you know that?"

"I knew. But you see, none of us chooses to marry again."

Rafe repeated the words to himself. To ask why none of them would marry again burned on the tip of his tongue. He had surmised a great deal about Sarah's marriage to Judd, none of it good. He let her statement pass.

"So, tell me why they gave you three the name."

The request was harmless enough, but Mary felt there was more to his questions than a way of passing time. He stirred strange notions that she had no business thinking about.

"Is it something shocking?" Rafe tried to keep his mind on anything but her soft, deft hands, playing with the ruffle of her gown. He wanted to tell her to stop, to point out that she was directing his gaze to the rise and fall of her breasts.

He had no business being drawn into sexual thoughts about her. Mary had done nothing to provoke them.

Maybe that was his trouble. She stood in shadow, giving free rein to his imaginings.

"Shocking? No," she replied seriously, "I can't think that our behavior was anything like that. Then again, we are all in our first year of widowhood, but not one of us will wear black, or gray if we can help it."

What about a year of mourning? He couldn't help but notice the absence of that word.

"I believe it was the music. And the laughter. You see, we're old friends, aside from Sarah being my cousin. We're happy living together. Before our marriages separated us, we sang a great deal, sometimes at parties. Now, in the evening when our chores are done, Sarah and Catherine will bring out their guitars and play. We sing favorite songs. With the memories comes laughter.''

Mary looked over at Rafe. She couldn't tell what he was looking at, for the candlelight was behind him and his face completely in shadow.

"Mr. McCade...Rafe, are you still in the same room with me?" she chided gently.

"I'm still here. I told you my luck changed for the better when I brought Beth to you."

She nodded and began working her way around the room, trying to get to the other side of the bed to check on Beth's fever.

"I hope we all live up to your faith in us."

"I have no doubts, Mary. None at all." He swung around to watch her as she bent over his child. "Here, give me the cloth. I'll freshen it. I should tell you that Beth has nightmares. Sometimes all that quiets her is the doll. It's fair to warn you that I'll be bedding down in here with her."

"In here? You can't. This is my room. I intended— no, I intend to sleep here to care for her."

Rafe looked directly into her eyes and felt something pass between them. Something, perhaps, that both of them didn't really want, or thought they didn't want. But it was there at this moment, between them, for the taking.

"No sense in wasting your breath to argue. I'm staying," he said softly.

Rafe had to look away from her eyes. Suddenly, he could not bear to see her green eyes watching him with a longing that he didn't believe she was aware of revealing to him.

As he stood there, he had the eerie feeling that if

he kept looking into those eyes of hers, he would fall
deeply into them, and never find his way out again.

"Is it your worry for Beth that makes you so stubborn and demanding?"

"No." Rafe closed his eyes for moments. He had
to tell her. It wasn't a matter of being fair, but of
issuing a warning that could save lives. All day the
thought had gone around and around in his mind, like
a dog chasing the fleas on his tail. He had narrowed
down his choices.

"Rafe, what is it? Something is wrong."

"There's something else you need to know. And
the others," he said with a nod toward the doorway.

His husky voice was no longer soothing. Mary
heard the hard edge underscoring his words. A ripple
of fear crawled up her spine.

He looked down at his daughter. For Beth's sake,
for her life, he had to trust these women. But he
thought of the danger he brought to them, too.

"Rafe, from your changed attitude, I know... I feel
as if—"

"Someone set me up. Someone paid those Apaches
to attack that army detail. Paid them, because they
knew I would be riding with them."

Mary looked not at him, but at Beth. She gently
cupped the child's fever-flushed cheek. "I hear the
belief in your voice that what you're saying is true. I
am not calling you a liar, but you must know that the
Apache have been riding the war trail all year. This
is the worst it has been in a long time. Wherever men
gather, and women, too, that is all they talk about.
Do you understand what you are saying, Rafe?"

"Better than you, Mary."

"But who would want a man dead, a child hurt?"
She had to look at him. "What kind of a man are
you, Rafe McCade?"

"A man with enemies."

She saw the heel of his hand brush against the butt of his gun. She didn't think he was conscious of the move.

Men who lived by the gun died by the gun. Mary had heard those words long ago, but couldn't remember where.

It didn't matter. Beth mattered. She mattered a great deal. What would happen to her if Rafe was killed?

"I won't be." He held her startled gaze with his own steady one. "Killed. Isn't that what you're thinking?"

"Who are you?" she asked again.

"A man grateful his child found a compassionate woman to care for her."

Mary became aware that he had taken hold of her hand. She made no move to pull away as their joined hands formed a bridge across the bed. She trembled as he bent toward her and lifted her hand to his lips.

The feel of his warm breath touching her skin made her close her eyes. She couldn't summon the will to ask him what he thought he was doing.

And then his lips touched her flesh, as softly and as gently as the kiss he had given to his daughter.

But Mary wasn't a child. She opened her eyes to look at him.

Who are you?

A man who has enemies. A grateful man.

She accepted the words as true. The shimmering warmth making her flush from the inside out left no doubt that whatever tags Rafe McCade added, he was all man.

Gentle, yes. But there was to her the danger of his overwhelming masculine presence, which awakened long-dormant senses. Mary snatched her hand from his.

Rafe made no move to stop her.

"I'm going to take a look around outside. Then I'll be back." He leaned over and kissed his daughter.

Mary didn't answer him. She gazed at the child. Her arms ached to hold her. The ache came from the fear Rafe had brought into the open, and her own desperate needs.

She wanted the child. But she was afraid to want the man.

Chapter Nine

Rafe passed Catherine on the stairs.

"That was a mighty nice gift you gave Sarah."

"No more than she deserved. Catherine, I'll be out for a while. Mary will explain, but sleep light and keep your gun handy."

"My gun?" But the words were met with no response. Rafe was already down the stairs and out of sight.

Catherine wasted no time, and hurried into Mary's room, whispering a demand to know what was going on.

As Mary spoke to her, Rafe repeated what he had said to Sarah, who had just come inside, brushing off rain from the light drizzle that had started. "No need for you to go out. I just checked the horses."

"I'll be doing more than looking around here. I want to go down to the saloons. News travels fast and free when men are drinking. I need to hear what's being said."

"Straight on the line, Rafe. Do you believe that someone trailed you here?"

"I don't know. I want to be sure, whichever way

it goes. I don't want my presence, and Beth's, too, bringing trouble here."

Sarah sensed his impatience to go. "Take the brown gelding. He's got no markings to make him stand out. And he's eight months off the range. Spooks like a devil when something's not right."

She blew out the lantern. Rafe opened the door with a nod of thanks for her savvy. If someone was waiting in the dark drizzle for him, he would have presented a perfect target silhouetted in the doorway.

"Be careful," Sarah whispered as he melted into the shadows. She bolted the door, took up her rifle, and after pouring a cup of coffee, she sat at the table to await his return.

Upstairs, Mary hurried to the hall window. There was nothing to see beyond the glass but darkness. She stood for a few minutes, searching the ground below, then turned away.

Rafe was no longer there. She had not seen one shadow move, but there was no doubt in her mind that he had gone.

"Go with God," she whispered, and returned to her vigil.

Someone wanted to kill him.

It wasn't until he stepped into the saddle and rode out away from the road that Rafe blocked all else from his mind.

Before he could look into his past, the future beckoned like a wicked temptress.

Who would benefit from his death?

The obvious answer was Beth, for she would inherit the bulk of his holdings. Eliminate Beth, and the trust set up to protect her dissolved into so many minor bequests only the lawyers processing the will would earn an extra dollar.

The trust itself was ironclad. Anyone attempting to control his daughter and his fortune had to buck men honed in hell, who walked away after supping with the devil.

He would trust each of the four men named as trustees with his life. Truth was, he had, and so had each of them in return.

The gelding stepped with care on the rocky ground of the east-running wash. Rafe deliberately swung wide of the town to come in from the north end. The cool rain held to an intermittent drizzle that posed no problem. Several times he drew rein and sat listening to the night sounds around him.

And he thought of the many times he had ridden through the night. There was a difference, though— he could not bring the fight to this unknown enemy. He would not, could not, leave his daughter.

Rafe rode into the north end of town. Approaching the Paradise Saloon, he paused to study the main street of town. Lights beckoned down the opposite side of the street, from the Red Horse Saloon.

He swung the gelding away from the hitching rail, into the middle of the street, toward the other saloon. Beneath the brim of his hat, his eyes moved along the shadows of hidden doorways and alleys.

Two reasons made his decision for him. The hitching rails in front and on either side of the Red Horse were thick with horses. More men drinking there meant more news. More men could also mean more trouble for a stranger, too.

But Rafe rode with the knowledge that he had ridden into more raw-at-the-edge cow and mining towns than he cared to number. And usually he'd been the stranger.

His other reason had to do with his unwillingness to confront the doctor he had needed. He didn't quite trust himself not to have words with a man intent on drowning his sorrows.

At the Red Horse, he pulled up and swung down. He glanced at the lights from the windows, then tied his horse and loosened the cinch.

Rafe stood for a minute, looking along the street. Then he hitched up his gunbelt and slipped the thong from his gun. Rafe knew he wasn't looking for trouble, but he was as ready as he could be if it came calling on him.

He pushed through the doors into the saloon and paused briefly to allow his eyes to adjust to the change in light.

The habit was so ingrained that he didn't even think about doing it. Just as he didn't look directly at any of the lights now. Coal-oil fixtures, like campfires, proved the death of men who tried finding an enemy in the dark or the shadows with eyes accustomed to bright lights.

Rafe swept the room with a comprehensive glance. It told him he knew no one there, and it was unlikely anyone knew him.

Choosing the empty place at the end of the bar, where the wall protected his back and the door remained a few steps at his side, he ordered a whiskey.

Only three men stood at the bar. One looked to be a drummer, from his derby hat and plaid box jacket. The other two were cowpunchers.

The bartender ceased mopping the bar and brought Rafe his whiskey.

The tables scattered over the sawdust-covered floor were mostly filled with men playing cards or deep in talk.

Rafe, seeing the looks directed his way as the curiosity offered any stranger, sipped his drink and listened to their conversations.

Railroads were the topic of a heated discussion at one table. Rafe's mouth held a hint of a smile when he heard about the money that could have been made since the Central and Pacific Railroad Company and the Atchison, Topeka and Sante Fe Railroad Company had opened traffic from Kansas City to San Francisco. He had made a tidy sum on the deal.

A cousin spoke of a letter received from family members in Council Bluffs, telling of the Union Elevator Company filing their articles of incorporation with half a million in capital in the Iowa city.

Rafe moved a bit closer to the end of the bar, for Council Bluffs was a major grain-buying center, and several roads terminated there. He didn't know Sidney Dillion or Hugh Riddle, two of the incorporators named, but had a passing acquaintance with Al Keep. He listened, for this was the way he had begun his fortune.

The crusty old miner at the table, who wore his years well, remarked, "Ain't ever seen the like of no half a million. Ain't likely to 'fore I meet my Maker."

Rafe listened to the old miner, gathering he had been out on the trail for some time. He spoke knowingly of California and Nevada capitalists, with their mining experts, visiting camps to look over ore and mining operations for investments.

Rafe motioned for another drink. The Cañón del Agua and San Pedro company, in which he had recently won a major share, had just had a new smelter put in, and yet he was hearing that they had suspended operations and had a large force employed in building fortifications around the mine, armed with the latest and most improved arms, including the explosive-shell cartridge.

The voices lowered, and Rafe couldn't hear what

they said, but it had something to do with the lone
man seated in the corner.

"Ask me," one of the men at the table said, "he
looks like a kid still wet behind the ears."

"Look again," the old miner warned. "That tied-
down gun don't make him a green kid. Hear he's been
offering fightin' wages up to seventy-five dollars a
day. Them boys up at the Cañón del Agua is fixin'
to fight."

"Well, I ain't but passable handy with a gun," another man said. "An' I'd want one of them New York
Life insurance policies like my sister got. Her man
got killed with Custer, an' they paid her two thousand
dollars 'cause he was an officer. Hear tell they paid
out close to forty thousand just to families in our territory."

Rafe took another, closer look at the lone man. He
had already decided to leave, since he wasn't hearing
the type of news he had come for. He thought about
finishing off his drink, and while he did, he saw that
he was about to have company.

A man wearing double holsters, tied down, was a
rare sight. Rafe always figured that if a man couldn't
do the job needed with one gun, he shouldn't be pack-
ing any weapon.

Rafe thought the young man resembled William
Bonney, but the outlaw people knew as Billy the Kid
had been killed in July.

The man set his drink on the corner of the bar, near
where Rafe stood. Slim, wiry, the man was better
dressed than most cowhands. Along with the double
tied-down guns, he sported polished black boots
dressed with fancy large-roweled Mexican spurs.
He was dressed entirely in black, including a flat-
brimmed hat similar to Rafe's.

The young man's cool brown eyes swept over Rafe

with a sharp glance. "Don't I know you?" he demanded.

Rafe shrugged, his own gaze expressionless. "You might."

"Passin' through?"

"Maybe. Ain't decided."

"Want a job?"

Rafe sipped his drink and found that conversations had quieted while gazes focused on the two of them.

"Asked you a question, stranger."

"So you did."

"Well? You any good with that gun, mister?"

"Maybe." Rafe pushed aside his glass. He could smell the type of trouble coming his way.

"I'm hiring for a mining outfit. We'll pay well...very well."

"What outfit's that?"

"Ain't important." The kid's voice grew sharp. "I'm doing the hiring."

"Good for you."

Rafe saw his mouth tighten, and excitement light his brown eyes. He knew what he was going to hear before the eager, aggressive voice was raised in challenge.

"I don't like your answer. I don't like it at all."

Rafe looked at him, sized up the youth, then looked away. Every man found his own path to prove his manhood to others. He offered no remark to the challenge, but then, his cool gray-eyed look was enough.

"Fact is, mister, I don't like you."

Rafe's hand curled over the edge of the bar. He took his time answering. The other three men at the bar moved away. The bartender found a spot at the far end of the bar that required vigorous mopping. The whispered conversations abruptly ceased.

"You hear me, hombre? I don't like you."

"Does it really matter?" Rafe asked in a soft drawl.

Rafe could feel the young man staring at him. He heard the scrape of chairs pushed back and the shuffle of feet as men moved away from them, to get out of the line of any gunfire.

Rafe thought of his own feelings the first time he had been challenged by a man older and wiser. There had been an icy chill down his spine that night. He had felt fear that never quite left him. Only a stupid man never felt it. He had remembered his father's words when he first taught him to shoot. It wasn't always the one fastest to draw and shoot first that walked away.

It was the man who made his shots count.

His father had long been dead, and Rafe remembered thinking he had to fight or be branded a coward. He spared a quick look at the kid's darting eyes. Yeah, he was feeling the same sort of fear.

But he didn't back down.

"I figure it does matter, mister. I'll make it matter." His voice broke over the last words, but his hand hovered over his gun.

The onlookers sent their tension crawling through the saloon.

Rafe tipped his hat back and looked directly into the kid's eyes, and then he smiled. There was humor in his gaze, not mockery.

"Well, kid," Rafe said, in a soft but carrying voice, "don't shoot me now. I ain't finished my drink."

Rafe deliberately turned to face the bartender. He motioned with his left hand. "Top this one off, then I'll be leaving. I ate all the dust I wanted this morning."

Men started talking, in whispers at first, and then

their voices rose as cards were shuffled and bets made.

Rafe picked up his full glass of whiskey. The kid moved to the other end of the bar.

"Mister," the bartender said, "he don't know how lucky he is. I'm of a mind that this wasn't new to you. Ain't so many men so sure of themselves that they could step casually aside."

"I had nothing to prove to him or anyone," Rafe answered. He lifted his glass, and as he did, he saw a square-shouldered man, his buckskin jacket barely covering his barrel-shaped chest, slide from his chair and go out the back door.

If the hostility in the man's gaze had been a bullet, Rafe would be dead. He said nothing. He had walked this path before. A quick glance around the room told him no one else had paid any attention to the man leaving.

Rafe swallowed his drink, turned quietly and went outside. Some of those men in the saloon would say he'd backed down, while others, like the bartender, might realize that he had avoided a shooting.

The bartender, Ross Durvarey, rarely debated with himself, but he did so now. He had half ownership in the Red Horse, after a life of drifting over freight trails and mining camps when his stint as a quartermaster in the Union army was finished. He set a fresh drink in front of the kid.

"I've stayed alive by keeping out of other men's business," Ross said. "You're real lucky. That hombre rode out of an Apache attack today. Not many could say as much. He brought in his kid on a travois. So drink up. Man ought to celebrate another night of living."

Outside, Rafe had stepped to the side of the building, where no light from the windows touched him.

He waited for the barrel-chested man to claim his horse.

When minutes slipped by, Rafe realized he was not coming.

If his horse was not one of those tied at the hitching rails, the animal was in the livery, or hidden in one of the shallow washes outside of town. It was where he would have put his horse, ready for a hard ride, after dry-gulching a man.

Not that he had ever dry-gulched a man. He'd never shot one in the back, or fired at an unarmed man. But he was aware of the thin line dividing those who would not, and those who could and often did.

Rafe could not shake the feeling that the man had known him.

Or was it the kid who had earned that hostile look for failing to draw him into a gunfight?

Rafe figured close to the minute how long he had been gone. He wanted to track the man down—no easy task in the dark. But the rain would wash away his tracks.

Yet he had to give some thought to this being a ruse to draw him out.

And there was Beth to consider. If she called for him and he was not there, she would be afraid.

Or would she be?

Mary was there with her.

The thought of Mary with his daughter settled far too easily in his mind, with a rightness he did not question. He never trusted quickly, but that woman, with her sad, lovely eyes had broken his guard.

Rafe suddenly felt anxious to get to the woman and the child he had left. For all he knew, the kid could have delayed him while the man he waited for went hunting.

He came out of the protective shadows and went to his horse.

The drizzle had let up. Rafe quickly tightened the cinch.

"Hey, mister." The kid stepped out of the saloon.

Rafe lowered the saddle skirt. He didn't betray the tension running through him. He knew how bad his position was to get off a clean shot. Caught as he was between the horses, his right side to the street, he would have to lose seconds to turn and fire.

Seconds cost men their lives.

"You could've killed me," the kid said. "I should have known you were handy with a gun."

"Likely."

"Well? Why didn't you do it? I didn't read you right off. Guess I was too busy talking, when I should've been looking you over. Careless of me."

"I didn't come hunting trouble. Still don't want any. But I won't run from it."

"Ain't gonna have any from me. Just wanted to set things right betwixt us. You should know, a man in there earlier—" he hitched his thumb over his shoulder at the saloon doors "—he was asking questions if a man rode in with a kid. That you?"

"Could be."

"You don't give away much, do you?"

Rafe caught the grin on the kid's lips, and for a second fought his own.

"Sometimes it's safer that way."

"I'm Shell Lundy. If you ain't interested in fighting wages and you're hunting a cowhand's job, get yourself north of Socorro, to the Rafter D. Food's good, pay's thirty a month, and you keep one horse from the remuda you help break."

"Keep it in mind." The offer of a job would indicate that Shell Lundy didn't know who he was. Rafe thought about that. He stepped into the saddle. Time to make his decision. Turn and ride out, offering his back as a target, or sit there and wait for Shell to make the first move.

"Ain't never shot a man in the back," came Shell's soft declaration. "Never had to."

Shell knew when a man had someone hunting him. He would be leery of strangers, especially those men who attempted friendship.

Like him. But this man had already shown his hand. Shell started to turn toward the saloon doors, leaving his own back exposed.

"Mister, you never said your name."

"McCade. Rafe McCade."

"McCade? Why, you're—" Shell stopped and spun around.

Rafe set his heels to the horse and rode hard on the road south of town.

Shell thumbed his hat back. He wasn't sure if he should give way to the laughter bubbling inside him or the rumble of fear that twisted his gut.

Shell stood there, his thoughts racing. He could ride out and hunt up the very job he had offered McCade. He could walk away.

"Loco fool," he whispered under his breath.

No one had told him the man's name, only where to find him. Rafe McCade owned a piece of the Cañon del Agua mine.

But where did Shell draw the line? He had accepted fighting wages, and a bonus on the side from the man's partners. Some of the money came from McCade's pocket, and McCade was the man he'd been hired to kill.

Chapter Ten

Yesterday's promised storm broke across the land. The rumbles of thunder rattled the windowpanes in Mary's room.

Mary stood watching the storm, and thought of the old Indian woman who had helped her around the house. Storms like this one brought forth the Apache saying that the Thunder People thudded their drums in the canyons and along the dark hills.

Eerie sheet lightning flickered bluish tongues of light against the blackened sky. The sight struck a wild responding chord within Mary.

A harsh wind had risen before the dawn, and brought with it blinding curtains of rain that swept the county with a liquid broom, from the Black Range eastward toward the Rio Grande, in successive blanketing gusts that filled the watercourses brim-full and then flowed over their banks.

Earlier, when she went down to the kitchen to replenish Beth's tea, she could barely make out the looming dark mass of their barn. Streams of water poured from the roof of the barn and the house. The yard was one big mud hole, and the lower half of the pasture always flooded.

She worried. Sarah and Catherine were still out in the storm. They had gone to bring the horses to shelter in the barn and move their few head of cattle into the corral, where the two-sided shed offered the animals some protection.

Mary rubbed her arms. Despite the woolen shawl wrapped around her, she was chilled from her own foray into the rain.

After she made tea and another pot of coffee, she had mixed a batch of biscuits. While they baked, she thought of Beth and the others needing something warm to eat. It prompted her to shred the leftover stew meat and vegetables and add beans and water to the pot. She soon had the hearty soup simmering on the wood stove.

She had learned to make do with every scrap of food, for Harry had been a tightfisted man with his money. He had never heard of taking food to sickly neighbors, and when he did, he had forbidden her to do it. Acts of charity had been as foreign to Harry's nature as they were familiar to Mary.

How could she have been so blind?

She dismissed the question, and thought instead of stretching the soup to feed a hungry man.

A few feet from the back door stood her garden. There were still carrots and onions in plentiful supply, and the herbs planted between the spokes of the old wagon wheels she had found. Adding those and dumplings would provide hearty fare for them all.

But her slicker proved to be little protection from the wind and slashing rain as she snipped herbs, bent low, and pulled root vegetables from thick mud. The fernlike leaves of chamomile were nearly buried as she replenished her supply for Beth's tea.

With her shoes covered in mud and water seeping

into the leather, she cut parsley, rosemary and dill, then took the last of the chili peppers for the soup.

She had left her shoes drying by the wood stove after stuffing them with the smallest lengths of kindling to prevent them from shrinking.

Drinking the last of her coffee, Mary glanced at the pallet where Rafe slept at the foot of the bed. He had refused to use the spare room, where Sarah had fixed the cot for him.

Rafe insisted on remaining near his daughter.

Mary stayed near the window. She did not want to wake him. His rest was as well deserved as his child's. Rafe had remained awake most of the night with her to help bathe Beth and keep her fever down.

Mary was unaware of the softening of her mouth and her gaze as she looked at Beth. She still held the topsy-turvy doll. Her cheeks held a fever flush, but the tea appeared to be working. The child no longer tossed restlessly and whimpered in her sleep.

Despite Mary's best intention not to do it, her gaze strayed back to Rafe.

He had not said a word about what news, if any, he had heard in town. She was sure that if there was danger to any of them, Rafe would have said so.

She was not certain where the thought that she was right had come from. Saying as much aloud would sound foolish. How could she know what another person would do or think on such short acquaintance?

After all, she reminded herself, what did she really know about Rafe?

He was gentle with his child. Tender and patient by turns. A man unashamed to reveal, by act and word, his love for his daughter.

This in a time when men set great store by the sons who would carry on after them.

She could almost envy the child.

Sleep did nothing to soften the strong, clean-cut lines of his handsome features. The dark growth of beard stubble intensified the impression of Rafe being a lone wolf.

He lay on his back, his left hand flung above his head. Earlier she had drawn the blanket up to his shoulders, but now it was pushed down to his hips.

On his right side, she saw his gun in its holster.

Even asleep, his right hand lay only inches from the butt.

Mary hesitated, then stepped closer. What was there about this man that drew her? She didn't know. Even in sleep, he appeared coiled tight as a bull-whacker's whip and just as ready to lash out.

She found herself looking at the back of her hand. The image of Rafe holding it, then pressing his lips against her flesh, rose in her mind. The heated touch of his lips had lingered long after he left her last night.

Looking at his hard, lean, muscled body aroused every feminine nerve.

It was too long since she had been held and kissed, since she had felt the quickening excitement of making love.

Shocked at her thoughts, Mary raised her hand to her cheek. Such shameful musings.

Shameful? Why should she condemn herself? She had needs, too.

She couldn't forget his kiss, or the few moments when her body had betrayed her.

And he had been aware of her reaction to him.

What would happen to her with his prolonged stay?

The mere thought was unsettling. But it couldn't stop her from imagining what his lips would feel like against her own.

What was wrong with her? She had met a few nice men in town. One had appeared interested in coming to call on her. Mary had discouraged him. She had never speculated about his kisses.

The sound of the back door slamming closed carried up the stairs. Her hand fell with guilty haste from her cheek to her heart.

She looked over her shoulder at the empty doorway. When she looked back, she found Rafe's penetrating gray eyes watching her.

"You're awake."

"Lord, I needed to hear your confirmation. For a minute there, I thought I was still dreaming. You're the prettiest sight I've awakened to in a long time. Pity if you weren't real."

It wasn't a lie. Her hair was softly pulled back from her delicate, cameolike features. The high neckline of her pale blue gown emphasized her slender neck.

The look in her eyes, radiant with sensuality and speculation, was enough for him to think of what it would be like to get beneath the buttons and cloth, to the sultry feminine flesh hidden from sight.

"Like I said, real pretty."

Gritty with sleep, his voice washed through her. The frank male appreciation trailed heat in its wake.

Mary couldn't respond. She wouldn't dare allow herself to think he meant a word of it.

But Rafe was waiting for her to say something.

"It's a wonder you slept at all on the floor. You couldn't have been comfortable. You should have taken the spare room across the hall."

"Bed's dry. Roof's snug against the rain. Smells like spring in here. And I've slept on harder places without half the comfort."

The look in his eyes wasn't hard. If anything, it was soft and heated. She admonished herself. Most likely it was a trick of the dim light.

But she could not pull her gaze from his, or think of one sensible thing to say to put him in his place.

"It's storming outside," she blurted out, motioning toward the window. *Mary, what is wrong with you? He can hear the rain for himself.*

The corner of Rafe's mouth kicked up. "It's not the only one. Or am I alone in feeling there's a storm every bit as strong brewing in here?"

Warmth shimmered and spread inside her, sending a sizzle through her blood strong enough to curl her stocking-clad toes.

"I am sure," she said, pulling her shawl tighter around her, "I don't know what you're talking about."

Rafe's grin became a full-fledged smile. "That coffee for me?"

Mary was so rattled it took her a few seconds to understand his gesture toward the empty cup she still held.

She shook her head. The spare motion sent her thick single braid sliding across the cloth covering her suddenly sensitive skin.

Wind sent rain beating against the windows. All Mary heard was the pounding of her heart and the mingled sounds of their breathing. All she could feel was the heat of his gaze.

The room seemed to shrink around them, as if they were the only two people there.

It could have lasted for seconds or minutes. Mary was not sure. With a start, she drew one deep, ragged breath, released it, then repeated the simple act to break the sensual snare surrounding her.

"I'll…" Her mouth was so dry she had to swallow a few times. "I'll fetch your coffee. Breakfast, too," she added. She backed away from him toward the door.

"Mary, wait."

Just the sound of her name spoken in his black-velvet voice stopped her flight.

"I don't want you waiting on me." He propped himself up on one elbow. "I never meant to sleep so long. How is—"

"You're exhausted. You needed the sleep. And you seem to forget that you were wounded. I'd like to—" *Touch you.* "You should let someone look at those wounds."

It would be so easy to ask her to touch him. He could imagine those lovely hands on his skin.

Abruptly Rafe looked away from her. "Just skin scratches. Nothing for you to worry about. I've had worse. But tell me, how is Beth doing?"

"Still sleeping. More comfortably, I believe. I've already changed her bandage. There's swelling and redness, but nothing more to indicate that infection has set in. It is still too soon for you to consider moving her."

Mary reminded him of the brown tabby he had discovered protecting her litter in the hayloft of the barn. All hiss and spit, ready to defend her own against a larger adversary.

Mary was not hissing or spitting at him. Not one bared claw in sight. But the tigerish light in her green eyes and the firm conviction in her voice warned of the fight he might have if he attempted to move his daughter before Mary thought the time was right.

If he had not been so touched by the depth of her caring for his lonely, wounded child, Rafe might have laughed.

Mary's fragile appearance was like that of one of the kittens. Fragile-looking, yes, but brave nonetheless. He hunkered down, hand extended to the kitten. He talked softly. Curiosity had drawn the kitten from the protection of his mama. Then, ears flat, the kitten had dared him to touch.

Out of respect for the tiny animal's courage, Rafe had backed away.

Mary deserved nothing less, but all he could do was to allow the intense arousal she caused to retreat before she became aware of it.

"Mary, I wasn't going to ask you about moving her."

"Yesterday, you couldn't wait—"

"Yesterday is gone, Mary. I can't go back and undo what's past." Rafe winced as he shifted his weight and felt the pull on his wounds.

"If I could go back, I'd know who was behind that attack. I'd know what I'd done to make someone hate me so much that they'd kill my child, too.

"No excuses. Guess I was more tired than I could admit to you or myself when I asked that foolish question about moving Beth."

"It wasn't foolish. I could see you only wanted your daughter to be safe."

"You do a little thought reading of your own? That was exactly what I wanted. Still do. I can keep Beth from any harm at my home. And I don't want the trouble that's dogging me to follow me here. I don't need another death on my conscience."

An odd look went over Rafe's face. Mary saw it as a shadow that she named grief. She wondered if he spoke of his wife's death.

Had Rafe somehow been responsible?

In the next breath, Mary recalled his hard, cold voice answering her few questions about Beth's mother. She thought then that her feeling of envy for the woman had been misplaced.

"No, Mary. I didn't kill my wife. For what she did to our child, I could have. But I didn't."

"I wasn't accusing you!"

"Weren't you?"

"No. I—"

"Papa?"

Beth's weak voice ended Mary's attempt to explain.

"He's right here, lamb. And I'll be back in a bit with some warm soup for you."

"And coffee for me?" Rafe asked, already at his daughter's side. "We're a matched pair, Beth and I."

Mary flung back her head and shot him a defiant look. "Don't remind me."

But she hurried away, still wanting the child and still very much afraid to want the man.

Chapter Eleven

"Tell me more," Beth pleaded.

Rafe, seated on the rocking chair, cuddled Beth closer. He was running out of stories suitable for a child's ears. He looked at Mary, who was busy changing the sheets on the bed. She nodded encouragement for him to continue.

"All right, one more. There was a white man who traded with the Sioux. Many of the Indians warned him to stop his cheating ways, but he wouldn't listen to them. One day, this trader was told there was someone who could cheat better than him. The trader didn't believe it. He demanded to see who it was.

"The Sioux at his store brought him outside and pointed to Coyote. Him, they said. He is a tricky-looking one. The trader thought he was the best cheater of all and went to talk to Coyote. The Sioux say you can outsmart me. Let me see you try. Well, Coyote told him he couldn't outsmart him. He didn't have his cheating medicine with him.

"Now the trader was excited. He wanted to be named the best cheater of all. He told Coyote to get his medicine. But Coyote said that he lived too far and had no horse. He asked if the trader would lend him his horse. And the trader agreed.

"Then Coyote said that the horse was afraid of him. If he had the trader's clothes, the horse would think Coyote was his owner and let him ride swiftly home. And once again the trader agreed. He was so sure he could beat Coyote's cheating medicine."

Rafe was distracted by a muffled sound. He glanced at Mary. She held her hand to her mouth. He grinned, then finished the story.

"Well, there the trader stood in his union suit, while Coyote made off with his clothes and his horse. There's a lesson here for—"

"Mustn't cheat, Papa?"

"That's right." Rafe smoothed back her hair. "Mustn't be greedy, either."

"Tell me more."

"Beth, honey, your tea's cool enough to drink." Mary saw the shadows beneath Rafe's eyes, heard the hoarseness of his voice. He'd been telling Beth stories for almost two hours, ever since they finished supper.

Rafe had begun with deeds of valor performed by mountain men and traders. Mary had enjoyed listening to those, but he had a talent for spinning an enchanted web when telling fables that taught a moral value. And the teaching had continued with the Indian tales.

Mary turned down the top sheet. She admitted to herself that she loved listening to his voice. Had the circumstances been different, she would have added her plea for him to continue to Beth's.

Just being with the two of them sent pleasure seeping inside her. She could pretend they were hers to care for, love and protect. It harmed no one. She would not make the mistake of thinking any of it was real.

But her pleasure was tainted with worry. Beth's eyes glistened with a rising fever.

Her gaze met Rafe's, and she saw that he shared her concern.

Beth wore the camisole Mary had altered to fit her as a nightgown. She cradled the soft cloth doll in the curve of her unwounded arm. Despite her plea for one more tale, the child's body remained listless in Rafe's arms.

"First you drink your tea, love. I'll tell one more, then into bed with you."

Mary, cup in hand, came to kneel by the rocker. She waited as Rafe gently cupped Beth's neck to lift her up so that she could drink. The effort proved beyond the child.

"I'll get a spoon." Mary rose to her feet. She ran the back of her hand over Beth's cheek. Once more she thought Rafe communicated a silent message for her to hurry. She felt the same need.

Although the fury of the storm had lessened, the rain continued unabated throughout the day. The house held pockets of warmth as Mary raced downstairs.

The kitchen was the warmest room, and there she found Sarah and Catherine working. Sarah was leaning over the table, the household accounts occupying her attention. Catherine was struggling to clean her boots.

"How is she?" the two of them asked at the same time.

"Weak. I came down for a spoon. Poor little love, she can't drink from the cup. And the fever's rising again."

"Mary, why not let one of us watch over her tonight?" Sarah suggested. It was not what she had intended to say to her cousin. True, Mary's eyes held shadows from too little rest, but she worried more that her cousin's heart had already been lost to the child. She knew she would hear a refusal of her suggestion. Mary didn't disappoint her.

"No. I want—"

"Sarah's right," Catherine said. She put aside her boots. "You should look at yourself, Mary."

"Getting the child well is all that matters, not my appearance."

Mary turned her back toward them to get a spoon from the cupboard. Sarah laid a hand over Catherine's arm. She warned her with a quick shake of her head not to press Mary.

Before she left the kitchen Mary checked the coffeepot. There wasn't much left.

"Go on up, Mary. I'll make a fresh pot and bring it upstairs."

"That's good of you, Sarah." At the doorway Mary paused, then turned to face them.

"I know you both think I'm being foolish to care so much, but I can't help myself. Since I'm the oldest, I'm perfectly capable of making my own decisions. And my own mistakes," she added in a whisper, and left them.

Catherine felt Mary had struck too close to her own thoughts. She loved finally having independence and would fight tooth and nail if anyone dared to try and curtail it. Glancing at Sarah, she couldn't help wondering what thoughts were hidden within her dark eyes.

"She may be older than you or I, Sarah, but I worry that Mary will be hurt. She's so wrapped up in that child. Rafe's going to leave and take his daughter with him. What will she do then?"

"Mary? She'll go on making a new life for herself.

Just as you and I are. But I admit I've never seen her so possessive about anyone or anything.''

"Do you remember when we used to play and Mary pretended she had a houseful of children? At least a dozen. She'd make a wonderful mother, too.''

Catherine picked up her boot and the rag spotted with bootblack. "Wouldn't it be wonderful if Mary could find a widower with a brood of children? Or,'' she added with a sly smile, "if Rafe fell in love with her?''

"Catherine! Get that dreamy look gone. My cousin may want a child, or a brood, as you said. Mary doesn't want another marriage. I don't know all the details of what Harry did to her, but he stole my cousin's laughter, and her spirit. What's more, the devil take him if he wasn't already dead, he made Mary believe that no man would ever want her.''

"You knew that and never told me?''

"There was no reason to. Besides, Rafe has enough trouble on his hands without taking on Mary's problems. You would be wise to let the matter die here and now.''

"He's handsome as sin, and he's a kindly man, too.''

"Enough, Catherine. You can't go about ordering people to fall in love because you think they'd make a good pair.''

"Oh, all right, I'll stop. But even you can't deny there's a tension between them. Have you seen the way he watches her? And Mary? My goodness, Sarah, you'd need to be blind not to see the longing in her eyes. Cooped up in her room, why, who knows what can happen?''

Sarah tossed her pencil down and folded her arms across her chest. "May I remind you, that there is a child up there with them?''

Catherine leaned forward. She smiled. "Yes, I know. And what stronger bond could there be to bring two people together?"

"I give up. You keep your fanciful thoughts to yourself. I've got work to do."

"Sarah, don't you ever get lonely? I mean sometimes, at night, don't you wish there was someone holding you?"

"Like a man?"

"Well, we're a little too old to want Mama's arms. Of course I meant a man."

"No."

"You don't!"

"That's what I said."

"Well, I do. I miss Louis. Well, that's not exactly true. I miss his visiting my bed. Don't you miss—"

"No. I like sleeping alone."

"Did you love Judd so much that no one can replace him?"

But Sarah had already bent her head over her accounts.

"It was a silly question, Sarah. Please, forgive me. I know you loved Judd, or you wouldn't have married him. Tell you what. I'll make the coffee for Rafe and Mary while you finish your accounts."

She had to be satisfied with Sarah's curt nod. But as she waited for the water to boil, Catherine's gaze strayed to the ceiling. Her thoughts were rich with possibilities for Rafe and Mary.

Long after midnight, Mary woke with a start. She soon realized she was lying on the pallet she had made for Rafe, without any idea of how she had got there.

The last thing she remembered was sitting near the head of the bed after bathing Beth's fevered little body. She must have fallen asleep there, and Rafe had moved her. The catnap had done little to relieve her exhaustion.

From the glow against the wall, she knew a fresh candle had been lit. Then she heard Rafe's voice as he whispered to his fretful child.

"And when you're better, Beth, I'll take you up to the magic lake where the Indians claim the bluebird got his color. The one where Coyote, too, turned a beautiful shade of blue, but then fell into the dirt and became so dust-covered, he remains brown to this day.

"I'll buy you the prettiest and sturdiest mountain pony. We'll ride the mountain trails where no one else has ever gone. Just get well, baby. Fight this fever. Come on, try and drink a little more for me. That's my girl. I love you, Beth. Remember that. I've always loved you."

Rafe said more in the same vein, and told another Indian tale. His husky voice soft as a murmur as he pleaded with his daughter to respond.

Listening to him, Mary felt herself an intruder, for Rafe was a man intent on baring his soul to that little girl.

It was wrong of Mary not to make some noise, to make some effort to alert him that she was awake to hear his every word.

She asked the Lord's forgiveness for her silence.

"From the first I couldn't believe we'd been blessed with a child. I'd rush from the diggings to get back to our cabin every night, just to hear about the storm you had kicked up while I was gone. The first time I felt you move, Beth, I thought an angel's wing touched me.

"When we get home, you'll see the cradle I began that very night. Sometimes I'd stop working and just

think about you. What you'd look like, what I'd do.
I never knew a man could hold so much happiness
without bursting from the sheer joy of it.

"Toward the end, I hated to go to the mine claim
I had staked. But it was all we had. Every day I went
off with a fear that you'd come along and I wouldn't
be there. Lord, baby, that was a hair-raising, heart-
thumping night. But when that sun came up, there you
came into my waiting hands."

Mary filled in what Rafe left unsaid. A lonely
cabin, no doctor, no other women around to help. But
Rafe had been there, eager to be with his wife as she
labored to birth their child.

Was it then that Mary's tears began? She wasn't
sure. It could have happened seconds later, when the
hushed quality of Rafe's voice told of holding his
tiny, squalling daughter in his hands. Of his own
breathless wonder as she took her first breath of life
and he saw with new eyes the very lovely miracle
that was his daughter.

"I held you, Beth. Your head was no bigger than
my palm. Red-faced, your eyes squeezed closed, a bit
of a nose, and your small pink mouth crying out that
you had arrived. I can still see those small fingers
curled tight and remember swearing that I'd always
be there to fight your battles for you.

"But that's when I got scared, Beth. I've faced
armed men with no more than a shovel in hand, but
nothing scared me as much as you. I felt so big and
clumsy handling your fragile body. Even when you
were wrapped up tight in your blanket. I wanted the
very best of everything for you, baby.

"And I wanted to be everything I wasn't—patient
and gentle, wise and kind, strong and rich. So much.
Maybe too much. But I looked at you, and I wondered

why I had ever thought I knew how to be a father, a good father.

"You humbled me, Beth. Humbled me and filled me with all the love I'd never given to anyone else."

Mary had to cover her mouth with her hand to still the sob that built inside her. Rafe was pouring out his heart. She had known from the first how much he loved Beth, but she hadn't fully understood the depth of his love.

"Ah, Beth, that fear never left me. I'd get up during the night to stand by your cradle and watch you sleep. All that time, I was questioning myself. How was I going to learn to be what you needed? Where would the knowledge come from to teach you the things that really matter? What if I failed you? What if all the love I had for you wasn't enough?

"Oh, but you were a beautiful baby, Beth. The first time you smiled at me I thought my heart turned over. It was a gift every time. Pretty brown curls, bright eyes, rosy cheeks and those toothless smiles. I treasured every image of you from that first year. Sometimes it was all that kept me going after you were gone.

"And it wasn't true, Beth, that I didn't want you. I didn't want to let you go. But I couldn't stop her from taking you away. I once thought it was because I couldn't give her much in those days and she was afraid of living in a lonely place.

"But let the Lord stand as my witness, Beth. Losing you was losing the best piece of myself."

Mary felt the hot sting of tears slide down her cheeks. Twice she heard Rafe's voice break, as if he were having a hard time holding back tears of his own.

What you're doing is wicked. Lying here, eaves-

dropping on what you have no business hearing. No business knowing.

But she didn't move. Didn't utter a sound.

"I'll never leave you again, Beth. I'll never let anyone take you away from me, either. But you have to help by fighting this fever so that doesn't happen. I've prayed so hard for you to get well, baby, that the words are all running together in my mind.

"I'll deal with the devil if I can see you smile."

Oh, Lord, help him. Help us all. Mary bit down on her knuckle. Her listening had become a violation of Rafe's most private thoughts and feelings. She cringed inwardly at the thought of alerting him now. Somehow, that seemed a worse violation.

What was she to do?

His desperate murmuring ceased for a few moments.

Mary strained to hear what he was doing. The sound was water dripping into the bucket. He was bathing Beth again.

"Hush, baby. I know it feels cold. And I'm not as gentle as Mary doing this. Your poor little body is so hot. But let me, love. It will help.

"What we need from the Lord is an angel. No. We already have one to help us. That's how scattered my thoughts are, Beth. That Mary's a lovely warrior angel, armed with so much compassion that she'd take your pain and fever and make them her own if she could.

"That's powerful medicine right there, love. You've got me and Mary ready to fight this battle right along with you. Only...only it's not...not up to us."

The creak of the rope spring beneath the feather tick mattress muffled Rafe's last words, and the sounds that followed.

Mary tried to stop crying. She rubbed her hands over her eyes, but couldn't control the tears. What should she do? What *could* she do?

The yearning to go to Rafe and gather him and his child into her arms was an ache that grew in intensity.

But then Rafe would know she had heard him.

They needed her. She couldn't pretend to be asleep when that need reached out and touched her.

She lay there no more than a minute before she gave in to the intuitive beckoning. She cast aside her blanket and stood up.

Candlelight gilded the dark thickness of Rafe's hair where his head bent towards the pristine whiteness of the pillow. She saw that his shoulders were shaking, and at first she thought it was a trick of the wavering light.

The faintest sounds gave her to understand that it was more. So much more.

She hesitated. This was beyond her capabilities. She had never seen a man express heart-wrenching emotion. The sight stirred her soul as no words ever could have.

Rafe named her a warrior angel. Mary had never felt less adequate to bear the title. Her store of healing skills was so small when measured against the need in this room.

Mary had once thought herself broken, and had fought to pick up the pieces and make herself whole once more. She had to find some way to keep Rafe whole. And that meant racking her mind for something, anything, she could do, for the sight of this man and his helpless child tore at her.

Her stocking feet made no sound as she glided closer to Rafe's kneeling body. Her hand hovered above his shoulder. Then, with a resolution coming from deep inside, she lowered her hand to touch him.

"Rafe? Rafe, listen to me. There's one thing I...I haven't tried. Do you hear me? We still have hope to break Beth's fever."

If he had jumped up and roared with fury at her, Mary could not have been more shocked than she was by the deathlike stillness that permeated his body.

Rafe called her compassionate. But while that well of compassion overflowed, it was something stronger, a feeling she would not name, that drew her hand to slide into his hair.

And the feeling that she would not give a name to urged both her touch and her voice to caress.

"Rafe? You're not alone. Please. I—"

"I woke you."

Whatever Mary expected, it was not to hear a mixture of resignation and accusation in his husky voice.

To deny it would be to lie to herself, as well as to Rafe.

"Yes. I...heard you."

"Then you know Beth's burning up. Tell me, Mary, what you have in your bag of tricks to help her now."

The bite of his mockery hurt her. Mary let it pass. She couldn't let him matter—only Beth.

"Down on the side of the house we have rain barrels. I want to take Beth there and immerse her."

"She's shaking from the chills and fever."

Mary let her hand fall away from his hair to her side. His voice chilled her. "I won't lie to you. I've done what I can. This is all I can think of. You trusted—"

"Trusted? Yeah, I trusted you."

He came to his feet in a controlled rush.

Mary hated herself for doing it, but she backed up a step, then took another, before she stood her ground.

Rafe was bathed in shadow. Dark. Dangerous. His

overpowering masculine anger blanketed the very air they were breathing.

"Are you drunk from lack of sleep?" he demanded. "It can happen. I've seen it."

"No. I think it would work."

"You think? What you propose to do could very well kill her."

"And if I'm right, Rafe," she answered, as calmly as she could, "this might break the fever and save her life."

He moved so quickly that Mary didn't have time to evade him. His fingers bit into her upper arms as he hauled her against his body.

"How did such a fragile-looking woman get so strong-minded?"

"Someone tried to break me once."

"And?"

"And I found I don't break."

"That's damn good to know. 'Cause the way you cloud a man's senses when he should be thinking of other things can make him forget how soft a woman you really are."

Mary tilted her head back. She stared up at him. All she could see, all she could feel, was the burning heat of his gaze.

Not a sound of protest at his tight grip passed her lips. She bore with his threatening dark visage, not as a sacrificial lamb—that was a role she refused to play—but as the compassionate woman Rafe named her, who understood the true source of his anger.

"You're wasting precious time, Rafe." The reminder helped Mary distance herself from the aching need to slide her arms around him and hold him close.

He lowered his head. Her breath caught. But it wasn't to kiss her. When he spoke, his words whispered across her mouth.

"And what if you're wrong, Mary?"

Despite the sudden trembling that beset her, she found the courage to answer him.

"I'm not. I can't be wrong. Besides, the Lord doesn't need Beth. You do."

Chapter Twelve

Rafe reluctantly let her go. "Tell me what you want done."

"Carry Beth. I'll bring the blanket and quilt. We'll need them afterward." Mary picked up the candle and led the way from her room.

Out of the dark hall came Catherine's whisper. "Rafe, what is going on?"

Mary was poised at the top of the stairway, and she turned, allowing the candlelight to spill on her night-gown-clad friend and the gun she held.

"There's no need for that, Catherine."

"Blame Rafe. He's the one who told me to sleep with it handy. Now, where the devil are you two going with Beth?"

When Mary didn't answer, Rafe did. "Mary has an idea how to break Beth's fever."

"And we are wasting time. Catherine, since you're awake, please come down and stoke the stove fire. We'll need heat, and coffee."

Mary went down the stairs quickly, and was around the newel post on her way to the back hall when she heard Sarah's sleepy query. Catherine was the one who answered her. Mary didn't pay them attention. She was praying.

By the time Rafe walked into the kitchen, Mary had her stockings off and was working on the buttons of her gown's bodice.

"What are you doing?"

Mary ignored him. This was no time for modesty. The bodice joined her stockings on the back of the chair. She went to work loosening the tapes holding her skirt and petticoats around her waist.

"Damn it! Answer me!"

"I can't put Beth in the barrel alone. I don't want to get her bandage wet if I can help it. Satisfied?"

"Don't snap at me. This whole idea is crazy." *Satisfied?* When hell froze, he might be. Did she have any notion of what she looked like by candlelight? Not that she cared that he was a witness. But it was a provoking sight to see her fiery dark hair tumbling over pale skin and the skimpy bit of cloth stretching over her breasts.

"Hell," he muttered, annoyed with himself for noticing her soft curves, her small waist, and the gentle flare of her hips. Annoyance gave way to anger. She was thoughtlessly doing what he had accused her of— clouding his senses just by being near, by simply breathing the same air as he.

"You agreed with me upstairs, Rafe."

Mary kept her gaze averted from him. She had the foresight to place the candle on the dry sink, leaving her out of the pool of light. But Rafe would have to be blind not to see her. Just the thought sent heat beneath her skin when she stood shivering in her camisole and drawers. The oft-washed cotton was thin as cheesecloth.

Then Mary looked at Beth. Her head lolled over Rafe's arm. Her skin was pale, but her cheeks were mantled with fever and her body was racked with chills.

Mary's embarrassment disappeared. She snatched up the rolled quilt and blanket and opened the back door.

"Better take the lantern with you, Mary."

"No." Rafe answered Catherine, who entered the kitchen. "We don't want to be a target if someone is watching the house."

"Like fish caught in a barrel. Lord, forgive that. I'm not really awake, Rafe. But what makes you think anyone's watching the house? What kind of enemies do you have?"

Rafe didn't answer. He followed Mary outside.

"We don't have to worry about rattlesnakes. We check the side of the house every day." Mary drew in a deep breath, for the air was bracingly cool after the relative warmth of the house. The scent was clean with a newly washed fragrance from the soapberry bushes planted as a screen around the barrels at the corner of the house. The tops of the large barrels reached Mary's chest. She lifted a small three-legged stool from its nail in the clapboard and placed it against the first barrel. She leaned over and pressed hard to anchor the stool in the muddy earth.

"I'll climb in. Then you hand me Beth."

"No. Drape the blankets over my shoulder and take Beth. I'll help you in."

Mary couldn't argue. She had to clench her jaw to stop her teeth from clattering.

But when she held Beth, she forgot the cold. "Sweetie…" she whispered, tucking one small arm beneath her own to angle the child's body so that her wounded shoulder wouldn't get wet.

"Ready?"

"Y-yes." For a moment, Mary closed her eyes

against the heat of Rafe's hands settling on her waist. The thin cloth offered no protection from the strength of his fingers as he lifted her. She bit her lip when her bare feet took the first shock of the icy rainwater. In her arms, Beth's body went rigid, her cry breaking the night as Mary immersed them into the water.

"How long?" Rafe asked.

"A f-few…min-minutes."

Mary had to hold Beth tight. The child thrashed in her arms. She struggled to keep as much of Beth's body as she could beneath the water. The child's cries faded to pitiful whimpers. The sounds tore at Mary, but she forced herself to remain firm in her conviction that they needed to remain a little longer.

"About two minutes gone," Rafe said.

"M-more."

"You're freezing." When she didn't answer him, Rafe ordered her to get out.

"A l-little m-more."

"You sure know how to make a man feel as helpless as a cow caught in a mudhole." But he bowed to her judgment and waited.

If Rafe had not been beset with worry, he might have realized he wasn't waiting alone.

Out beyond the cottonwoods near the pasture fence, Shell Lundy grabbed hold of the rifle from the man he had knocked out with his gun butt. He didn't hold with dry-gulching, or back-shooting a man, and he damn well wasn't killing a kid and a woman. He rolled the man over, stuck the rifle barrel down his pants and grabbed hold of his shoulders to drag him back and away.

Shell was so furious at not having been told all the facts before he had accepted the bonus money to kill McCade that he wasn't thinking about the tracks he left behind.

He just wanted to get off by himself and think this job through before he proceeded.

Back by the barrels, Rafe figured he'd waited long enough. He was about to haul Mary and his daughter out when her shaken whisper came.

"N-now."

Mary could barely manage to stand. Rafe took Beth from her into his quilt-draped arms.

"Can you get out by yourself?"

"Go."

"Blanket's on the nail. Give me your hand."

"J-just...go."

His daughter needed him to get dry and warm. Mary needed help, too. He couldn't rush into the house and leave her. Beth shook in his arms, her cries reduced to mewling noises. Mary struggled to get out of the barrel. He heard the audible click of her teeth as her pale hands slipped off the barrel's rim each time she attempted to lift herself up and out.

"G-go," she repeated.

Rafe shifted Beth's quilt-wrapped weight to his shoulder and held her there with one arm. He dipped the other into the water, grabbed hold of Mary around her waist and hauled her over the rim.

He held her tight for a moment, then let her body slide down the side of his until her bare feet touched the ground.

Rafe snatched the blanket from the nail, clumsily wrapping it around her shivering body, then slipped his arm around her shoulders. He was drenched from the water and the press of icy bodies by the time he got them all inside.

"Get Mary whiskey or brandy, whatever you have," Rafe ordered Catherine. He hooked the bottom rung of the chair with his boot to pull it away from the table. With his hand he pushed Mary on the seat.

"There's no liquor in the house," Sarah answered. "I don't allow it. But the coffee's good and hot."

"I'll get it for Mary. You get Rafe and Beth upstairs and out of those wet things."

Mary barely heard Catherine. She didn't see Rafe leave with Sarah. She could hardly help Catherine strip off her soaked undergarments or use the heated towels to dry herself.

Mary thought she would never be warm again. But once she had put on the nightgown, stockings and thick woolen shawl that Catherine thoughtfully heated on the stove, the feelings returned to her near-frozen limbs.

"Where did you get such a hare-brained notion from, Mary? I never heard the like of what you did to Beth."

"I did. Truth to tell. Once."

"Did it work?"

Mary didn't answer her question. "I need to go upstairs. I want to be with Beth."

"Mary, you've done all you can."

"No. I can still pray."

Mary met Sarah on the stairs. "I was just bringing this quilt down to dry. See if you can get Rafe to change. I put a pair of pants and a shirt of Judd's on my bed for him. They should fit."

Mary merely nodded and started to pass her, but Sarah caught hold of her arm.

"You're not alone. We'll do what we can to help."

"I need to be with her, Sarah. Don't ask me to explain. I can't."

Mary came to kneel beside Rafe. Sarah had piled quilts and blankets on top of Beth, but Mary felt the child's shivering when she slipped her hand beneath the coverings.

She sought Beth's hand and covered it with her own. If she could, she would impart her strength to this child who had woven her way into her heart.

Rafe's breathing kept cadence with hers. Then his hand, larger and warmer, enfolded theirs.

"Go change," Mary whispered.

"She's been so quiet since Sarah gave her a little more tea."

"You won't do Beth or yourself any good if you get sick. Sarah left clothes—"

"Yes. She told me. Can't you understand that I don't want to leave her?"

I understand so well that I ache for you. The words remained unsaid.

"I have no pride. All I can do is beg the Lord to let her live. I'll give everything I own."

"I'll pray every bit as hard for both of us while you're changing." Mary leaned against him, her head touching his shoulder, offering a silent message that he wasn't alone.

Rafe's fingers tightened over hers. "Mary, what I said before, I didn't mean—"

"Later. There'll be time enough for talking. Go on. I'm here with her."

She looked at him. Tears shimmered in her green eyes.

Rafe didn't think it strange that he wanted to brush a tear from the corner of Mary's eye, or that he should bring it to his lips. He didn't question where the strength to leave his daughter—however briefly—came from. After all, he had Mary's assurance that she would be there watching over Beth.

After he returned to Mary's room, it seemed right

that she should lean on him as much as she had supported him through these trying hours.

Together they held Beth when the chills racked her body. In tandem they bathed her yet again, and spooned both the tea and the broth that Sarah supplied into the child.

They prayed together, sometimes aloud, sometimes in silence. And the act seemed right again.

Rafe watched her as much as he watched his daughter. Mary never lost her patience, no matter how exhausted she grew. She never flagged in her belief that Beth's fever would break. Her voice, murmuring or humming some soft tune, soothed his frayed nerves and calmed his restless child.

His admiration for Mary grew when she made no move to force a discussion about what she had heard earlier in the room. Admiration, and something more that he refused to name.

Her gaze, meeting his, offered constant hope. Her touch was both comforting and encouraging. And he found himself wondering if she felt the bond that had formed between them.

Mary had never known she could be so sensitive to another's needs and moods. The night stretched endlessly, yet she was helpless to stop the rich strands that wove a bond around her heart. Rafe was restless, as she was, but he never became impatient with the repetition Beth's care demanded.

Each time her gaze met his, she took courage from his silent look. His unshakable belief, now that the ice bath was over, fed her own. His very presence lent her strength and calmed her when she felt despair.

His strength combined with gentleness forced her to remember past dreams. And she wondered if he felt the bond forming between them.

Catherine and Sarah were ghostly presences coming and going throughout their vigil, offering a touch, a word of comfort, bringing sustenance.

The room grew lighter as dawn broke on a new day. Mary lifted her head from the side of the bed. Eyes burning, she raised the cloth from Beth's forehead to wet it again.

Befuddled, she stared at the already soaked cloth. Had Rafe—? A glance showed that he was still beside her, one arm flung across Beth's legs.

Exhaustion made her struggle to remember who had last bathed Beth. She even turned to see if her cousin or Catherine was in the room again.

But she and Rafe were alone with Beth.

"Rafe? Rafe, wake up. Look at me." Mary shook her head. To her ears, her voice sounded slurred. She turned toward him, took hold of his shoulder and gently shook him until he groggily lifted his head.

"What? Mary, what's wrong?"

"I need your help. I must have spilled water all over Beth's pillow and the sheets. They're soaked."

"Go rest, Mary," he mumbled, rubbing his eyes. "I'll take care of it."

Rafe grabbed hold of the footboard to pull himself to his feet. He stood swaying, blinking his eyes and tried to remember what Mary wanted him to do.

Meanwhile, Mary had turned back the covers. When she felt the dampness of the wool shirt wrapped around Beth, she couldn't hold back a cry.

Rafe froze. His blood seemed to turn to ice. His heart skipped a beat. In a second, his throat and mouth were as dry as a desert in summer. He couldn't move, couldn't utter a sound.

He could only watch Mary's hand touching his daughter's cheek. And he learned he had not yet tasted even the tip of fear, for what encompassed him filled him with an unknown dread.

Rafe started to reach for Mary, then yanked his hand back.

Mary looked at Rafe. She tried to smile, but her lips trembled. Joy glittered behind the tears. Rafe didn't understand. How could he? His eyes were closed, his face was a mask of anguish.

As much as Beth required her attention, Mary knew Rafe needed her more.

She rose unsteadily and went to him. Instinct guided her. She raised her hands and cradled his dark, beard-stubbled cheeks.

He cried out at her touch. "No!" It was a whisper torn from deep inside him, agonizing and defiant.

"Rafe, look at me. Listen," Mary pleaded. "The fever's broken. We won, Rafe. We won."

Her thumbs spread of their own volition to the corners of his mouth. She watched his thick lashes lift and read the disbelief in his gray eyes.

"Say…" He had to stop and moisten his lips. "Say it again."

"We won. It's over, Rafe."

"Over? Beth's safe?"

"Yes," she murmured, feeling the joy bubbling up from deep inside. "Yes," she repeated, louder this time.

Rafe caught her up in his arms and swung her around.

Mary pressed one hand over his racing heart. She could hear the pounding of her own. She was crying and laughing when he suddenly stopped. Time disappeared in the moments when he held his gaze on hers. Slowly, then, he lowered her to stand in front of him.

Rafe traced the curve of her chin with his finger.

"Your laughter's as sweet as your songs." He held her with a few inches separating them. One of his strong hands splayed over her lower back, the other slid along her spine, into the thick wealth of her tumbled hair.

Mary offered him no resistance. She wanted to give him all the womanly solace and compassion her heart held. She closed her eyes briefly as he drew her against his hard body and gently rocked her within his embrace.

Rafe lowered his head, and she felt the moisture touch her cheek where his rested. The tears were hers alone. Tears of relief, joy, and thankfulness.

Mary savored the moments he held her. She slipped her arms around his waist. It had been too long since she had her simple need to be held like this met.

She found unmeasured serenity in the silent communion. The shared agony was over. Happiness could have free rein. Mary tilted her head back as he lifted his.

"Mary."

Her smile faded when she heard her name in that black-velvet whisper. Her lips parted. Her pulses pounded to life. A subtle tension strummed her body. She wanted to close her eyes, but the force of his gaze wouldn't allow that retreat.

Mary had seconds to avoid what came. Her breath caught, and she did nothing to stop him.

Heated dampness bathed her mouth as Rafe's lips covered hers. She welcomed the kiss as one of celebration. Welcomed it and eagerly surrendered to it.

But the meeting of their lips didn't offer any comfort.

Mary could give it one name. Need. And it had nothing to do with Rafe being Beth's father, grateful and sharing. The kiss had everything to do with Rafe, the man. It was as raw and savage as the heightened emotions that had bonded them together through the night.

She kept her hands around his waist, shocked at how much she wanted to use them on him. To test the muscles beneath his shirt, to drag them through his hair.

Rafe felt no restraint. He relished her sigh, the small hitch in her breathing, the passionate warmth he laid claim to. He knew her strength, and found fire in her soft, lovely mouth. She opened for him as if they'd shared a hundred kisses. Her taste held a glory all her own. The press of her body against him was discovery and homecoming in one.

His fingers tangled in her hair. He tugged her head back to deepen his kiss. He savored, and learned what it meant to be savored in return.

The desire came at him like lightning. It jolted him to want her this much. Then he became aware that she was trembling like a leaf caught by a strong wind, her hands no longer kneading his back, but pushing him away. He let her go.

Mary stumbled backward. She raised shaking fingertips to her mouth. He had brought to life a passion she had never known. She wanted more.

And it terrified her.

"Beth," she managed to whisper. "She needs me."

Need. The woman didn't know what the word meant. But Rafe did.

It was running inside him, heating his blood, leaving him poised on a blade's edge when she turned away from him.

Chapter Thirteen

Early the next afternoon, Rafe carried Beth down to the parlor. Catherine was going to amuse her while Mary cleaned her room.

Rafe had just settled his daughter on the settee when Sarah sought him out.

"I'd like you to come outside with me, Rafe. There is something you need to see."

"Go on," Catherine urged from where she sat on a stool near Beth. String lay in her lap. "Cat's cradles," she said to Rafe's questioning look. "Beth and I will be just fine." She smiled at the child, who lay wrapped in a quilt, clutching one of Mary's dolls. Beth tired easily, but Mary wasn't worried. She said the little girl would be weak after the bout of fever.

"And," Catherine added, with an imp of mischief dancing in her blue eyes, "we are going to sing nursery rhymes. I intend to teach her 'Mary, Mary, quite contrary.' Remember, Sarah, how we teased her with that one? And it came true, for she loves to grow things." Catherine faced Beth. "It will be a surprise for Mary."

"I can see I'm going to have a spoiled little girl on my hands."

"No, Papa. No more."

"Seems like you've had a talk about this already," Sarah remarked.

"Once, it wasn't enough. If she gets out of hand, don't forget the word *no*. Beth is learning she'll be hearing it."

"Often, to judge by your expression. But she's a little sweetie with me. Aren't you, love?" Catherine asked.

"Promised Mary to be good."

Rafe smiled to hear that, and Catherine laughed. Sarah touched his arm and left the room.

"Beth," Rafe explained to Sarah, "had an army of servants catering to her wants. A few more *no*'s in her life will build character. At least that's what I tell myself until it's time for me to say it."

"That was never a problem for my cousin. Saying no, that is." Sarah opened the kitchen door and stepped outside. The wind was soft as a woman's sigh, and the air dry as a kiva oven. False summer weather, before the true start of fall.

"When we were little, Mary kept me and Catherine out of trouble. She never broke the rules."

"Why does that sound like a warning? And where are you taking me, Sarah?"

"Over to the other side of the pasture fence. And maybe I am warning you. Be careful of my cousin. Mary's strong, despite her delicate appearance. But don't be fooled. Inside, Mary's as fragile as a desert flower. There are some flowers that bloom but once.

"Do you have any notion of how much water it takes for the desert to bloom? Gallons, and what's more, everything has to be perfect before that flowering happens."

Rafe didn't pretend not to understand Sarah. He

wasn't going to deny his attraction to Mary. But perfect? And he said so.

"Perfect, Sarah? I don't know anything that happens between a man and a woman can ever be that way."

Sarah tossed him a look beneath the brim of her hat. Rafe had taken her warning, but issued one in return. He was right, she supposed. Whatever happened was between him and Mary.

As they rounded the pasture fence, Sarah noticed the dust kicked up by their boots. For all the heavy rains, the earth had soaked up the water and was already thirsty.

"There's a spot over here you need to see."

Rafe followed Sarah to a clump of cottonwood saplings. Long-tailed magpies flitted about. In the distance Rafe saw the bronze-red hills, and the green clouds of leaves that seemed to float above their base. The rich color of the hills reminded him of the lovely shades in Mary's hair. And thoughts of Mary reminded him of the guarded manner she had adopted with him ever since he kissed her.

"Well, Rafe, what do you think it is?"

Rafe set aside his musings about Mary. It was hard to do. She confused him. He looked at where Sarah pointed.

The dried clumps of churned-up mud didn't appear to be much of anything to him. Then he spied the broken matches.

He stepped closer, but didn't touch, just stared down at the matches. They hadn't been cleanly broken, merely bent in half, with a sliver of wood holding the ends together.

It was an odd thing for a man to do.

But not odd for a nervous man, one bored with waiting and feeling the weight of time passing.

Rafe hunkered down. He closed his eyes for a few seconds and blanked his mind.

There was no question the disturbed earth pointed to the night of the storm. He picked up one chunk, and it crumbled in his hand.

"Rafe?"

He looked up. Sarah's face was a study of concern. He grinned at her. "It's a good thing for me you're not a screaming lily."

"I don't scare easy, Rafe. But I won't ignore this. Someone waited here. A good long while."

"Yeah. I figure this was done while it rained. Not after the storm."

"And there's more, Rafe. Something was dragged away from here. I started to follow the tracks—"

"Not a good idea to do it alone, Sarah." He came to his feet.

"McCade, what do you think I did before my cousin came to live with me? What do you think I'll do when you're gone?"

"When I'm gone, Sarah, you won't have this kind of trouble to worry about."

She shook her head. "Rafe, as long as men walk this land, women have trouble to worry about."

But Rafe didn't respond. He was thinking about that night after the storm. Mary, his daughter and himself, exposed as targets. His rage was building, hot and furious.

Turning at an angle to Sarah, Rafe stretched out his arm, pointed his index finger with his thumb extended upward. Rafe then sighted the length of his arm as if it were a rifle barrel.

His targeted projection centered on the back door of the house.

Ghostly fingers raced up his spine. He dropped his arm. "Go back to the house, Sarah."

"Pardon?"

"I said go back."

Boots planted slightly apart, Sarah stood her ground. "McCade, no one hearing you could deny you're a man accustomed to giving orders and having them obeyed. But if I've got a copper-colored snake hiding under a rock out here, I not only want to know where it's hiding, but I aim to—"

"You won't do anything, or put yourself at risk, Sarah. This isn't your fight."

The cold, deadly tone of his voice was reinforced by the hard look in his eyes. Sarah had no trouble believing Rafe meant every word. She dug her boot-heels in a little deeper.

"No way, McCade. We had a mule once that could be reasoned with a heck of a lot easier than you. But this isn't a question of whose fight it is. Since you brought it up, I'm going to tell you a few home truths."

"Now, Sarah—"

"Now button your lip, McCade and listen. We're talking about fear. Not the kind a man like you, or any man, could ever understand. But women would. Especially those women who live alone. The three of us made a choice. We live alone, but we are not going to live scared of shadows. Real or imagined.

"If one hombre—just one, mind you—figures he can get this close to the house and watch us, the wind can have all the reasons why. It's trespassing, and it's a violation against us. If he did it once and got away with it, tell me what's going to stop him or the next man from thinking he can come inside?

"We don't have a town sheriff yet. Hillsboro still has growing pains. And if there's a county marshal within hailing distance, I haven't heard about him. Wouldn't do us a lick of good, anyway. By the time someone fetched the law, it would be all over except for the burying."

"Sarah, I hear—"

"No, you don't hear me. Or if you do, McCade, you're not ready to believe me. Don't deny it. Your eyes make potent silent talk. Look at my rifle. I don't carry this or a sidearm with me everywhere for show. I can and will use it. I've run a few varmints off, and it's likely I'll do it again."

Sarah shifted her weight and braced herself for their silent clash of wills.

Rafe thought Mary a warrior angel, soft and womanly, but strong. Looking at Sarah's slim form put in his mind a very stubborn, prideful one.

If the matter before them wasn't so serious, Rafe might have been amused at her attempt to stare him down. Well, he had to admit it to himself, it went beyond an attempt. Those black eyes of hers didn't waver once.

And her reasoning made sense. He was learning more about women in these few days than he had in half a lifetime. And he wasn't ashamed to admit it.

"Tell me, Sarah, do you play poker?"

"Not lately."

"That's real good to know. Sets a man's mind at ease. Should I ever be so foolish to suggest a game between us, don't accept and play."

"Why?" Her brow wrinkled with confusion.

"You'd likely win."

Sarah inclined her head as graciously as any gowned lady accepting a pleasing compliment.

"McCade, you'll do. It's a rare man who admits a woman is right." She peered up at him, thumbing back the hat's brim. "You're not afraid of a strong woman."

"No. Should I be?"

"Most men are."

"I'm not most men. I do try to keep an open mind. But I'll tell you something I've never told anyone. I learned what real courage and strength are. The kind most women are born with. Beth taught it to me when she was a baby starting to crawl.

"She'd be moving along when her arms and knees gave way, and she'd get this surprised look. I'd want to rush over and pick her up to set her world right again. Even when she didn't cry. I stopped myself when I realized the generations of women who stood by while a child learned for themselves to crawl, walk and stand tall. That's when an understanding of the different kinds of strength came to me. Can't measure them.

"This fever of Beth's taught me more. I could've faced an armed man with nothing but watching, being helpless." He shook his head. "I don't know if I'm explaining this right. But women have lived with that kind of fear, too. For their children, their men, and, as you said, for themselves."

"And find the strength to do it?"

"Yeah, Sarah, they do. So, show me the rest of the tracks."

And where was your wife, McCade? Sarah bit the words off before she asked him. She led off toward rocky soil that held a sparse growth of creosote bushes and grass.

Inwardly she heaved a sigh. Rafe wasn't the first man she had had to prove herself against. But she wished, for her peace of mind, that he would be the last.

Sure, and wish the rifle you're toting was a parasol, while you're at it.

On the one hand, Rafe's admission disturbed her, for it was so rare to hear a man speak of such things.

On the other hand, Sarah had to admit that it comforted her a great deal. Mary, if Catherine was right, might find what she longed for with him.

By the thick trunk of an ancient cottonwood tree, Sarah stopped.

"Whatever was dragged stopped here. The bark of this branch is scraped. The horse was tied for a while and shied. But there's tracks of a second horse. I don't think it was here too long."

Sarah turned around and saw that Rafe wasn't with her. She took off her hat and fanned herself. Something had caught his interest in the tracks that were clearly visible in the mud.

Rafe lingered behind. He studied the tracks, several times bending low to look at them closer. He had learned his tracking from a variety of men. Two of the best there were at hunting game or men. One had scouted with the army for almost twenty years. Staying alive for that long proved the man's ability to survive. The other man had been a Pima Indian. He could tell how heavy a man was and which side of his body he wore his gun on, and come within a quarter of an inch, using only his eyes, of telling how long a man's stride was and thereby judging his height. Uncanny how many times the Pima had been right.

What Rafe read bothered him. The man dragged had been heavier than the one pulling him. Heavier, and either dead or out cold. His boots were worn, but the other man was of slighter build, and had nearly new boots. Boots and a pair of fancy spurs. The thin, sliced depression had dried clearly in the mud. Rafe knew he wasn't mistaken.

He thought one man waited with the horses and the other snuck up to the house. Nervous while waiting, he had a habit of breaking matches. There had been no signs of lightning strikes anywhere nearby.

Puzzled, he looked back to where Sarah patiently waited.

Maybe it wasn't two men. It could have been the man who had ducked out of the saloon. That kid Lundy had warned that he was asking questions. But who had removed him?

"Rafe? Rafe, what's wrong? Did you find something?" Sarah asked her questions as she walked back to join him.

"You were right. There were two men here. Not much more to tell. We'd better get back. I've been thinking today would be a good day to go into town and do some shopping for Beth and myself. We both need clothes. I'll look down at the livery for a few packhorses, too."

"That's it? You go into a brown study over these tracks, and that's all you have to say?"

Rafe tugged on his hat brim. The move concealed his wry smile. "That's about it."

"McCade, remind me never to play poker with you."

Near the house, Sarah turned off toward the barn. Rafe went into the kitchen, thinking that he would ask Mary to ride into town with him. She needed to get out of the house and, selfishly, he wanted some time alone with her. He'd hold out the lure—a most truthful one—that he needed her advice about what clothes to buy for Beth. He'd never known a woman who could resist shopping. Especially when a man was paying the bills.

The parlor was deserted. He went upstairs.

Catherine sat in the rocking chair, mending a froth of something white. Beth lay on the bed, sound asleep. There was no sign of Mary.

Rafe motioned to Catherine. She rose quickly and joined him in the hallway.

"Beth," she said in a whisper, "grew tired. Mary and I thought she would sleep better up here. You'll be pleased to know she ate almost a full cup of maple custard, too."

"Any sign of appetite is good." Rafe's gaze drifted to Beth. Earlier, when her bandage was changed, he had seen less swelling and redness around the still-open wound. He should stay with her, but the matter of their clothing was a pressing need.

And he wanted to send a few telegrams.

"Something smells like spring in here," he remarked.

"Oh, Mary freshened the bowl of potpourri she makes. She trades with everyone who grows something she doesn't. Or for treats like maple syrup."

"Where is Mary?"

"Oh, she had to go into town. She promised Mrs. Mullin—that's the owner of the dress shop—one of her dolls for Nita's granddaughter's birthday. Only Mary didn't have the doll to give her."

"It's the one she gave Beth."

"Yes. But not to worry. She's going to buy one of the dolls back from Mr. Crabtree."

"The owner of the emporium?"

"Hmmm... That's him."

"Something wrong, Catherine?"

"Oh, you'd understand if you met the man. He's so tight-fisted, he would squeeze water from rock if there was a profit to be made. Mary has a problem dealing with him. Her husband— Oh, I've said too much."

"Tell me. Please. I'd really like to know."

"I've said all I'm going to, Rafe. But if you were going into town yourself, Nita Mullins's dress shop is two doors down from the emporium." Catherine looked right into his eyes and winked.

"I can't impose on your good nature, to say nothing of your time—"

"Rafe McCade, do you play poker?"

"Funny you should ask. It's the second time someone has mentioned poker to me today."

"Really? Who asked first?"

"Sarah."

"Oh, I would love to know why she did. Of course, being a gentleman, you wouldn't tell me. But you haven't answered me. About poker?"

"Something tells me I may regret admitting that I do play."

"Don't regret it. But you should never play while thinking or talking about Mary, much less if she's anywhere near you. You get this gleam in your eyes that reminds me of the funny look my rooster gets when I introduce a new hen to the flock."

Rafe had to smile. Catherine's pert grin and the sparkle in her eyes allowed no offense to be taken at her observation.

"I will keep your sage advice in mind."

"Now, before you ask me," she began, straightening away from the wall, "Beth is no trouble. And if you hurry, you can catch up with Mary. She's walking."

"Walking into town? Why? Can't she ride?"

"Mary? Her father was a blacksmith. She grew up around horses, and could ride just as soon as she found something high enough to climb on a horse's back.

"No," she continued thoughtfully, "Mary said she had to walk to sort through a host of things that needed to be put in their proper places."

"I see." Rafe looked away from her.

"Ah, I hoped you would. So, what are you waiting for?"

"But Beth—"

"Rafe, you'll be back. After all, it's not as if you were planning to run off with Mary. Your daughter will be all right."

Catherine wasn't about to give him time to argue with her. She shooed him toward the stairs.

"Can I bring you something from town?"

"Surprise me, Rafe. I love surprises."

Catherine settled down to her mending as his boots hit the stairs like those of a man in a hurry.

Mary, she thought, wasn't the only one who knew how to plant seeds and nurture them a bit. She could just sit back now and watch her seeds grow.

Chapter Fourteen

Mary had not lied to Catherine. Her walk into town provided her with the time to sort through the problems plaguing her.

She spent the first few minutes marshaling her bartering skills for the confrontation with Mr. Crabtree. Always an unpleasant chore. He was not going to allow her to buy back a doll at the same price he had paid her for it.

While this was not the most important item on her mental list, it was the shortest. Thinking about Mr. Crabtree also gave her the opportunity to start forth on a somewhat positive note.

The next problem she couldn't ignore.

What was she going to do about Rafe?

Letting her guard down with him had proved the worst mistake she could make.

That's it, Mary. Close the oven door after the bread's been baking for a while.

Self-directed anger churned inside. She added a good dose of anger at Rafe, and she walked faster.

How dare Rafe make her admit how much she had missed the special closeness that only happened between a man and a woman!

She couldn't get that kiss out of her mind. At odd moments she caught herself remembering the firm feel of his lips enticing her mouth into a deeper kiss. His masculine scents that filled her with longing.

She had expected the heat. If anything, it had surpassed her imagination.

But she had not thought to lose all sense of self in surrendering to her own need.

Rafe made her feel...

Hungry?

No!

"Yes," she whispered. "There's no sense denying it."

The clear, bell-like song of meadowlarks rode on the soft breeze. The sounds, like the mild weather, made for a serene day and mocked her agitation.

She had run from the house when she longed to be with Beth, run to escape thoughts of Rafe and his seductive kiss.

She could admit that Rafe and his daughter made her hungry to fill the emptiness of her life.

The sound of approaching riders sent her to the edge of the road. Mary didn't recognize the two men who rode past, but their appearance served to set aside her musing.

She set her market basket down to retie the brown ribbons of her natural straw bonnet and straighten her shawl. She shook the dust from the hem of her dark brown calico skirt and petticoats. With a touch to the small cluster of ribbon roses at the banded neck of the long-sleeved white muslin blouse, she continued into town.

Mary had to step carefully once she reached the wooden sidewalk. It was built two feet above the dirt street. The heavy rains turned the street into a fast-flowing stream, and the moisture had warped the boards.

The sound of hammering came from behind Abel Nieven's tobacco shop. He also served as the town's undertaker. A few horses, tails flicking to chase flies, were hitched along the rails lining the street.

Across the way, Dolly Hudspeth stopped sweeping in front of the tailor shop she and her husband owned to return Mary's wave. Dolly's brother, Thomas Hoffman, was the new minister. He held Sunday service in the Paradise Saloon until the church could be built.

Next to Dolly's shop was Will Nelson's telegraph and Wells Fargo office. Mary inclined her head to acknowledge Buck Purcell's greeting in front of the First Bank of Hillsboro. She stopped against the wall of Murphy's Café when a shouting group of men spilled from Waterman's Assayers. Mary had to smile, despite the colorful suggestions men made to the two in the center. The miner's ore must have proved rich, to judge by the amount of liquor they intended to buy, as well as the nightlong visit to the little house set back behind the livery.

As one of the respectable ladies in town she was not supposed to acknowledge the existence of that house or its occupants, much less to know what went on there. But it was a topic of conversation for the ladies' sewing circle that met once a month.

She skirted the stacked nail kegs in front of J. P. Crabtree's Dry Goods Emporium and stepped inside. The air was musty and the light dim, but the store had no overpowering smell of brine from barrels of salt pork and pickles like Marcus Jobe's family grocery.

Mary saw J.P. behind the counter, totaling the order of two men she pegged as miners from their dress.

She chose to wait until J.P. was free before she approached him.

It could be a while. J.P., like the other business owners in town, acted as a clearinghouse for news. At least the men called it news when they passed it along. Women gossiped.

Miners talked of weather in the mountains, Indian troubles and conditions on the trails. Happenings from murders to claim jumping to new strikes in mining camps were passed along in saloons, cafés and boarding houses. From the livery stable, information about men's horses filtered down. She had even heard it said that you could tell a gunman's horse from any other. Those men tended to have the best grain-fed horses.

She imagined men who lived by their guns needed animals that could be depended upon to ride fast and far.

Wandering the aisles, Mary shook her head. How did J.P. ever find what someone wanted? The goods on the rough board shelving were partly obscured by hanging farm implements, horse collars and bridles. Hickory chairs hung above the shelves on thick wooden wall pegs, carpetbags next to a barrel filled with ax heads. Goodness knew where the ax handles were stored. Kerosene and lamp oil, leakage making their odor pungent, took up a large part of one wall.

Iron kettles, enamel pots and soup ladles were mixed with lanterns, boxes of candles and coils of rope.

In a small alcove, a drummer stood tallying an assortment of weapons. Kegs of blasting powder, fuses and caps were piled to one side.

Mary, looking down the aisle, saw J.P. alone. He was fishing a piece of rock candy from the covered crock on the counter. J.P. generously allowed anyone spending a dollar or more in his store one piece of candy.

Mary wasted no time in hurrying down the aisle.

"Afternoon, Miz Inlow. Saw you come in. What can I do for you this fine day?"

"Mr. Crabtree, I need to buy back one of the dolls I sold you." Mary found three dolls sitting on the cluttered shelf behind him. Her eyes widened when she saw the price he had posted.

"You're charging more than three times what you paid me for the dolls?"

"That's right." J.P. hooked his suspenders with his thumbs. "An' don't you get in a flutter over it. Supply an' demand is my law, Miz Inlow. Truth to tell, I done you a big favor taking them dolls on in the first place. Fact is, I only sold two last week, to one of the drummers. Ain't got much call for fancy presents for little ones. Girls, that is.

"Boys, now, are a mite easier to please. Fishing hooks, pocketknives, a good rifle or a pair of boots do a boy just fine. Girls tend to get as finicky as their mamas over what they get. Fact is, Miz Inlow, I don't much cater to women's trade."

Mary couldn't help herself. She swept a disdainful gaze over the clutter behind him. "I couldn't doubt the truth of your statement, Mr. Crabtree. But I supplied the dolls. You aren't thinking of charging me—"

"Now, now, I got to. Folks would hear I'd gone soft. No arguing. That's my price. Two dollars. Cash, mind you. An' don't," he said, freeing one hand to point a finger at her, "be telling me you ain't got the money. I sent that fella what was needing help for his little girl to you. Ain't gonna tell me you ain't charged him for what all you done, and board. Ain't gonna believe—"

"Mr. Crabtree, what I did or didn't do is none of your business. But you would benefit greatly from a dose of Christian charity."

"Not when it costs me money, I ain't. Miz Inlow, things are a mite tight."

"It's a pure wonder you don't strangle on them," Mary muttered, under the guise of a cough. She set her market basket on the counter and opened the cord tie of her drawstring purse.

"I am prepared to pay you sixty cents more than I received, and not one penny more, Mr. Crabtree. If I didn't need the doll for Nita's granddaughter's birthday gift, I wouldn't purchase it at all."

"Nita, you say?" He rubbed his chin, then turned around to look at the dolls.

"That's right. Besides, doubling your money should help cushion your bank account, but it won't do much for your conscience. Nita shared the amount of contributions the businessman in town made to the church building fund. I can't tell you how disappointed the ladies' sewing circle was to learn you made one of the smallest pledges. And you a founding father of the town."

"She had no right—"

"Yes, she did. She's keeping records for the minister. He mentioned something about putting up a plaque, a brass one, with all the names of those who made the church building possible."

Mary lowered her gaze and counted out the money from her meager store. Laughter bubbled inside her. Mr. Crabtree gazed heavenward, stroking his chin, and she could almost hear his greedy mind at work, thinking of his name being the first on that plaque. The Lord would forgive her lie, she was sure. After all, the church would benefit from it.

She pushed the money across the counter to him.

She glanced at the big crock of candy and thought how much Beth, and Catherine, too, would enjoy having some. Stingy Mr. Crabtree would only allow one piece for her sale. A small one, most likely.

He reminded her so much of her husband that she found it impossible to remain and bargain over the cost of candy with him.

"I'd like the doll in the middle with the blue satin skirt. And please wrap my piece of rock candy."

Mr. Crabtree handed over the doll and, with a quick twist, paper-wrapped a chunk of the sugar-sweet candy. Still thoughtful, he peered at Mary. "How come I ain't heard nothing about this here brass plaque?"

"It's to be a surprise. If you tell, I'll know. And Mr. Crabtree, rest assured I will share the news of your newfound generosity with the ladies' sewing circle."

"Ain't said I was gonna give—"

"Why, just think, they might consider putting your name on a pew. One right in the front of the church, Mr. Crabtree."

Mary put the doll and candy into her basket. He offered a vague hand wave as she wished him a good day. Mary was occupied with convincing Nita and the other ladies that her idea of plaques had merit. They would encourage a little competition and garner larger donations. She bumped into a man coming into the store.

"I beg your pardon," she said, then attempted to step around the barrel-chested man.

Her apology was greeted with a snorting laugh that sounded like a hog at the feeding trough. Wrinkling her nose at the odors of liquor and unwashed body, Mary repeated her apology. The man was unshaven, and his food-stained clothing and the rings of dirt above and below his neckerchief were repelling.

"I'll ask once more. Please, excuse me."

"You're just the little lady I've been looking for."

She looked at his face. Thin lips, thick mustache, a long nose and small ice-blue eyes with no more warmth in them than the head of a nail made her back away.

He hooked one hand on the basket handle. The other rested on the butt of his gun.

"I can't imagine why you would be looking for me. We do not know each other. I want it kept that way." Mary yanked the basket, but he wouldn't release it.

"Name's John Balen. Friends call me Hog. On account of my laugh. You got—"

"Mister, we are not friends. We are not even chance acquaintances. Let go of my property and let me pass."

"You call attention and you're gonna get someone killed. Just listen. You got a man out at your place. You tell him to come into town. I'm waiting on him."

Mary's eyes widened as she looked above the man's square shoulders. Before she could utter a sound, Rafe spoke.

"Where I come from, when a lady asks politely, a man's smart to move."

"Then go back where the hell you came from stranger. Butt out. This ain't your affair."

"Oh, but it is." Rafe knocked aside Balen's hand and lifted his gun, while using his other hand to spin the man around.

"You can deliver your message in person. To me."

Chapter Fifteen

Rafe rode Rebel into town. His first stop had been at Bott's livery, to hire a wagon for the supplies he intended to buy.

Will Bott was a giant of a man, topping Rafe by a good few inches. The livery owner admired good horseflesh, and Rebel was that. The big sandy-haired man asked a fair price to rent his wagon and a team. Rafe agreed, then asked if any dead or injured man had been found.

"Funny you should ask. Found a fella in the stable this morning. Had a lump on the back of his head the size of a shot glass. Said his horse got spooked and threw him. Didn't appear to me to know how he got here. Wouldn't know anything about it, would you?"

With all honesty, Rafe said he knew nothing about it.

"That man was cross as an old grizzly. Wouldn't want to meet up with him again today."

"You appear a man who could hold his own and then some," Rafe remarked. He thought about the tracks. The feeling came back that Shell Lundy had something to do with the barrel-chested man.

"Like to wrassle some. Ain't much good with a

gun. Not to say I couldn't use one if the need was there.'' He eyed McCade's lean body with a wide grin. ''Ain't had me a good man to tussle with in a while.''

''I can hold my own, but unlike you, I'm better with a gun. That man hanging around town?''

''Saw him go over to the Red Horse. You mind what I say. Be careful. He's a mean-looking hombre. And I'll bring the wagon around back of Jobe's grocery for you.''

''Appreciate that.'' Rafe handed over the dollar rental fee, then added another dollar. ''Don't know if I can get your wagon back tomorrow. I'll need pack-horses, too. Four. Mountain-bred, if you've got them.''

''Got three mustangs. Ten dollars a head. Trail-broke, but I ain't saying they're good for more.''

''Tie them back of the wagon.'' Once more Rafe counted out money, this time two twenty-dollar gold pieces. ''I'll be needing saddle packs for the horses. If the charge is more—''

''Plenty here. Stuff I got ain't new. But say, you're the fella with the little girl. J.P. said she was hurt. Apache attack, right. How's she doing?''

''Better. I've got things to—''

''That Mrs. Inlow's a mighty fine and knowing woman. She took care of my Bessie—that's my wife—when she stole a honeycomb from the wrong hive. Had so many bee stings, a man couldn't count them all. Them widows come by every day to tend her and the chores. Fine—''

''Yes. I know. I'll see you at the grocery.''

Rafe led Rebel by the reins and walked into town. Hearing Will talk about Mary wiped every thought but those of her from his mind. But he had to go to the telegraph office before he found Mary. He had to know what was happening at the Cañón del Agua mine.

Unconsciously he must have been looking for the square-shouldered man from the saloon. His gaze lit on him blocking the door of the emporium. That was where Mary had gone.

Hearing Mary's demand to pass, set Rafe to moving with a deadly fury.

Now, holding the man's weapon on him, Rafe repeated, in a deadly-cold voice, a request to have the message delivered to his face. "Only we'll step around back. Mary, did he hurt you?"

"No. But, Rafe—"

"I had a wagon sent over to the grocery. I'd be pleased if you'll meet me there. This won't take long."

"Now, you hold on there, McCade. I ain't going nowhere with you."

Rafe clicked back the hammer of Balen's gun. Then he smiled. "I have Samuel Colt's word that you will do exactly what I tell you."

Mary's gaze followed Balen's down to the gun barrel that nudged his stomach.

"I've heard that Colt's impatient. And you're straining mine. Move."

Balen glanced at the men gathering in front of the store. He made a move to turn around. Rafe stopped him.

"No. Walk backward. I want you to face me at all times. I don't shoot men in the back, as a rule. Of course, there's always a first time for everything."

Mary clutched her basket to her chest. How could Rafe sound so calm, but speak with a deadly menace that left no doubt he would shoot Balen as soon as talk to the man?

Rafe crowded Balen. The man moved backward along the uneven wooden sidewalk.

Mary followed them. When Rafe disappeared into the side alley, some unseen and unheard signal passed between men she knew—Dolly's husband, Chad, Abel Nieven and Ollie Walker—to block not only her view but her passage.

"Be best if you go on with your shopping, Mrs. Inlow," Chad suggested. He took hold of her arm to turn her away. "Ain't for a lady to see."

Mary didn't waste breath arguing with him. Since they wouldn't let her pass between them, she'd go around them. A loud grunt came from the direction of the alley. All she could think was that Rafe might get hurt.

Someone shouted that there was a fight. Before Mary took a step, men appeared from the saloons and shops, all running to see. Their backs presented her with a solid wall of male resistance.

She refused to be defeated. Hurrying along the sidewalk, she intended to go around the buildings from the other side. Nita came out of her shop. She caught hold of Mary's arm.

"What's going on? Who's fighting?"

"Come and see." Mary tugged free and ran.

Brush and broken bottles, assorted wooden boxes and puddles slowed Mary's progress. But she managed to get around, with Nita hot on her heels.

Rafe had tossed aside Balen's gun. His first blow sent Balen staggering, the second doubled the man over.

"That was for the disrespect you showed Mrs. Inlow. How many more blows you take depends on the answers I get."

"Ain't telling you nothing," Balen snarled. He wiped his cut lip. He was shorter but heavier than

McCade. And he knew every dirty trick to beat a man senseless. He came up swinging.

Balen's hardened fist caught Rafe on the chin. Rafe's punch sent Balen to his knees. He started to get up, and Rafe swung again, once more forcing Balen to his knees.

"Ain't nobody ever whipped me with fists," Balen boasted. "Ain't no one making that claim." He charged Rafe like a maddened bull, butting his head into Rafe's midsection, until he pinned him against the wall.

Rafe landed a few blows, just enough to get Balen to back off. He brought up his knee and drove it into Balen's belly, swinging his right fist into the man's chin.

The fighting was cold and furious. Rafe caught as many punches as he landed. He tasted blood, but grimly hung in. He had to get answers from Balen.

Excited voices spewed encouragement and advice. Rafe heard it all as a muted roar. Balen tripped him, sending him to the ground, and followed him down.

"You're gonna die."

Silently Rafe made Balen the same promise. Jerking his head to avoid the thumbs Balen aimed at his eyes, he bucked, attempting to dislodge the heavier man.

Balen fumbled for Rafe's gun. Rafe rolled, crushing the other man's leg beneath his body. He saw Balen's mouth open, but couldn't hear what he cried. Balen had his knee pressed into his ribs. Rafe risked the blows to get his hands on Balen's leg. He heaved and sent the other man sprawling.

Rafe sprang up, lunging at Balen. All his rage at his daughter's suffering added strength to the blows he delivered without mercy.

Balen tried to get away. His punches were wildly

PLAY "LUCKY 7" AND GET
FIVE FREE GIFTS!

HOW TO PLAY:

1. With a coin, carefully scratch off the silver box at the right. Then check the claim c
to see what we have for you—**FREE BOOKS** and a gift—**ALL YOURS! ALL FREE!**

2. Send back this card and you'll receive brand-new Harlequin Historical™ novels. The
books have a cover price of $5.99 each, but they are yours to keep absolutely free.

3. There's no catch. You're under no obligation to buy anything. We charge nothing—
ZERO—for your first shipm
And you don't have to ma
any minimum number of
purchases—not even one

4. The fact is thousands of readers enjoy receiving books by mail from the Harlequir
Reader Service® months before they're available in stores. They like the convenience
home delivery and they love our discount prices!

5. We hope that after receiving your free books you'll want to remain a subscriber. B
the choice is yours—to continue or cancel, any time at all! So why not take us up on
invitation, with no risk of any kind. You'll be glad you did!

YOURS FREE!

You'll love this exquisite
necklace, set with an elegant
simulated pearl pendant!
It's the perfect accessory to
dress up any outfit, casual
or formal — and is yours
ABSOLUTELY FREE when
you accept our NO-RISK offer!

NOT ACTUAL SIZE

NO COST! NO OBLIGATION TO BUY!
NO PURCHASE NECESSARY!

The Harlequin Reader Service® —Here's how it work

Accepting free books places you under no obligation to buy anything. You may keep the books and gift an return the shipping statement marked "cancel." If you do not cancel, about a month later we'll send you 4 additional novels, and bill you just $3.94 each, plus 25¢ delivery per book and GST. * That's the complete price—and compared to cover prices of $5.99 each—quite a bargain! You may cancel at any time, but if you choose to continue, every month we'll send you 4 more books, which you may either purchase at the discount price...or return to us and cancel your subscription.

*Terms and prices subject to change without notice.
Canadian residents will be charged applicable provincial taxes and GST.

0195619199-L2A5X3-BR01

HARLEQUIN READER SERVICE
PO BOX 609
FORT ERIE ON   L2A 9Z9

thrown, missing his target. Rafe ducked and weaved his way clear of most of the blows. Balen feinted and caught Rafe with a solid punch to the belly, then tried to land another with his left fist.

Rafe knocked his arm aside. Civility fell away. His punches were fueled by every hour of Beth's pain, his own fear of losing his child, and the agony of it all.

Balen's knees gave way. He started to fall, but Rafe grabbed hold of his collar and jerked him upright. Three more punches landed before Rafe staggered and let Balen go.

The man fell face forward on the ground. He didn't get up again.

Rafe stood over him. He wiped the sweat from his eyes and the blood from his mouth. His chest heaved with every breath he drew. He stood there by sheer force of will, and fought his body's urge to sway.

He nudged Balen's side with the toe of his boot. He wanted to issue his warning with witnesses. He didn't know if one or all three partners in the newly acquired Cañón del Agua mine wanted him dead. If he was wrong, Balen might slip with another name.

"Listen to me so you can tell Vargas, Trent and Malhar they're on notice. Buy-out talk could've opened this ball. They made music with bullets and men like you. I won't dance to any man's tune. I find you or any men they send on my trail and I'll have bullets waiting."

Balen's grunt could have meant anything. Rafe hid his disappointment, but he also hoped Shell Lundy heard him. He'd get the message.

Men crowded around, slapping him on the back, offering to buy him a drink, although none knew the real reason Rafe had fought.

Their faces were a blur to Rafe. He looked for only

one. And when he saw that pale face framed by red-gold hair and met a green-eyed gaze, he forced himself to move.

Mary, too, was trying to reach him. With Nita's help, she pushed aside men who tried to keep her from Rafe's side.

Someone had handed Rafe his hat. He held it when she broke through the circle surrounding him and had her first closer view.

Her stomach rolled over with a twist and a jerk. She fought down a cry, fought the first impulse to fling herself into his arms and make sure he was all right.

She could not give way to feminine needs in front of these men. She would still be living here long after Rafe and Beth were gone. More important, for Rafe's sake, she could not shame him.

No tears allowed for his bruised state, she warned herself, taking another step forward. No scolding for the rips in the shirt she had carefully mended for him. No recriminations that he might have been injured or killed, and what would she have told his daughter..?

The fight had been short, but vicious. Rafe stood like a proud warrior, waiting for her. In his silent gaze she read what he wanted from her.

"You give a hard lesson in manners, Mr. McCade."

"We'll hope it takes."

"Proud of yourself, are you?"

"I'm still standing."

"Yes, there is that." The calm of her voice was at odds with the emotions flaring inside her.

"You gonna reward him?" someone shouted. A few hoots and whistles greeted the suggestion.

"If you'll come with me, Mr. McCade, I'll tend to your battered face."

"Go on, McCade," several men encouraged.

"Yeah, she's gonna kiss it all better," another yelled.

Rafe tried to appreciate the lovely shade of pink Mary was turning. He found it difficult to do with one eye beginning to swell.

"Hush up, the lot of you," Nita shouted, "before you end up with a dose of lye soap for your mouths! Come on, Mary," she said in a softer voice, "let's get you inside before you blush brighter than Grandpa's new union suit."

Nita used her elbows to clear a path. She went first and opened the back door of her shop.

Mary, accepting Rafe's arm, walked alongside him. Nita scolded the men who attempted to come inside, then locked the door.

Mary never had a second alone with Rafe until they were riding home in the loaded wagon. Rebel and the three mustangs Rafe had bought were tied to the tailgate of the wagon. Rafe had his rifle by his side.

When Rafe pulled up just past the turnoff for the farmhouse, Mary turned on the wooden seat to face him.

"Why have you stopped here?"

"We need to talk, Mary. Here we can without interference, and without my compromising your reputation." But now that the time had come for Rafe to put into words the idea he had been mulling over for a few hours, he found himself delaying.

The late-afternoon sun had already faded into the deeper shadows that warned of approaching dusk. Above them, magpies settled into the treetops. Flies buzzed annoyingly around the horses.

Mary faced front. "It's rather late for you to consider my reputation. Not after the way you shopped."

"You disapproved?"

"It's not my place to—"

"Of course you did. Mary, you don't need to say a word. You convey a wealth of opinion in your carriage and every glance you sent my way since we entered Nita's shop, to say nothing of the daggers flying in the grocery."

"As I started to say, it is not my place to approve or disapprove of anything you do." She managed to sound prim, when inside she was quaking. Why? she begged to know. Why must you leave so soon? There was no other explanation for the amount of supplies he had bought and the presence of the extra horses and pack saddles.

"Mary, I can't help enjoying spending money. It wasn't what I bought, but how much."

"Are you asking or telling me what I think?"

"Temper? Fine. Let's have this out first. You didn't mind choosing material for clothes for my daughter. You had a good time until I doubled everything. You balked when I wanted the length of wool for you. Let's ignore the color being perfect for you. You can't say you didn't admire it, too. I thought you'd rub a hole in the spot you kept fingering. I admit I wanted to buy you something special, something you wouldn't or couldn't buy for yourself. You don't condemn a man for that, Mary. I won't let you do that to me."

"You bought too much."

Rafe heard her tight little voice, and gazed down at where she clenched her hands together in her lap. He had resisted the urge to take her hand into his. If he touched her now, he'd never get any of this said.

"So what if I did? Some dress lengths for the three of you? A few shawls? Some—" He had to grin, and it hurt him when she shot a glaring look his way. "All right, unmentionables."

"You spent too much. You paid Nita a ridiculous amount to sew. You swept into Jobe's grocery as if no one else might need to shop this week. Buying sacks, cases, barrels." She took a breath, holding one hand up as she ticked off more.

Rafe watched the deep breath she took, and wished he was sitting in a big, comfortable chair, so that he could pull Mary onto his lap, lean back and let her rip into him. She had shown spirit, but this was temper, her face flushed, sparks lighting her eyes, and her back so rigid he thought a move might make it snap.

He wanted to kiss her senseless. And he needed to know all the secrets she hid behind sad eyes.

"You were saying?" he prompted.

"Eight smoked hams? If you had nothing else to eat for a month of Sundays times twelve, you couldn't finish those. And between the sides of bacon and links of sausage, I lost count. If you fed Beth half of those sugarloaves, you'll rot her teeth."

"You had every bit as much fun as I did, Mary. And I'll call you a liar if you deny it."

Mary made the mistake of looking at him. His lopsided grin infuriated her. She lost track of where she had been with her complaints and twisted around to glance at the loaded wagon.

"No one uses a full barrel of dried apples. Unless, of course, you were planning to cook for a bunkhouse full of men. And three sacks of dried peas? Really. The amounts— Oh, what could you do with all that rice and those jugs of molasses? And the spices." Mary closed her eyes briefly, one hand on her heart. "I swear, you must have money to burn to have bought so many."

"And so much of each spice. You don't want to forget that part, Mary."

"Don't poke fun at me. This is serious. You

were...were reckless. I don't know what poor Marcus made of you. Firing orders at him. Keeping his three sons racing from one end of the store to the other. People must think we're harboring a madman.''

"That might not be far from the truth.''

"What?'' Her gaze clashed with his, but then she saw that deepening smile and huffed her opinion of his teasing.

"You're not mad. After all, you purchased a sensible amount of beans. The only thing that was—''

"Actually, I hate beans, Mary. They're necessary, but I ate my fill of them, day in and day out, for more times than I ever want to remember.''

"I see.''

"I don't think you do. Not really. You would have to have been so hungry that your belly and backbone met more times than not. But all that was a long time ago.''

"Rafe, I'm sorry.''

"Don't be. It's in the past. I won't look back. But you did forget a few things,'' he said, wanting the sadness gone and her prim, starched manner returned. "I seem to recall decidedly pursed lips when I added another case of canned tomatoes to the one you ordered.''

"I don't like tomatoes.''

"Well, there you have it. Common ground, Mary. We each have something we don't like. Aside from my spending habits, that is. Now, since we've achieved a level of honesty, tell me that you did have fun.''

"You are a very persistent man, Rafe.''

"When I want something, yes. Will you answer me?''

Mary looked across the road and spoke softly. "I admit it was fun. I was married for ten years to a man who demanded an account of every penny I spent. It was humiliating to have him go to the storekeepers and check my bills. When my father died, my husband sold the property left to me and kept the money.

"But it wasn't just money. It was accounting for my time, for who I spoke to, for a hundred small things that made life hellish. I don't mean—"

He brushed his fingertips over her bent and bare neck. "Mary, take a lesson from me. Put it in the past and forget it. He's dead. You're very much alive."

She hunched her shoulders, pulling slightly away from him. Rafe gave her a few minutes to collect herself. He had gotten more than he thought he would.

But he'd be damned before he let some ghost steal her happy mood. He found himself glancing back at the full load in the wagon's bed. He mentally listed the items purchased that Mary had taken him to task over. One or two remained.

"Tell me, Mary, how do you feel about cornmeal?"

She jerked around, swiping one hand over her eyes. "Cornmeal?"

"Yeah. Do you like it?"

A smile lit her face. Impossible man. Anyone listening to him would believe he asked her opinion seriously. But she, too, wished to forget the memories that spoiled her mood. His silly game required attention.

"I like it. But that French milled soap—"

"Expensive? But scented like a flower garden?" *And you stood sniffing it with such a look of rapture on your face, I had to buy it.* Rafe left those words unsaid and thought of what he'd seen in his mind while she stood holding a bar. Mary, pale skin flushed with the water's heat, slicked with scented soap, that glorious red hair tumbling... He had to shift in his seat. And his hat was put to better use in his lap. If Mary looked down, she'd run.

"I liked the soap, Mary."

"Well, so do I!"

"I'll make you a gift of it," he offered in a very soft voice, while trying not to laugh at her indignant expression.

"You've done more than enough, thank you."

"No, Mary, I haven't. I couldn't do enough for you." Rafe leaned forward and caught her chin within his hand. "Look at me, Mary. Can you deny that winter's coming?"

"What?"

"Winter? As in cold weather? The need-for-plenty-of-stocked-rations-and-warm-clothing kind of winter?" In spite of the silliness of the game they had played, it was worth pushing a little more to see her puzzled attempt to understand.

"Mary?"

"No. Yes. I'm not sure." She couldn't be expected to pay attention to what he said. She was far too busy doing as he wanted—looking. At him. And storing the memories against the time he would be gone.

Despite his slightly bruised features, the warmth of his gaze sent an equally warm butterfly sort of a feeling to spread from her breasts to the toes curling in her shoes.

"Your poor face," she whispered. Lightly, her fingertips grazed his cheek. And the feeling inside her grew in intensity.

"Going to kiss me and make it better, Mary?"

Rafe braced his hand on the back of the wagon's seat. The tip of his nose touched hers. There was a questing, teasing play to the up-and-down motion he made.

Mary couldn't resist responding in kind. She rubbed the tip of her nose against his in a side to side motion.

"What contrary messages," he murmured. "Is that regret in your eyes, or can I hope for a maybe? Lips ready to say no. But wait, Mary. What's in your mind? Your heart?"

Her whole body was urging a *yes* past the smile on her lips. Her eyelids wanted to close and hide from the kiss already darkening his eyes.

"Sweet Mary, you made magic with me once before. Kiss me now. Let me taste your magic again."

Her mind—as befuddled as could be—latched on to one word. *Magic.* Lord, had Rafe bought that, too? He didn't need any. She should tell him that. And she would. In just another moment or two.

Right after she savored the quickening anticipation that filled her.

But her attempt to whisper of magic of his own became mere breath floating across his parted lips.

There was none of the fevered mating she expected and had longed for despite the fear it brought. Rafe sipped so delicately at her mouth, his touch so tender and soft, she could not tell when the kiss truly began. With leisurely moves, he shifted the angle of his head, while the coaxing ply of his mouth kindled her desire.

Chapter Sixteen

Rafe had no intention of kissing her. But this close, she was irresistible. Lethal, for she clouded his thinking. But her luscious mouth had been set in disapproving lines, and he wanted her smile.

And another taste.

Her lips were sweeter than memory, but headier with the dark spice of passion. He stopped thinking and lost himself. Lost himself to sink into that soft, wet mouth, to tease it with his tongue, until her lips parted and granted him freedom to explore.

The taste was darker. Deeper. Exciting, and desperately arousing.

He held slender strength in his arms. Her muscles taut, even as small, firm breasts yielded against him. The scent of her, that of a cool spring morning, stirred his blood. He used his teeth on her lower lip. She came up hard against him with a shudder.

"Not contrary at all," he whispered, and crushed her mouth in a kiss of devastating intensity. Heat ran through him, tempting and tormenting.

Watch what you wish for. It was a rational thought. One of the last Mary formed. She had wanted to taste the fevered hunger of that first kiss.

But she wasn't prepared to defend herself. His kiss simply destroyed her. Heat and need. Give and take. A bone-threatening trembling beset her. Sensation after sensation battered her, too many to deal with at once.

Again he took from her. With the smooth, skilled demand of his mouth. Took with the hard, confident hands that molded her body to his. Gave back excitement with every breath she drew of his masculine scent.

She could only feel.

Some soft, accepting sound rose from her throat. Her hands tangled in his hair. She couldn't stop the kiss, she couldn't stop the trembling or contain the bewildering need to let everything she was melt into him.

Rafe had what he wanted. There wasn't a disapproving bone left in her body. She couldn't meet passionate demand with needs of her own if she wasn't as blissfully drunk on pleasure as he was.

He could have tasted her mouth endlessly. He was simply absorbed with the soft, silky melding of her mouth against his. He fed on her sweet moans. And he eased deeper, aroused past the point of caring.

She did this to him. Mary. Breath catching in her throat as he skimmed his palms over the sides of her small breasts.

He swallowed her gasp, touched her again, and let her shudders sink into his body.

Mary's hands slipped from his hair to lie limp on his broad shoulders. She should stop him.

Her head fell back. His hand took the weight from her neck.

Rafe studied her face. Her cheeks were flushed, her eyes were closed, her breath as ragged as his own.

Her lips were moist and parted, fully colored with passion.

And he thought she would look just like this lying beneath him. His body clenched with need until he ached.

She opened her eyes, and he saw they were dazed, and held a little fear. He could easily understand the fear. He had a dose of it himself.

Mary struggled free of his arms. She had to regain her balance, emotionally and physically. She practically— No, there had been nothing practical or sensible about the way she threw herself at him.

"Mary, I—"

"Please." The word was an effort to speak. She shook her head when he repeated her name.

Rafe ran his hand through his hair. He scooped up his hat from the floor of the wagon. Hell, for all the attention he had paid, someone could have shot him and he'd just be getting around to noticing.

"I swear I didn't stop here for this. I really wanted to talk to you. About my leaving."

He'd confirmed what she already knew. She stared straight ahead at the deepening shadows that crept across the road.

"Mary, did you hear me?"

"When?"

He lifted his hand to touch her at that choked sound, but dropped it to his side. If he touched her again, now, he wouldn't trust himself to stop until he had all her secrets and had made her part of him. Another glance at her told him the barriers were in place.

"If Beth is well enough to travel, the end of the week. I want to explain why I can't wait any longer."

"I told you, it's not for me to—"

"I said *I want* you to know."

She hitched her shawl around her shoulders and nodded.

"That man Balen is hunting me. Sarah showed me tracks out past the far pasture fence. I think Balen waited there the night we were outside. He had a clear field of vision to the back door. An easy shot with a rifle. Only someone stopped him."

"A friend of yours?"

"I wish I could say for sure. But no. Not a friend. Someone who may have been paid to do the same job. I can't keep risking your life, or Sarah's and Catherine's, with this kind of trouble hunting me. I need to get my daughter where she'll be safe."

He's leaving. He is going to leave and take Beth away. Mary sat straight-backed and calm-faced, refusing to feel any emotion. She had no right. Beth was his child. Not hers. She could never be Mary's.

And she would learn to live with the emptiness they would leave behind.

A week. He said that long. It was something to cling to.

"We should go up to the house. They'll be wondering what happened to us."

"I'm wondering the same thing, Mary." But Rafe took up the reins and turned the team around.

She shot him a quick, startled glance. There was no denying the ring of honesty in his voice. But Mary had to protect herself. For the second time, Rafe McCade had shown her how vulnerable she was to him.

"There is nothing to wonder about. There is no 'us.'" She wrapped her arms around her waist. The heat of passion had suddenly become encompassingly cold.

Rafe decided it was unfair to pursue her denial, but

he could, and did, continue to explain his worry for all of them.

Mary listened. She had no choice. It had nothing to do with being a captive audience, but the sound of his voice called to her on some deep level.

She heard of how Rafe had won his share of the Cañón del Agua mine and of his decision to leave day-to-day operations to the other three partners when he was notified of his wife's death.

"There was no time to go north and meet the men. I had to get Beth. Valerie's family didn't want my daughter. Not when they learned the generous allowance I gave my absent wife stopped with her death."

"Poor Beth. Oh, Rafe, did she know her mother's family didn't want her?"

"She knew. I'd always paid Beth's expenses after I made my first strike. But even then, Val refused me a chance to visit with Beth. She kept putting me off, begging for a little more time, for Beth to be older so she would understand why I didn't live with them.

"I never knew Val hated me so much that she told Beth I never wanted her. But you heard most of this, Mary. And believe me, it doesn't bear repeating."

"Beth's nightmares—"

"Val's death triggered those. She didn't spend much time with our child, but she was Beth's mother. And me showing up didn't help. That's why I stayed in the East so long. My daughter didn't know me. At least Val used my money to set up her own house. That's where I stayed. And Beth has this feeling that she didn't try hard enough to stop Val from going out in the boat the day she drowned. But we're working on that."

"I'm sure you will succeed once Beth feels secure in your love."

Questions burned the tip of his tongue. How had

Mary—without children of her own—become so wise? But he wasn't about to bring the sadness back to her eyes.

"It was about two months later that I got a telegram saying there was trouble up at the mine. Ore shipments had stopped. I sent a man I trusted to find out what was going on. He ended up dry-gulched. A few days after he was found, the man I'd won the share from was shot in the back."

Rafe brought the team to a stop in front of the barn doors. Light spilled from the kitchen window.

"Rafe, do you believe these men, the ones you named to Balen, are responsible for the attack, too?"

"Makes the most sense to me. It's not hard to pay a renegade band in guns and whiskey to do your dirty work for you. No one benefits from my death but my daughter. If anything happened to Beth, only the lawyers get rich. But Val's death happened too close to my winning the share of the mine. I haven't had time to add a codicil to my will."

"But they can't know that."

"My point, on the money. That night I went into town, a man named Shell Lundy claimed he was hiring men for fighting wages. That's more than double what a cowhand earns in a month. Earlier talk in the Red Horse led me to believe it was the Cañón where the trouble was."

Mary faced him. She placed her hand on his arm. "Do you think this man is working with Balen?"

There was no question that he could trust Mary with the little he did know. Telling her his suspicion about Shell could save her life, or the others.

"I want to say yes. Shell tried to goad me into a gunfight, then backed off. But those tracks Sarah and I followed showed the second man wore a large, fancy spur on his boot. I noticed Shell wearing spurs like that.''

Rafe tied off the reins and jumped down. He came around the wagon to Mary's side to lift her down.

''Wait. I've listened and I've thought about this, Rafe. What I don't understand is why these men didn't offer to buy you out?''

''You think I didn't ask myself the same thing? I'm a wealthy man, Mary. People get funny notions about those who have money. The only reason that makes sense to me is, they were afraid that I'd do the buying and they'd end up with nothing. How can I know what's in their minds?''

''Couldn't you notify them that you'd sell your share? Once that was done, they'd leave you alone.''

''It's not that simple, Mary. They tried to kill Beth. No one is walking away from that. If I did, what's to stop any business partner from hiring someone to kill me if they are too cowardly to do the deed themselves? They'd all think I was the coward. That's a brand no man can live with. Either that, or they'd ruin me with threats against my child and run me off after paying a penny on a dollar owed.

''Money's a god to some men. You said yourself that your husband demanded an accounting of every penny. I admit I enjoy having it, not so much for what I buy, but for the freedom it's brought to me. But when I weigh it against Beth, it's an empty reward without anyone to share it with. And without you asking, I confess, I'd give it away to have the chance to see my daughter grow up.''

''They don't know that, Rafe.''

''No one does. You're the only one I've said that to.''

Despite the painful reference to her husband's miserly ways, Mary felt a warm glow at the knowledge that he trusted her enough to share a confidence. She sorted through what he had said, some words with anger, others with pride. Rafe wasn't a man to wear the mantle of a coward. In a strange way, she understood. He couldn't go to the law with suspicions. He could do that only with proof. And the wheels of justice turned too slow in a land where men often made justice their own in an instant. Someday there would be civilized law to settle such matters. Until then, a man, and a woman, too, had to be ready to defend life and home against any who would take, regardless of right or wrong.

"Let's get you inside before Sarah and Catherine fall out of the window. They've been twitching the curtain back and forth by turns."

Mary reached for him as his hands clasped her waist to lift her down from the wagon's seat. For a moment, she remained close to him, her hands on his broad shoulders, her body pressed against his.

The cold seeped from her body.

"It's not easy for you," she murmured, unwilling to let the moment go and yet knowing she had to.

"You're a very special woman, Mary. Easy to talk to. Sorting through this helped me clarify things. Trust is one of the strongest bonds between two people. Once it's been betrayed, no matter how things get patched, it's never the same. But I've trusted you with things I've said to no one.

"Is that part of your special magic, Mary?" His hand stole between their bodies to tip her chin up. "Don't judge all men by what your husband did. No," he whispered, tightening his arm around her, "I'm going to say my piece and not let you go until I do.

"He must have loved you to distraction. Only another man could understand that. You're a lovely woman. You have a good heart. There's strength of purpose and kindness that earned my admiration. A man who loved such a woman would very selfishly and possessively want to keep all of her to himself. I know I would.''

She had closed her eyes, now, eyes opened, she saw his head angle lower.

You're wrong! she wanted to scream.

She couldn't stay within his arms. This close, with her heartbeat pounding, desire flaring to life. No! One devastating battering to her senses was all she could stand.

She tore herself free of his arms.

''You're wrong, Rafe.'' She clasped one hand to her mouth. She hadn't meant to say it. But a small, hard-built dam had been cracked by his words.

''Very wrong. Love had nothing to do with it. Harry—'' She stopped and backed away. She couldn't tell him the real reason. She could not lay bare her soul—her secret shame.

She barely managed to raise her hand to ward off his forward move. ''Don't,'' she demanded in a choked voice.

She wasn't the woman he had spoken of in a voice warm with admiration. She felt as if he had thrust a knife in her belly and twisted it. It was the only way she could think of the pain.

Half a woman. Worthless. She heard Harry's voice shouting in her mind.

But she would not run. Not from herself or from her past. She had learned that she couldn't. But she could and did turn her back on Rafe.

She heard nothing of the vicious, self-directed swearing he muttered while caring for the horses.

What had he done? What had he said to make her vanish like a ghost? She had not disappeared in quite that way. Physically, she had walked into the house. But the woman he had kissed, the woman he had praised, had gone.

What had she said? He was wrong. Very wrong. *Love had nothing to do with it.*

How could that be true? How could any man not love her?

Chapter Seventeen

Rafe carried Beth upstairs after supper. Had he been the only one to sense the undercurrent of tension between him and Mary?

If he had wanted to put aside his thoughts about her, it was impossible. Her scent surrounded him in her room, and she was right behind him.

Beth was half-asleep, and Rafe veered from the bed to sit in the rocker with his daughter on his lap. "Little sleepy puss," he bent to whisper, pulling off her boots.

"I missed—" She stopped to yawn. "Missed you. And I missed Mary."

"But you knew I was coming back to you."

Her small arms stole around his neck. "I hoped and hoped."

"I'll always come back to you, love. Always." Above her head, his gaze met Mary's. She turned away and began placing the few items of ready-made clothing he had bought for Beth into the top bureau drawer.

Rafe watched Mary. Twice he caught her looking into the mirror at him.

Catherine had changed the bandage, and Mary now

made short work of getting Beth undressed and into one of the new nightgowns. The hem trailed a good two inches too long.

"We'll take care of this tomorrow. If you feel up to it, Beth, we can try on a few of your things. That way I can make whatever adjustments are needed." Mary held Beth close before she gave her turn to Rafe.

"What's my little girl's pleasure tonight? A story?"

"Will you rock me, Papa? Then Mary can sing to us."

"Mary's tired, Beth." It was all he could say, when he knew she wanted out of his presence. But he hoped she would stay.

"No. I'm fine. Really." And Mary wasn't sure why she agreed, when she wanted to flee.

She brought her shawl to Rafe and watched him wrap it around Beth and her Muffy. It seemed foolish for her to sit on the bed or stand to sing, so she settled herself on the floor, close enough to touch Beth's hair.

Mary sang "Lorena," a haunting love song that had made Confederate soldiers so homesick there were desertions after the song was heard. Someone had told her the name had become so popular that for years after the end of the war baby girls were christened with the name.

"Jeanie with the Light Brown Hair," an old Stephen Foster song, became, with little effort, "Bethie," and that brought a sleepy grin to the child's face.

Long before Mary had finished the song, Beth was asleep. Rafe tucked her in bed, and kissed her.

Mary was waiting with a whispered good-night when he turned around.

He couldn't argue with a woman who had backed

into a shadowed corner. Rafe left, but instead of going across the hall to the spare room, he went downstairs.

He needed answers. Sarah was his choice to provide them.

"Beth asleep?" Catherine asked when he came into the kitchen.

"Mary's with her."

"Coffee, Rafe? Catherine and I were just going to sit down and figure out where to store—"

"I want to take a look around outside. Come with me, Sarah."

"Sure." Sarah shared a puzzled look with Catherine. Sarah shrugged, grabbed her rifle, then followed Rafe. He was halfway to the corral when she caught up with him.

"A nice night for a walk," she remarked, wondering where the fire was. She had a long stride for a woman, or so she had been told, but she was hard put to keep pace with him.

"Rafe, do you ever look up at that vast black sky and wonder how far away the stars are? Or where they come from?"

"A time or two. Sarah," he said, stopping abruptly to face her, "will you tell me about Mary? About her marriage?"

Sarah shivered, despite her wool shirt. "Why are you asking me?" There was more than curiosity in her question. Sarah had to protect Mary.

"I want to know. Need to."

"That's not good enough, Rafe. You're asking for what I can't give you. I'd break my word. But I can't deny that I'd like to know why it should matter to you."

Rafe started off again, and Sarah walked by his side, around the corral, where their presence made the horses restlessly pace with them. Sarah thought he wouldn't answer her. But he did, and his voice was soft with anguish.

"It matters to me. It's important. And don't ask me why. It just is." He probed the shadows behind the barn, with his other senses more than with sight. When Sarah didn't respond, he stopped. "Didn't that satisfy you?"

"Not enough. I don't understand why you need to know anything. You said you'll leave at the end of the week if Beth can travel. Mary's past has nothing to do with that. Or with you."

He barely restrained himself from taking hold of her arms and shaking what he wanted to know from her. Coming up around the far side of the barn, he leaned wearily against the siding.

"Mary told me a little about him. Her husband sounds like a first-class bastard."

"He was. He's dead, remember?"

"I said some things that—"

"What?" Sarah clutched his arm. "I swear, McCade, if you hurt my cousin after I warned you, I'll shoot you where you stand. She's had enough pain to last two women a lifetime. Tell me," she demanded, digging her fingers into his arm.

"That's just it! I don't know, Sarah." He had gone over the conversation, repeating what Mary had told him, what he had said in return. Before he stopped himself, he told Sarah a little of it.

She released his arm when he was done, and sagged against the barn. "Damn you, McCade." But there was little heat in her words.

"I don't know if I can make you understand what it was like for Mary. Have you ever begged for pennies to buy a new bar of soap because you were reduced to a sliver that wouldn't wash a mouse? No, of course not. I doubt you ever begged anyone for

anything in your life. That's what Harry did to Mary.
By the time he died, my cousin was an empty shell.
It was months before she laughed.''

Sarah tilted her head back and closed her eyes. She
had not meant to tell Rafe, but the words whispered
past her lips.

''She needed constant reassurance. Did I like supper? The coffee? Her bread? Was I really sure I didn't
mind that she bartered a few loaves for material to
make kitchen curtains? It wasn't that she told me
things as much as what I pieced together. My cousin
didn't believe she had any worth at all, not as a
woman—'' Her voice broke as she swallowed a sob.
She turned aside. Raking this up for Rafe had raked
up her own past, and she had to fight to keep memories at bay.

Rafe touched her shoulder. ''I'm sorry, Sarah. I
swear I didn't ask to hurt her or you.''

''Lord,'' she said, with a sob caught in her throat
and a bitter laugh following, ''save me from men and
their good intentions. He made her life a living hell,
and when he died, Harry left her nothing. Mary came
here—''

''She told me he'd taken the money from the sale
of her father's property.''

''He stole everything from her. Mary was the one
who wanted a home and a dozen children, a man to
love and herself the beloved. So simple a dream.
Harry fooled everyone.''

Sarah looked at Rafe, but he was nothing more than
a shadow within the shadows.

So simple a dream, she had said. Wasn't it the same
one he had shared with Valerie? Sarah was wrong,
though he wouldn't admit it to her. He had begged
Val for one more year to work his claim and amass
enough gold so she'd never want for anything again.

But Val wouldn't give him the time. And he'd often wondered, after she left with Beth, if she had ever loved him at all.

"I've satisfied your—"

"A little," he said, cutting her off. "Mary is the only one who has the right, if she will, to tell it all."

Sarah straightened. "You just remember what she said to you, Rafe. Love had nothing to do with it. Love doesn't mean the same thing to men as it does to women. When women love and marry men who turn out to be bastards, their love keeps hope alive that the men will change. There's always tomorrow. But changes don't come.

"Men, to flip the coin, cut their losses and move on. Love to them is just a word used as means to an end." She started to walk away from him, but his soft, sincere utterance stopped her for a few seconds.

"You're wrong. Men can love with hope, too."

She didn't answer him. She didn't believe him.

Mary lay awake long after Beth had fallen asleep. Rafe was the only one who had not come upstairs to bed.

She thought about the things that Rafe had told her. His wife hadn't really wanted Beth. Every womanly sense flared in outrage. How could a woman not want a child?

And she, who longed for a child, remained with aching heart and empty arms.

She warned herself not to dwell on such thoughts. Life had enough pain to drag one's spirits down. If one allowed it.

Pain had ruined too much of her life already. She refused to let it spread and darken her hours again.

But the day had been a series of shocks for her. The vicious fight, the shocking delight of Rafe's reckless spending, her own abandoned response to his kiss. *Oh, more than a mere kiss.*

Fear and forbidden longing had melded in that moment when she lost herself in his kiss. Did passion truly have a taste all its own? Was there a scent to yearning? Surely she was wrong to think that potent mingling of strong emotions, darkness and passion lingered on her tongue?

But if that was true, why did thought evoke those minutes when her every sense had been fully aroused?

"Don't," she whispered. But the warm sound of his approval replayed in her mind. Vulnerable now, Mary couldn't stop remembering the shocking intrusion of her past that forced her to understand once more how thin was her protective armor.

She shied from thinking about it and turned to the scene after supper when she'd been alone in the pantry with Sarah. She had mockingly grumbled about the smallness of the pantry and its inability to hold Rafe's generously given half share of the foodstuffs he'd purchased. To find enough room was a housewife's bane and blessing.

And then Sarah's confession of the debt Rafe claimed he owed to her, and his promise to make it good.

A shock in and of itself. But then Sarah had admitted that she had kept this deliberately from her, for fear of coloring Mary's perception of Rafe.

As if anything could.

Nothing would come of her growing feelings for him. Not only was he leaving, but she could never allow any man to have a say in her life again.

She rolled onto her side, and smoothed one hand over Beth's head. She listened to the quiet of the night and the child's breathing. Here was a blessing to think about, a child who was healing. All too soon, Mary's eyelids grew heavy. She couldn't mark the exact moment when she fell asleep.

Or the moment the dream began.

Her fierce struggles. The overwhelming need. She had to reach the child to stop the frightened cries. Helpless. The bonds that held her back. The cry was louder, more urgent in summoning her aid.

Only the cries weren't in her mind. They were real.

"Beth!" She held the child's shuddering body within the shelter of her arms. "Hush, baby. I'm here with you." Mary hugged her, and repeated that she wasn't alone. It was long minutes before the child seemed fully awake and the shaking subsided.

"Sweetie, can you tell me what frightened you?"

Beth sniffed and rubbed her eyes. She nestled closer to Mary. "The ghoulies came."

"Ah, very frightening indeed." What monster had scared her with such talk? The question went begging for an answer. She had to calm Beth. She could feel the child's fright, understand it with aching clarity. It was not so different from her own terrors.

Beth whimpered. Mary rocked her and brushed the tangled hair back from her face. "It's a bad dream, little one, and bad dreams go away. Let me light the candle—"

But Mary's move to turn had Beth clamping her arm around her neck. "Don't...leave me."

"I won't leave you." What terrible happening haunted the child's sleep? Should she question her? It wasn't her right to pry. But the trembling was not lessened.

"Honey, can you tell me why these ghoulies came? We could find a magic to make them go away."

Beth was silent, but for an occasional sob, for so long that Mary didn't think she would answer her.

Then she said, "Mave said they come at night. To

eat little girls who ask for too much. They like to hide in the dark.''

"Then we need the candle lit. The light will help us to chase them away. Come, turn with me so we still hold each other tight.''

Mary managed to scoot up a bit, so that she was almost sitting. Beth lay on top of her. It was awkward at best to try and strike the match, but two tries and the candle was lit.

Beth squeezed her eyes closed and, no matter how Mary coaxed, refused to open them.

Careful of Beth's wounded arm, Mary pulled the quilt up to the child's shoulders, making sure it was snug about her.

"Are you warm enough? That's important, Beth. First the light, then feeling safe and warm. I'll keep my arms around you, too.''

"Muffy's scared, too.''

"We'll tuck her under the covers, then. She can hide while you and I try to find the right magic to get rid of these ghoulies. After all, we know how brave you are, but Muffy isn't as old as you. She needs you to protect her.''

"Like a mama?''

"Yes, sweet, like a mama.'' The pressure of Beth's arm around her neck said as much as the look on her face. Trust. A wondrous gift from anyone, more special coming from this child.

"Do you have ghoulies, Mary?''

"Everyone is afraid of something, Beth. Even me.''

"And Papa?''

"We'll have to ask him.'' Mary tilted her head to the side, her eyes awash with tears. Beth stared back at her. Her gray eyes, so like her father's, were impossibly expressive, and too wise for a child of six.

"Do you want to tell me what you asked for?"

"It's a secret. I told God. And Muffy."

"Ah, a secret. Then you mustn't tell. Now, we can find some magic words, so if these monsters come again, you can chase them."

"Magic words?"

"Yes, my sweet. First we say the words, then, why, we hunt up the magic...er..." Mary struggled to recall what was in her wardrobe. "A cane. That's it. My papa's magic cane. We'll hunt the ghoulies out of shadows and from under the bed. That's where they're hiding?"

Beth sucked her thumb, eyes solemn, as she nodded.

"Now you say this. 'The Lord loves me, Papa loves me, and Mary does, too.' And we mustn't forget Sarah and Catherine.

"Ah, yes, and the mommy tabby with all her kittens. Catherine's chickens and Papa's horses. All the birds. Oh, and Muffy, too. She loves you almost as much as your papa does."

"I loved Mama lots. She went away. I wished and wished she wouldn't go. She said having me wasn't enough. She...she needed more...more love."

"Oh, little one." Mary rocked her from side to side, begging for the wisdom to ease the child's troubled mind.

"Mave said the ghoulies always know when you wish too much." Beth lifted her head, her eyes reaching deep into Mary's, that steady gaze disquieting.

"Mave was wrong, Beth. Love isn't what makes people go away. No one can have too much love. And your wishes had nothing to do with your mama going away. You weren't punished for that. Sometimes the Lord needs more angels to help him. He knows your papa needs you more than anyone."

Mary felt herself drowning in deep waters. If Beth truly believed she had placed her mother in jeopardy and caused her death, what could she do to help her?

"Beth, shall we tell your father about this? He's a brave man. He loves you so much, sweetie. Your papa would slay all the ghoulies and monsters in the world to keep you safe."

"Can't tell. He'll be sad again. He...he cried," she whispered. "I told him Mama said he didn't want me."

"But you know that isn't true, Beth."

"I know. Will you sing to me?"

Mary hummed a lullaby. Little by little she felt Beth's body relax against hers, the child's breathing even. She never knew what made her look toward the open doorway. It wasn't a noise.

But Rafe stood there, and when she would have spoken to him, he pressed a finger to his lips.

This was one time Mary was glad she couldn't see his face, couldn't look into his eyes. She was filled with enough anger and sadness of her own at what Beth had told her. She couldn't deal with Rafe's emotions, too.

But she wanted to. Lord, how she wanted to go to him.

Rafe lost track of how long he stood watching Mary and fighting his need to gather her and Beth into his arms. He knew that, given time and enough love, he could slay all Beth's dragons. But Mary's...

He would carry the picture she made, bathed in candlelight, framed by a cloud of red-gold fire he would gladly singe his hands on just to touch. The pale, luminous sheen of skin, cream against the pristine white of her nightgown. Her lips reddened where she had bitten them, and her eyes, a brighter green brimming with emotion.

He added the missing pieces left unsaid by Mary and later by Sarah. He thought of what she had given Beth and wished, as he rarely did, for time to slip back. An hour was all he wanted with Mary's husband. One segment of time to beat an understanding into the man of what a truly worthless wife was.

It wasn't a woman like Mary.

There was an abundance of love within the woman holding his daughter. There was passion there, too. More than he had thought to find.

But he had to struggle with an idea that formed— to struggle for the trust involved. An issue that went beyond the confidences he had shared with Mary, and was a hundred times more important. Beth stood at its heart.

And he couldn't trust his own. He'd been wrong once.

Beth had suffered with him. He would never knowingly put his daughter or himself through that agony again.

He had another consideration to weigh, and one that was equally important to him. Mary's pride.

Money had proved to be a touchy issue between them. She would get her feathers ruffled if he dared offer her a gift of money.

The woman presented all sorts of problems for him. A week before he had to leave, he had told her.

Given the challenge Mary presented, he could surely move one of her mountains. Maybe two.

Rafe lingered for a last look at Mary. And he knew she was a woman worth attempting a mountain for.

Chapter Eighteen

Rafe lingered over his coffee at the kitchen table. A splash of sunshine warmed his back. Beth was still sleeping, and while he had to go back into town, he wanted to see her first.

Mary, lovely to watch, was putting the last of their breakfast dishes away after refusing his offer to help. Just as she had turned aside his attempt to thank her for what she had done with Beth last night.

Yesterday he had seen the barrier set in place between them. Through supper she had remained distant, even when the other women pressed her to describe materials and styles chosen for new gowns. He'd never known a woman who wasn't thrilled to shop for new clothes. But he was learning that Mary wasn't like other women he'd known.

This morning Mary had shored up the barrier into a solid wall. He was readjusting his first planned foray to scout the obstacles in his path when Catherine joined them.

"Done. Hall, stairs and front foyer swept," she announced while putting the broom in the pantry. "And see, Mary," she said, waving the feather duster in the air, "I did use it in the parlor this time."

Mary, with hands on hips, surveyed the few dust smudges on Catherine's white apron.

"Ah, mum, don't be looking at me so. Am I not dusty enough to be believed? Ye can't be knowing how you strike terror in my heart with that fierce gaze that picks a speck of lint from the carpet." Catherine posed with feathers tickling her chin. She sneezed, then made a deep curtsy to Mary. "Now, mum, will ye be wantin' more from this poor hardworkin' lass this fine an' glorious morn?"

"There's a good lass," Mary returned, stifling her need to laugh. "If you're in a mood to clean—"

"Never!" Catherine declared, pressing the feather duster to her heart and flinging her arm to her forehead. "Woe to me, for ye's a cruel woman."

Mary couldn't contain her laughter, and between fresh bursts she claimed that Catherine would never change.

Catherine agreed and laughed harder. They both glanced at Rafe. His puzzled expression sent gales of laughter to fill the kitchen.

"Will one of you share the joke with me?"

Mary recovered first. "It's the cleaning," she began.

"Aye, the infernal cleaning," Catherine added.

"None of us like spending the entire morning doing it, but we all like a clean house. Catherine tends to skimp where she can get away with it."

"And, to my sorrow, I caused Mary embarrassment when the ladies' sewing circle met here. Do you know there are women who poke their gloved fingers on moldings and mantels to discover how well you clean?"

"It's not been my experience..." Rafe started to say.

"Well, it's been mine. I'm careful not to neglect

my chores since then.'' She looked at Mary. ''Did you ask him?''

''Ask me what?''

''Catherine wants to take Beth to see the kittens in the barn. She found a mousehole for the mother cat to explore in the tack room. That should keep her out of the hayloft long enough for Beth to play with the little ones.''

Rafe was aware that while Mary spoke she had moved closer to his side. The deep breath he drew to steady his reaction to her nearness had the opposite effect. Her scent made him lose track of the conversation.

''Rafe, this is just what Beth needs.'' Mary placed her hand on his shoulder, unaware of the havoc she caused him, because she was dealing with her own unsettled feeling. A tingling heat raced from her hand to spread through her body. For Beth she had to convince him to say yes.

''You do understand it is important to her?''

''Her?'' He was ready to blindly agree to whatever Mary wanted for Beth, and yet, at the same time, he wanted to keep her close to him.

''Please let her pick out a kitten for her own. They are almost ready to be weaned. The kitten would not only be a comfort to her, but will teach her responsibility, too. You said your home is isolated, and with winter coming, Beth must have things to occupy her. And she's such a loving child. She would adore having a kitten of her own.''

''A kitten?'' He struggled to display some reluctance, knowing he was torturing himself.

''She can have her choice of five,'' Catherine said. ''I picked out a darling marmalade male for myself. She can have more than one. Two or three. Cats like the company of other cats. Well, some do.''

"And I know we have a basket around here that she could use to carry the kitten. It wouldn't be a burden to you, Rafe."

Mary's hand pressed against his shoulder. He wanted to cover it with his own, but not with Catherine watching. "I'd be condemned for meanness if I tried to stand against such earnest pleas. How can a man refuse when you're right?"

When Beth woke up, Rafe insisted on taking care of her by himself. Mary gave him a salve that would help Beth's wound heal and keep the skin soft, along with clean strips of linen. She felt hurt, as if he were already forcing the parting to come.

She swore it was hurt and not resentment she felt when she went to work in her garden. She had no right to be resentful. She should be happy to have her daily routine back. But for once the peace she found in weeding around her plants, in the enticing scents released into the air, failed her. Rafe was Beth's father, her only parent, and he loved her. She was a friend at best, and at worst someone to be quickly forgotten.

Work was what she needed to occupy her. And Mary attacked the weeds that had sprung up after the rain.

Upstairs, Beth could hardly contain her excitement over picking out a kitten. Rafe, patiently working through the intricacies of dressing his daughter, wished he hadn't been so curt in his refusal to let Mary help. He'd make it up to her, he silently promised. Right now, he had to talk to Beth.

"Yes, love, we'll go as soon as I get your boots on." Rafe tugged them on her small feet, for she didn't have much strength back yet. But her appetite improved each day. He wished the shadows beneath her eyes would soon fade.

Rafe surveyed his daughter. The calf-length blue dress and white pinafore were large for Beth. The wide shoulder straps of the apron slipped off one shoulder, but he was glad he'd listened to Mary when she suggested the larger size to accommodate Beth's bandage.

"Up you go." He lifted her with a short swing that made her squeal and perched her on top of the bureau. "Now for this little bird's nest." Rafe took a deep breath and picked up the new hairbrush he'd bought.

"Ouch, Papa."

"Sorry, love. But this is the worst tangle. I've a good mind to cut a heap of this off, Beth. Then we both wouldn't suffer."

"Oh, silly Papa. You can't cut my hair. I wouldn't be a pretty little girl."

Rafe bent over and touched his nose to hers. Beth's giggle was worth his attempt to cross his eyes. "Far as I can see, you'll always be a pretty little girl to your papa."

But when he resumed his brushing, Beth cried out again.

"It hurts. The brush is so hard."

"That's because it's new."

"Use Mary's. She said I could. She likes sharing things with me."

"Then how will we get rid of the stiffness in your brush, miss?"

"I can use it for Muffy when my arm's all better."

"Sweets, I hate to tell you this, but Muffy doesn't have any hair."

"Silly papa. She will. Mary promised me some."

"Ah, Mary's going to cut off some of yours."

"No. Oh, no, Papa. She'll sew yarn on Muffy's head."

While Rafe brushed out her hair as gently as he

could, he told Beth they would be leaving at the end of the week to go home.

"I know how much you'll miss Mary—"

"Oh, yes. And Catherine and Sarah, too."

"Will it make you sad to leave them, Beth?"

"They are very nice to me, Papa. But if we go away, who will take care of me?"

"I will." *And do a better job of it this time.* Rafe tied a bow in the ribbon he had wrapped around the end of the single braid, then stood back to look at his handiwork. "Not too bad, Beth. I'm getting better. All the ends are tucked in this time."

Beth attempted to twist around to look in the mirror, and cried out when the movement pulled at her wound.

"Not so fast." Rafe scooped her up in his arms. "We need to be careful for a while longer."

Beth laid her head against his chest, and he rested his chin on top, resisting the urge to squeeze her tight. She was so precious to him, he sometimes thought he'd never have time enough to show her how much she was loved.

"Papa? If you take care of me, who takes care of you?"

"We'll take care of each other."

"I wish we could stay here. Mary will be all alone and very sad without me. But I want to go home, too."

"Did she tell you that, Beth?" Swift anger rose inside at the thought that anyone would try to manipulate Beth's feelings.

"Oh, no." She pressed her hand over his heart. "I feel it. I wouldn't tell her. She might be so sad that she would cry."

Rafe cleared his throat. He should have known better than to suspect that Mary would try to use his child. But it never ceased to surprise him how Beth reasoned things out for herself.

"Then this will be our secret. We don't want Mary to cry."

Beth rubbed her cheek against him. "I have a secret with Mary. And I have a big wish. I wish Mary could come with us. She doesn't have a little girl of her own. If she did, she told me she would wish her to be just like me. But I'm your little girl, Papa."

"Yes, love, forever and ever."

"If Mary came home with us, we'd be like a family. Wouldn't we?" she asked in a very soft voice, almost as if she were afraid to ask, and more afraid of the answer.

Rafe had wanted to know how Beth felt about Mary, and now he knew. To say anything to his daughter before he spoke to Mary would leave the path open to hurt.

"I think we need to talk more about this, but for now, let's go look at those kittens."

Mary, working at the far end of the garden, looked up when Beth called her. She straightened slowly, smiled and waved, but stopped herself from going over to them. Beth was wrapped in a shawl against the cool morning breeze. Rafe's new red wool shirt drew her eyes. The cloth fit his body as closely as a glove made for it. Like her, he was bareheaded, and he wore his gun. She remembered thinking he would look naked without it.

Catherine stood waiting with Sarah near the open barn doors. Mary turned back to gathering sprigs of herbs and their flowers to replenish the dried ones she intended to give to Rafe for fevers, wounds and a hundred other uses.

The thought of Beth or him getting hurt and being alone preyed on her mind. The smallest of cuts and scrapes could cause serious complications if not treated properly. To say nothing of falls and broken bones. Even the simplest sprain could swell longer than necessary unless wrapped with linen soaked in beaten egg whites.

"Mary?"

She glanced up. Rafe was crossing the yard toward her. She stood there and waited.

Rafe had never known a woman could remain so still. She was wearing the same faded gown she'd had on the first time he saw her, covered with a large apron, slightly soiled from her morning's work. She was bareheaded, and without a shawl, despite the chill breeze. The red-gold fire cloud of her hair had been subdued to a dull glow, and he blamed it on the neat cornet of braids.

She stood and waited—straight back, lifted chin and face devoid of expression. Unless he drew close enough to see her eyes. Expression was alive there. Pride and a bit of fear darkened their green color.

"Could you come inside? I need to discuss a problem with you."

"If it's about last night, and why I didn't come for you—"

"No. Come inside to the parlor." Rafe didn't pause to make sure she followed him. He went through the kitchen, down the hall and into the front parlor. There, he stood by the doors. He wasn't going to give Mary a chance to refuse him before he said his piece, he wasn't about to allow her to put him off until later.

He had no intention of taking no for an answer, and he couldn't wait.

Mary barely glanced at him as she stepped inside the room. She heard the doors close, and his invitation to sit. She looked at her favorite wing chair, but some inner voice warned that this was not a time for comfort. She chose instead one of the straight-backed, armless side chairs next to the settee.

She started to fold her hands together in her lap, but didn't. Rafe wasn't sitting. He paced the thread-bare carpet. The stalking grace of his tall, lean body put her in mind of a caged animal—predator, not prey. She was to have the role of tethered lamb. Despite her mind's refusal to play it, she gripped the chair's seat with hands hidden by the folds of her skirt.

He stopped and faced her, making her the target of a steel-gray gaze. The blackish, purpled bruise surrounding one eye should have softened his look. She found it added to the force of it, and remained still.

Waiting. Praying nothing painful was to come. Hope dying when he spoke.

"Mary, I have an offer to make to you. Before I begin, I want your promise that you will consider what I say carefully before giving me an answer."

She looked away from him. He was asking her to trust him. No matter how he phrased his request, the underlying question remained one of trust.

Could she do that?

They are only words.

But words had the terrible power to wound.

"Mary, is what I asked so difficult to grant?"

"For me? Yes, it is."

"Then, will you listen for Beth's sake, and leave us—"

"All right." She cut him off quite deliberately. She did not want to hear him pair the two of them in any way. He was leaving. They couldn't be a pair.

She listened, her gaze focused on the lamp sitting in the center of the table before the window. Her gaze narrowed on the lamp's hanging crystal prisms. The sunlight caught within the cut glass flashed rainbows of color.

Her mind was drifting. Thus she had sat through Harry's trials. But Harry was dead. Rafe was here, very much alive as he demanded her attention.

Mary started to find him so close. He knelt on one knee, his booted foot taking the weight of the other bent leg. The spread of his thighs pressed against her legs. The warmth of his body penetrated her drifting state. He lifted her hands from the chair and held them within his own.

"Mary, did you hear one word?"

"Yes. I heard you." She didn't look at his face. His hands were much larger than hers. Months away from hard work had softened the calluses on his palms. Strong hands, with long fingers whose touch made her tremble with desire.

But he hadn't spoken of desire. He was offering a business arrangement.

"Tell what I said that made you withdraw."

"You wish to employ me. For six months. At a salary I could not earn in a year of sewing. There are hardships, mainly the isolation. You painted a clear, stark picture of the terms you are offering me."

"I thought they would meet with your approval."

"You are quite right." *And wrong.*

"I can't find a bit of assurance in your voice, Mary."

The softening in his husky voice as he said her name pierced her guard.

"Can't you look at me?" Rafe's voice was coaxing, but he had to work to keep a lid on the temper beginning to simmer.

"Can you tell me what it is I've said that makes you withdrawn?"

"Nothing. I'll do as you asked and consider this."

Even though he was freshly shaved, a dark shadow made his features appear even more chiseled and somewhat harsh. Mary attempted to pull her hands free from the grip of his, but he tightened his hold. The implacable set of his face warned her that Rafe was not going to be easily dismissed.

She sensed his frowning concentration totally focused on herself. It was unnerving. She glanced down at her lap. She wondered if the air between them really did pulse with tension, or if only she felt it.

Rafe thought furiously through what he had said to her, and how he had said it. What had he done to make Mary pale? Difficult as it was, given her natural fairness, it was happening before his eyes. He couldn't ignore it.

He'd deliberately left one issue unspoken between them. He had hoped to let it remain ever in his mind, but unsaid on his lips.

Now it was no longer a question of his risking outright refusal. He had to know.

"You haven't taken a notion that the money I offered you included having you share my bed? Do you think I'd insult you with such an offer?"

"I never thought—"

"If I wanted you for a mistress— No! That's much too polite for what you're thinking. A paid whore, isn't it?"

His control was slipping. Rafe moved before she could stop him. He rose in a rush and hauled her to stand in front of him. He forced himself to hold on to her hands, when all he wanted to do was shake some answers from her.

"You're a woman, Mary, not a green girl. You've been married. I assume you shared your husband's bed. Surely you know when a man wants you?"

"Stop!" She struggled, but he wouldn't let her go.

Each word fell upon her flesh like a knife prick. *Not like you. And I've never wanted the way you make me want.* She bit her lip to stop her confession from spilling forth.

"You're so damned skilled using silence as a weapon. Don't answer me," he said in a taunting voice. "But what's between us has nothing to do with my offer. I'm not a callow boy. I'm a man, Mary. And passion will not rule me. I'm not an animal who'll force your submission the moment I have you away from the protection of your home.

"Do you hear me?" He almost growled the words. "No force. No rape."

"Don't say such things. Stop it," she moaned, tugging against his fierce grip. "I never thought that. You don't know what's in my mind. You can't possibly know."

"Why? Is it so different from my thoughts? I'd have you in a heartbeat, if you'd come to me willingly. You must know I want you."

He whispered the last over her lips, losing the battle with the temptation to forget everything and remember only the taste of her.

"If desire isn't what you're afraid of, then tell what it is."

She shook her head, the movement brushing her hair against his lips and leaving him filled with the scent of her.

"Marriage, then? Did you expect me to offer you a marriage of convenience?"

She couldn't get away from him, and she refused to hide any longer. She lifted her head, and met the heated, fierce gray-eyed gaze he pinned on her with all the courage she had.

"No. Never that. I wasn't expecting a proposal of marriage. I wouldn't accept. I won't marry you or any man. Marriage involves total trust. I couldn't give that to any man again.''

It all came down to trust. And he found himself saying those very words to her, even when he knew they held true for him.

''You...you were right to think only of Beth.''

Beth? She had been driven from the center of his thoughts the moment he took Mary into his arms. If he had not caught the betraying tremor of her voice, he might have believed her.

''Oh, no. You won't use Beth to hide behind. We were talking about us. About trust and lies. Beth has no place here. It's between you and me, Mary. This is about need and denial.'' *And temptation.*

''You need, Mary. Deny it all you want with words, but you can't hide the need I see in your eyes. You can't taste it in your kiss. I do. This time you'll know, without a doubt lingering in your mind, that I do want you.''

She could have stopped him. There was a pause so infinite as his words died away before he lowered his head. Time enough for her to turn aside. Time enough to say no. Rafe was right. She could and did deny her own need. She wanted his kisses. Wanted him. But giving voice to her need meant giving power to it. She simply couldn't.

But the lips that met his were not cool and unresponsive, as he feared. They were parted. Hot and seeking. Hungry as his own.

Heat soared like an exploding keg of black powder, the blast engulfing them in its inferno. The bite of her fingers in his back urged him to take, and take, and take.

Rafe broke the kiss as suddenly as it had begun, but did not release her.

''Say you want me, Mary. Give me that much.''

She held his gaze with her own, searching past the blaze of passion darkening his eyes to the truth of his need for her. And she knew the lie would no longer serve.

Twice she parted her lips to speak, and twice he kissed her into silence, using teeth and tongue to claim her mouth, his hands stroking her body, claiming that, too, as his.

Mary, cradling his face within her hands, forced their lips to part. She gave in to the longing she had had from the first, and lifted one hand to brush back the wayward lock of hair from his forehead.

"I want you," she whispered, looking into his eyes. She felt the thunderous race of his heart, matching measure for measure the pounding of her own.

There was no air to breathe without his scent. Her body had softened to mold the hardness of his. No question, no doubt, lingered about where this passion would take them. Her breasts were swollen, the tips aching for relief. Moments ago, the rocking thrust of his hips against her belly had sent heat pooling between her trembling thighs.

And she said it once more, wanting to be sure, needing to know that he heard her. "I want you." Her arms lifted to his shoulders, his moved in a slow journey from her hips to the span of her waist, then slower still, to shape her rib cage. Each nearing touch intensified the ache that filled her. Her fingertips dug into his shoulders, a throaty sound escaped her. Her eyes closed when he used his thumbs to torment the tips of her breasts.

She discovered she had never known the true depth of passion. She, who had shared her husband's bed for the years of her marriage, had not truly been touched by the force of desire singing in her blood.

Moments later, she cried out his name. When he

kissed her, she was prepared for anything but lips tempered with a tenderness that made her heart ache.

It ended all too soon.

He pressed her head against his chest, rubbing his lips over her hair. "Mary, I want your trust. As much as I want you, lovely lady. But to gain one, I'll forgo the other— Leave me."

She trembled like a startled doe. "No. I—"

"Leave me, Mary," he ordered, in a voice husky and dark with passion. "Go. Go, before I lose what little control you've left me and take you here."

Rafe didn't give her a choice. He swept her into his arms and brought her to the door. "Open it. For both our sakes, open the door."

A faint hint of color mantled his high cheekbones. Beneath her hand, she felt the tautness of his body, and his eyes, staring down at her, were dark with need.

Signs that didn't lie, couldn't lie to her. *I want your trust. As much as I want you…to gain one, I'll forgo the other…*

She didn't know what to feel. Emotions ranged like predatory beasts seeking out the carefully built walls and scaling them to show their power.

Suddenly afraid, Mary opened the door.

Rafe set her on her feet in the hall. He wanted her trust so badly. He closed the door and pressed his shoulder against it. He closed his eyes and saw Mary standing there, watching him, those eyes hiding secrets from him. Was she angry that he had aroused them both to a fever pitch and then ruthlessly denied her? And himself. Surely she couldn't forget that. He saw her lips, moist and reddened, slightly swollen from his kisses, and desire prowled deep. Staggeringly deep, into his body, to run through his blood until he didn't trust himself not to go after her.

Trust. This was about gaining her trust.
But to what end?
Rafe couldn't put it into words. Not even to him-self.

Chapter Nineteen

There was a dreamlike quality to the autumn afternoon. Mary was late getting her bread ready for baking. When she had the dough kneaded for the second rising, she looked out the window. Clouds, thick as bursting cotton bolls, floated across the sky and cast thick shadows on the ground. The day had grown warmer. The last mild days would soon be gone, replaced with an intense heat to fill even the cool valleys before winter came.

Time. Two days had flown by for Mary. Rafe hadn't pressed her for an answer, but he soon would.

Last night, Beth had another nightmare. Rafe had come into the room and joined her in soothing the child back to sleep.

This morning, Mary had become aware that Beth knew nothing of her father's offer. Mary should have known that Rafe wouldn't tell his daughter about it until he had her answer. He wouldn't want Beth hurt or disappointed in any way. But Beth, with that sweet, hesitating voice, had asked on her own if Mary could come and live with them.

She glanced in surprise to see that she had shaped

all her loaves. She set them in their baking pans to rise one more time.

That word again. Rafe had bought three army mules to carry the heavier supplies. He was going forth with his plans to leave, and spent part of each day in town. The mules, he claimed, were a lucky buy. The army was closing a few of the smaller forts, now that more Indians had been brought into the reservations.

There had been little opportunity for her to be alone with him since the morning he asked her to join him in the parlor. Such a simple request. He had an offer to make, and would she listen?

She really didn't want to think about it, and yet could do little else. She didn't want to remember the hour she had listened, or the offer itself. She felt as if she were teetering on a seesaw. Sometimes she wished she had simply and adamantly refused him.

But she had not. She had stayed to hear him, and she had agreed to consider his request.

A business arrangement, he called his terms. But it wasn't true. Could never be true. Her heart was very much involved.

And the temptation he held out to her... Oh, she couldn't stand firm against its lure. She would have Beth. A child to give all the love she had stored these many empty years.

And Rafe... This desire she felt for him was new. And painful. She wanted to lie with him, a man not her husband, all pretense stripped away. She wanted him in her bed, and in her body, man and woman together. And she would not feel ashamed.

How could she admit that and not trust him?

If she accepted his offer, she would be Rafe McCade's paid employee—companion to his daughter, housekeeper of his home.

"What are you mumbling about, Mary?" Sarah asked, tossing her gloves and hat on the table. "Lord, but it's getting hot enough to fry eggs out there."

"I'm late getting my bread to rise."

Sarah noticed the pensive look of her cousin. "What's wrong? And don't tell me nothing is troubling you. You're as bad as Rafe. He just rode in. He's had no word of where Balen and Shell Lundy disappeared to, but he swears he's not worried. No one in town has seen either man since the fight."

Sarah drank thirstily from the dipper in the bucket. She refilled it, and offered it to Mary.

"Sarah, would you let Beth stay with us? If Rafe agreed?"

"Mary—"

"She'll be no trouble." She rushed on, the idea forming as she spoke. "She could winter with us. Rafe would be free to hunt down those who would kill him. Beth would be safe. She could attend church services, have Nita's granddaughter to play with, and go to school."

"And your heart and arms would be filled to overflowing. Oh, Mary, did you need to ask? Could I say no?" She went to her cousin and hugged her. "But Rafe won't agree. You know he won't. Don't set yourself up for heartbreak."

"He offered me a position, Sarah. With more money than I've had—"

"But I have enough—"

"No." She pulled back to see Sarah's face. "It's yours. I need my own security. But first I must ask him to consider leaving Beth."

"Then go. Catherine's still over at the boarding-house. She's dickering with Mrs. Harkins about supplying eggs, since she'll have more than enough with the new flock of chickens."

"Listen for Beth. She's sleeping in the parlor." She stepped away to strip off her apron.

"Mary, caution. Rafe's a generous man, and I admit my opinion of him has changed considerably since he's been with us. But don't mistake his generosity for softness. That man's a hard case. And I've seen enough of them to know."

Mary rushed to the door, then turned. "Sarah, would you trust him?"

"As far as I'd trust any man. But we're not talking about what I'd do, are we?"

"No. This is my decision."

Mary found him in the corral. He was working, as he had each day, with one of the mustangs carrying a loaded pack. Rafe had mentioned he wanted to be sure of the well-distributed weight each horse could carry.

She stood for a few moments watching him. He stood in the center of the corral, working the mustang on a lunge line. Two circles by the horse and he signaled for a faster pace. Small puffs of dust kicked up by the horse's hooves settled on his boots and pants. He wasn't wearing a vest today, and sweat stained his dark blue shirt, molding it to his body.

Sunlight spilled on his black hair. Mary drank in the sight of him. She didn't fight the quickening breath, the soft, warm rise of desire. It had become a foolish exercise to try.

She wasn't aware that she had done anything to attract his attention, but she lifted her gaze to see that he was looking at her.

She appeared calm. She'd made her decision. Rafe suddenly didn't want to hear it. He drew in the lunge line, and grabbed hold of the mustang's headstall. Without saying a word to her, he stripped off the pack, freed the horse and hefted the heavy weight to

his shoulder. He came toward her, searching her face
for a clue, but Mary, as he well knew, kept her secrets—unless she was responding with a passion he
had never dreamed he would find in a woman.

"Your cheeks are flushed bright as Indian paint-
brush," he teased, and set aside his burden.

"Beth's napping."

"Good. She needs the rest."

So easily, he reminded her that Beth would have
little rest on the trail.

"That's what I've come to talk to you about,
Rafe."

He stripped his neckerchief off and wiped his face.
He ran his hand through his hair, looking back at the
horse standing at the far side of the corral. Delaying
tactics.

She was glad he didn't look at her. It made the
words easier, but when she finished telling him that
Beth would be safer and better-off left with them,
Mary felt as if she had been plunged into an icy pool.
His eyes were that cold, coming to bear on her.

"No."

It was flat and hard and hateful to hear. "Please,
we can talk—"

"You have my answer, Mary. I'm not willing to
wait another day for yours."

Her uncertainties, all the danger he presented,
rushed to fill her mind.

Watching her, he knew what flashed through her
mind. He had his own doubts, and the added worry
of wondering where Balen and Lundy were hiding in
wait for him to make a move. He didn't think for one
minute that the beating and the warning he had issued
had chased either man off his trail.

But he couldn't share that with Mary. Not until he
had her answer.

"What's it to be, Mary? Yes or no?"

"Sarah warned me not to make the mistake of confusing your generosity with softness. I never did."

His breath caught painfully in his chest as every muscle in his body tensed. It was akin to the moment he'd found the color he was searching for in broken rock. Anticipation building to the excitement of discovering a deep vein of gold. Every second fraught with the fear that he couldn't trust his own sight and instincts. That he was wrong...

"You win, Rafe. I accept your offer."

She turned before he released his breath. He let her walk away. *There's no winning for me alone, Mary. Only time will teach you that.*

Mary had lied to him. She had lied to Sarah and to Catherine. Rafe was not the one who had won. She had. She could tell herself, and the others, that she was going with him for Beth, for the independence the money would give her.

It was part of the truth, but not all.

She glanced at the bed where Beth cuddled her doll and slept with a smile on her face. She thought about how much love a heart could hold. Into her vision came the image of Rafe's face.

Love was the true reason she had said yes.

The following days were a flurry of activity for Mary. Now that her mind was made up, she refused to allow doubts to come creeping in.

Rafe checked over her sorrel mare. She was not young stock, having been a last gift from her father the year he died.

"Her name is Owl," Mary said, watching his hands move slowly over fetlock and flank. Rafe's quirked brow had her adding, "Even as a three-year-old, she had a wise way about her. She's steady and dependable, but doesn't lack spirit, and she will ride her heart out if asked.''

Mary and Beth joined Rafe while he performed a minute inspection of Mary's saddle gear.

"This cinch is just worn enough to be replaced."

Beth spied the cat with her kittens and took off for the far stall. She had made her choice of a tabby kitten that resembled its mother. She had agreed to let the kitten spend a good part of the day to learn necessary survival skills, but naps and bedtime found the kitten sleeping with Beth or in the lined basket Mary provided for her.

"Not too long, Beth," Mary called out. And she said to Rafe, who was watching his daughter skip down the center aisle, "She's growing stronger every day."

"Thanks to your care, Mary. I'll bring a new cinch back with me. Is there anything else you need?"

She smiled. His warm praise made it easier to ask for the few items she needed. "Boots. I don't have any. Two pairs of pants. It will be more comfortable to ride in them. But I want you to take the cost out of my salary."

"I wouldn't think of doing anything else, Mary." His grin and the gleam in his eyes gave the lie to that. "You could ride in with me. Check on Mrs. Mullins and see how far along she is with the sewing. And the fit of a boot is not something I can do for you."

Rafe set the saddle down, and stood up. "Mary, in less than two days you are going to ride off with me and my child. You can't avoid being with me—"

"I'm not avoiding you. There's been so much to do. I—" She stopped at the touch of his hand cupping her chin, and she looked up to see him shaking his head.

"Have it your way, for now. Let's go trace the sole of your shoe, and I'll see what I can find to fit you."

The relief in her eyes warned him not to push her. What he felt for Mary was more than desire, although that was there, too. This was something tender. And that tenderness spurred his need to dispel her wariness. He wanted to tease her, and hear her laugh.

He startled her by putting his hands on her waist.

"What are you doing?"

He lifted her easily, then set her back from him. Sheer devilry lit his gaze. "Measuring your waist. Can't expect me to buy pants so big they'll be a danger to you. I don't want you to fall. I want every step you take to be on firm ground."

She would have responded to the underlying message, but his hands slid down to measure the span of her hips. Her breath caught.

"Mmm. Just what I thought. Boy slim, woman soft, and pleasing as heaven to touch." He stepped back, laughing at her vexed expression. But he got what he wanted. She smiled.

"Rafe McCade, your road to heaven is going to be a long haul."

His laughter ceased. "That's me, Mary, a man for the long haul. And I never claimed to be a saint."

"Nor I." She wanted to recall the words, but it was too late. He had heard them and what they implied.

"And I'm a happy man hearing you admit that you're not a saint," he whispered. "Sinnin' it's said, can be a pleasure all its own. Wanna sin with me?"

I do. In my dreams, awake and sleeping. You're always in my thoughts. She wouldn't say the words to him. She was enjoying his teasing flirtation too much.

"At the risk of losing out on a pair of boots?"

"I'll buy you a dozen pairs to make up for it."

"I think not."

"You wound me. Leather's only good for the soles of your feet. But sinning with me, Mary, ah, that would be good for your soul."

"You offer temptation like the best of the snake-oil drummers, but I—"

"But you decided that today's not the day you're buying anything I have to sell."

He was serious and teasing at once. Mary had to answer him honestly.

"No, not today. But women are known to change their minds." That said, she left him. But she was still smiling.

Supper that evening was merry, noisy and a feast. Mary and Catherine had cooked a good part of the day. Rafe had contributed freshly caught catfish that he'd bought in town. Crumbs of the cornmeal batter that had coated the fried fillets were all that remained on the platter.

Laughter's afterglow lasted through a round of singing to the accompaniment of guitars. Rafe joined in with his rich, deep voice, until he took Beth upstairs to put her to bed.

The three women were alone. Sarah suggested they go into the kitchen so that their voices wouldn't carry up the stairs.

Catherine put the kettle on to boil for tea. Mary placed the cups and a plate of cookies on the table. Sarah relit the coal-oil fixture.

"This will be our last night together, cousin, since you'll be in bed by this time tomorrow night to get that early start."

"Oh, Sarah, I hadn't thought—" Mary skirted the

table and hugged her cousin. "This is the hard part. But I won't be gone that long."

Over Mary's shoulder, Sarah met Catherine's gaze. She had a feeling Mary wouldn't be back at all, but wisely didn't say that.

"Of course you will. And we'll manage through the winter. I'll even look after your garden, so when you come back in the spring it will be ready for planting."

She hugged Mary tight, and whispered to her. "You're so happy these days. I wouldn't care if he was taking you to the far ends of the world to hear you laugh like you did tonight."

"I can't explain, Sarah. I feel like once I decided to go, a burden was lifted." Sniffling, she pulled away. "That doesn't make any sense, but it's what I feel."

The kettle whistled. Catherine poured the boiling water into the cups and filled the three tea balls with the loose dried tea leaves.

"I, for one, refuse to have this turn into a handkerchief session. This is a tea party, ladies, a time for...well, tea."

And laughter once more filled the cozy kitchen, softer this time, tinged with the sadness of parting, but the talk stayed on practical matters.

When it came time to say good-night, the hugs they shared were a little tighter than usual, the wishes were for good dreams, and no one blamed the others for the moisture in her eyes.

Mary wasn't aware that she remained awake the longest. But she had Catherine's last whispered message to turn over and over in her mind. And Sarah's.

"Give Rafe McCade a chance. Give yourself one, too. That's a powerful lot of man that smiles only at you. Don't throw it away, dearest friend."

"This will always be your home. Always. But if you find happiness with Rafe, take it. No one deserves it more, cousin."

She whispered it then. The secret she kept even from herself until now. "I love him."

But Rafe wasn't offering her love in return.

Chapter Twenty

Dawn spread a golden mantel as Mary turned back to see Sarah and Catherine at the edge of the road. She waved a last farewell, holding a handkerchief as sodden as theirs, then settled in the saddle for the first day of the journey. Excitement tumbled with trepidation.

Rafe led off, Beth half-asleep on his lap. She would ride with her father for the morning, then switch to sitting in front of Mary. Rafe had the lead rope for the three mustangs, carrying half their supplies. Mary rode behind them, the lead rope stringing out the three mules tied to her saddle. Rafe had been adamant that if trouble came, she was to slice the rope with the knife he had given her and let the mules free.

As if she could. Her precious quilt, sewing and herb baskets were tied to those mules. She wasn't about to lose them, or the soft wool gown of a deep wine color that Nita had delivered last night.

This morning, he'd teased her every time she said she had forgotten something important. But there was no teasing when he came into the kitchen and saw her dressed in her pants.

Washing shrunk the pants, she had explained,

blushing when she realized that mentioning it brought his gaze back to the close fit of cloth.

Rafe's voice had been all sincerity, dripping sympathy that it was a poor bargain for her. When she reminded him it had been his money wasted, he said it was a pity he hadn't bought more.

It still felt strange to wear them, but she loved the freedom of movement they offered.

Catherine had traded her barely worn best boots for the new ones, to prevent blisters. Mary had made sure Sarah had a large supply of the herb mixture that helped her headaches, and also a plentiful mix to relieve Catherine's monthly cramps.

Small gifts that they gave each other, but they were filled with love. She would miss them both.

There were other gifts. From Rafe. She looked at the gloves he had insisted he put on her hands. Fine tanned pigskin, thin as her tape measure, but made for hard use.

Even her hat was worn, one J.P. had taken in trade. Barter was the way most folks supplied themselves with what they needed when new goods were not available.

Her hair was tucked beneath the crown, and it was a good fit. From afar, Rafe had told her, no one could tell she was a woman. Safer for them all.

Beth had fallen into the spirit of looking like a little boy by rubbing dirt on her cheek. She remembered the boys at the army fort always had dirt smears on their hands and faces. On their clothing, too, she'd added, but, thankfully, she'd stopped at her father's order.

There was no arguing with the child's logic. Later, when Mary mounted, Rafe tucked a handgun and a box of .44 shells in her saddlebags, despite her telling him that she knew little about guns. He'd said he hoped that Mary hadn't been fooled by Beth's illness. His child was as much imp as she was sweetness.

No, she hadn't been fooled. Beth had confided so much of her mother's neglect that Mary could only rejoice in every act that proved she was healing from all her wounds.

They were still following the road north. Rafe said they would for an hour or so, then veer off for the Black Range. She glanced to her left at the open land and saw the long, sinuous shadow the mountains cast.

Mockingbirds sang their endless song in the cottonwoods. From far off she heard the clear, bell-like tone of the meadowlarks greeting the new day.

The sight of a white-tailed deer bounding into view made her look closely at the brush the animal sprang from. She had to remember that this was no Sunday ride into the hills and keep a sharp lookout for the men Rafe was sure would follow them.

A sobering thought. One she kept foremost in her mind throughout the day. By the time they made camp in a deep-sided dry wash, Mary was far more exhausted by the tension that had ridden with her than by the physical strain of hours in the saddle.

Darkness had not quite closed in on the land, and the moon, which had been increasing in size with each night's passing, had not yet risen. The night was warm, but before morning, she knew, they would all be glad of the thick wool blankets that made their beds over the ground sheets.

Rafe dumped a load of deadfall branches he had gathered after staking the mustangs and mules in a stand of trees a little distance from the camp. Rebel and Owl, stripped of their saddles, were picketed close by, eating grain from their nosebags.

Mary was stacking the smaller pieces of wood when Rafe hunkered down beside her. He scooped out the sandy soil, lined the pit from the pile of rocks they had cleared from where they would spread their beds and had a fire started before she unpacked what she needed to make supper.

"The fire'll burn hotter and longer with the heat reflecting off the stones," he said. "But never pick up a rock bigger than your hand."

"You shouldn't worry that you need to remind me to beware of rattlesnakes."

"But I'll worry about you anyway, Mary. 'Sides," he added, grinning, "you're not trail-broke."

"Yet."

"Yet," he confirmed. "Always act on the side of caution. It can save your life."

Mary followed his gaze to where Beth sat against his saddle and fed her kitten tiny pieces of ham.

"I'll beware of all danger, Rafe. She's become precious to me, too."

"Then you understand how I feel." He took up his rifle. "Where's the handgun?"

"In the saddlebag."

"Get it. Keep it within easy reach. I'm going to scout around."

He waited until she got the gun, then helped her lift the heavy lined-canvas water sack to fill the coffeepot. By the time she added the coffee grounds and set the pot on the fire, Rafe was gone.

Mary looked, but the wash was deep enough that even standing on tiptoe she couldn't see where he had disappeared.

She moved around the fire, keeping an eye on the horses. They would be the first alarm if danger in human or animal form approached.

Leaving the skillet filled with ham slices on the fire, Mary went to Beth. She had solved the problem of keeping the wound clean, since she'd have no time to change and wash out the linen wrapping.

"Let's take care of you while we're waiting for your father and supper."

"Look, Mary, my kitten's already sleeping. I put Muffy in the basket with her so she wouldn't be lonely."

Mary smiled and quickly pulled up the blanket over Beth. She opened her jacket and shirt. Untying the knot of the linen wrapping, Mary loosened it just enough to slip out the pad. A fresh square of linen with salve slipped into place, and she was done.

"Does it hurt, Beth?"

"Just a little."

"Have you thought of a name for the kitten?"

"Papa said I shouldn't rush. Names are important, you know. I'm Elizabeth Mary Victoria McCade. But Papa likes Beth best. I told Papa I shared your name. Sarah told me."

"I hadn't thought to ask. And my middle name is Elizabeth."

"Were you named for the queens, too?"

"No, love. My grandmothers."

"I have only one. She let me play with her pretty gold watch that had a tiny diamond swan on the case. *Grandmère* said I could have it when I was a big girl, but Mama said it belonged to her. *Grandmère* didn't like Mama much. They used to fight. *Grandmère* called Mama a red woman."

"Red woman? Beth, that couldn't be—"

"Was too." She frowned, trying to remember. "She yelled at Mama. Bright red... No, a scarlet woman is what she called her. That's a bright color, Mary, and Mama didn't like bright colors."

"Oh, sweetie, I'm sure your *grandmère* didn't mean to yell at her." Mary struggled to explain without detailing exactly what a scarlet woman was. "Beth, sometimes people fight, but that doesn't mean they don't love each other."

"Do you fight with Papa?"

"Not as much as she'd like to," Rafe answered, stepping into the firelight. He met Mary's worried gaze with a quick shake of his head.

She didn't hide her sigh of relief that he'd found no signs they had been followed.

After they finished supper, Rafe banked the fire. Mary stretched out next to an already sleeping Beth. Exhaustion begged her to close her eyes, but she waited until Rafe came to his bedroll on the other side of Beth.

Far off a coyote yipped in a frantic, broken cry, the call drawing eerie replies from others close by.

Mary moved her arm protectively over Beth's small body and encountered Rafe's hand, moving with the same intent. A trembling warmth and feeling of safety filled her with his hand over hers. She fell asleep with the thought that Beth was more than a bridge between them—she formed the strongest bond.

Rafe lay awake long after the sounds of child's and woman's breathing warned that he needed rest, too.

He wondered if he should have lied to Mary.

He had not done it with words, but he hadn't mistaken her sigh of relief. She believed he had found no sign that anyone trailed them.

But he had.

One man. Traveling light.

Balen? Shell Lundy?

He didn't know. But he wondered where the other one waited.

Two days later, Rafe was still looking out for the place of ambush.

And Mary had been told.

She was riding with Beth this afternoon, thinking how this nameless canyon reminded her of narrow, rugged Percha Canyon, where it seemed a dozen hideouts were waiting above them. Mary had tried to remember some landmark, but Rafe told her he had doubled back over North and Middle Percha creeks. She wasn't sure she could find her way back to the few mining claims scattered along their banks.

In these few days on the trial, they had spoken to one old prospector who shared coffee with them. He told them that, despite the renegade Apache Victorio's presence in the range, miners were flocking to the area.

Rafe was glad of the warning, even as he swore later. More men meant less chance of spotting one.

And Mary's tension dived deeper inside her, until she half expected a bullet between her shoulders.

At Thief Creek they stopped to eat cold cornbread and the last of the ham. They refilled the water bags. Rafe put two canteens on each of their saddles. He warned her again to cut the pack animals loose if shooting started.

The trail he led them to had been made by animals. Each twisted, sharp turn took them higher into the mountains.

Scattered clumps of juniper, cedar and scrub oak mixed with pine grew in the bottoms of canyons. A land by turn beautiful and terrifying.

Before nightfall, Rafe promised, they would climb the crest of the Black Range.

Rafe signaled a halt. He rode back and handed over the lead line for the mustangs. Twice before he had done this, and left them for a little while.

"I'll ride ahead. Look around." She nodded, her gaze calm. But Rafe caught her tightened grip on the reins. Catherine's boast about Mary's riding skill hadn't been an idle one. And she learned trail savvy after being shown once. Last night she had picked out their campsite in a cluster of thick-growing pines, a hundred feet from a clear-running stream. Two small things, but ones that could save a life. He knew that well. Never camp near water, for animals and humans headed there first. Build a fire beneath the thickest covering you could find, for the spiraling smoke would disappear through the spreading growth of branches.

Looking at Mary was a distraction he couldn't indulge now. She made him think of the fire's glow on her hair, flushing her pale skin. He wanted to be the one to heighten her color with a fire of his own. If it wasn't for Beth…

"There's shade here for a short rest. And it's safe," he added. He knew she was worried, despite her repeated denials.

"We'll be fine. You be careful." Mary noticed that he no longer kept the powerful army field glasses in his saddlebag, but rode with the strap wrapped around the saddle horn.

"Half an hour, Mary."

"We'll be waiting for you. Won't we, Beth?"

"And as quiet as mice, Papa."

Rafe backed Rebel clear of the mustangs before he spurred the horse up the trail. He carried the sight of their smiles with him. And his own deep-seated worry.

Mary lifted Beth down, saw the way she clung to her basket and suggested she sit under the trees. Beth went to a towering pine and took the kitten from the basket.

"Keep her close, Beth," Mary warned. "I don't want to chase after her like this morning."

Mary tied off the reins and lead ropes of the pack animals, keeping a sharp watch on Beth. A feeling of unease as if she were being watched, sent chills up her spine.

She thumbed her hat back, and gazed at the dense forest of trees that lined the narrow trail. Where she could see clear to the canyon wall, only stunted pockets of growth and holes too small to be called caves broke the wall of rock.

She saw no sign of life.

If Rafe had come back at that moment and asked why she was removing the handgun he'd given her from her saddlebag, Mary couldn't have answered him. She tucked the gun into the pocket of the jacket. She wasn't sure what good it would be. She had warned him she was a poor shot.

She slipped one of the canteens from her saddle horn, looked long and hard at the horses, but saw nothing to alarm her.

With the intention of sitting with Beth, she turned. Only the basket remained under the pine.

"Beth," she called.

Mary wasn't aware she dropped the canteen and took off running into the dense brush. "Beth! Answer me!"

Up ahead, she heard Beth calling her kitten. She pushed on, unable to shake off the fist of fear that closed around her. It was almost like her dream, racing to get to the child.

"Mary! Kitty's hurt!"

"Stay where you are," Mary shouted. She broke through the trees into a rock-strewn clearing.

Mary's stomach became one knot while her heart raced in alarm. Beth was not more than five feet in front of her, clutching her little kitten. There was nothing wrong with her pet.

A cougar's cub was pinned beneath the massive limb of a tree. A second cub whined while it pawed the earth near the injured one.

Mary saw the torn edge the deadfall branch had made coming free of the pine's trunk. She surmised that one cub had been climbing out on the dead branch and its weight had caused it to fall. From the faint spots on the cubs' sandy, shaded coats, she judged them to be about six months old.

Mama would not be far away.

Much as it pained her to see the glazed eyes of the cub, Mary had to get Beth out of there.

"Listen to me, Beth," she whispered. "We can't help the cub. I want you to walk backward toward my voice. I don't want you to make any noise, Beth. Just obey me."

"But he's hurt, Mary. It cried just like my kitty when I hold her too tight."

"Beth! Don't argue with me. Please. You're in danger there. Move."

Mary started forward. Sweat dampened her body. Fear dried her mouth. She was afraid to move her gaze from the scene in front of her. Afraid of what else she might see.

The uninjured cub turned and snarled at Beth.

Mary pulled the gun from her pocket. It wasn't until she attempted to cock the hammer that she saw her hand was shaking so badly she couldn't take aim.

She clamped her left hand over her right wrist to hold the gun steady. "Beth, come to me."

Another step forward. She could almost feel the child's fear growing and keeping her in place. The scream for Beth to move lodged in her throat.

The cub snarled again.

One more step. Just one step, and she would have Beth's shoulder beneath her hands.

Nothing prepared her for what she heard.

An inhuman scream of rage. A shower of small rocks tumbling into the clearing. Beth turning, her foot slipping. Her startled cry. The loud report of the gun going off before the huge cat on the rocks above could make a life-threatening leap.

Mary missed. Splintered rock flew up and brought another feral cry of rage from the big cat. One her cub seconded.

Mary fired blindly, filling the small clearing with a rolling explosion of sound until the gun clicked. Empty.

She yanked Beth behind her. "Run! Get down to the horses!"

Mary couldn't spare a moment to see if the child obeyed her. Her gaze locked with that of the cat. She still held the empty gun as an extension of her hand. It was all she had between her and certain death.

She knew that if she moved too fast, the cat would be at her throat.

If she didn't move, the cat might kill her anyway.

She strained to listen for Beth's passage. All she wanted was the child safe.

And then came the sound of someone crashing through the brush behind her. Her muscles clenched against the stillness she imposed on them. The sound wasn't away from her. Someone was behind her.

Someone? It could be only Rafe.

Was that a whimper? Mary drew her right foot back. One small step to safety. That mewling noise was coming from her own throat.

Beth was safe. She'd gotten away.

The rifle blast forced a scream from her. The shot caught the big cat in flight.

Mary stumbled back, turning her head away from

the fallen cat. The clearing rocked with another rifle blast. The cub fell over on its side.

Mary sprang into the shadowed forest behind her.

"Rafe! Thank God!" she cried, flinging herself at him.

At the last possible second, she recoiled and threw herself to the side.

"Balen!"

Chapter Twenty-One

The twisted, stunted cedar wasn't much cover for a man as tall as Rafe, but he'd had made do with less. With the cedar at his side and a flat slab of rock beneath him, Rafe had a good view of the surrounding terrain.

He fit a shield of hard leather over the top of his field glasses to prevent the reflection of sunlight hitting brass. An old buffalo hunter had shown him this, for such small things kept a man alive. That old man had blackened every bit of metal that could give away his position.

The rim of the canyon where he'd settled wasn't the highest point around, but it served as he worked the field glasses slowly over rocky spires and mesas. Bighorn sheep scrambled up the Buckhorn, a lone buzzard circled overhead. Thick stands of juniper and pine gave way to meadows, but showed no signs of human life.

He knew the long climbs out of the deep valleys, the rugged, rocky canyons, knew the seeps and water holes and remote streams. Scattered stands of golden-leafed aspen and spruce forests required the longest time to study. But nowhere did he see a lone horseman.

He had done what he could to hide their trail when possible, doubling back, riding into streams, then coming out the same side he'd gone in. Most men would go out the opposite side. Each time he alternated, so there was no pattern to follow.

Instinct said Balen or Lundy were still on his trail.

His telegrams had not garnered much information about Shell Lundy. But he learned that Balen was a man-killer by choice. He had been a scout for the army, as Rafe had, but had been dishonorably discharged. Balen had ridden as a paid gunhand for the big cattle outfits in Texas, then turned manhunter. Every bounty he collected was for a dead man.

Rafe made a quick scan over the same land again. Nothing moved but the wind. He lowered his left hand and carelessly brushed the rock. Exposure to the sun made it burn like hot metal. He should be moving on, yet he stayed.

He used the glasses again, studying the bottom of the canyon they would need to cross. A jackrabbit bounded from brush near the canyon's mouth. Rafe went still and waited.

A few minutes crawled by before an Apache warrior started his iron-gray horse out of the brush. He kept his animal to a walk, following the very trail that Rafe had to cross. If Rafe had ridden on without stopping, he would have been caught halfway down the game trail with no cover to hide him.

He sensed more Apache before he saw them. They rode out of the brush single file. Two boys, another warrior. A small band of hunters, he hoped.

His breathing was shallow. He waited, as still as the rock he lay upon. He was careful not to look directly at the Apaches, for fear he might draw their notice.

When Rafe was sure they would keep moving and not camp in the canyon below, he crawled backward off the slab of rock. He ran in a crouch to where he had left Rebel.

The sound of a shot bounced off the canyon's walls. Thick brush and trees distorted the noise. As much as it pained him, he had to wait again. He couldn't see the place where he had left Mary and Beth. The trail leading down to them twisted by two sharp turns and cut them off from his view.

If Mary had shot at a rattler, it was the devil's own timing, with the Apache this close.

Rolling explosions of repeated firing filled the air. Unless Mary or Beth had disturbed a nest of snakes, they were in even deeper trouble.

If he heard the shots, the Apache had, too.

Rafe grabbed Rebel's reins and flung himself into the saddle. He couldn't wait to see if the Apache were already climbing to the canyon's rim above him.

Right now, the Apache were a secondary danger to be faced.

He swore that he had to keep his horse to a walk down the trail. He reminded himself that the shots had been rapid repeating fire. And the silence. He had to remember how still it was. Mary wasn't fighting off an attack.

He stopped thinking about the one reason why she wouldn't be able to fight.

The silence sent his hand to free his rifle from the scabbard. He guided Rebel with his knees as he slipped the thong from his holstered gun.

He discovered that fear had new, deeper levels on which to attack a man.

Rafe rounded the last turn. The pack animals and

Owl stood where they were tied. None of the horses shied at his cautious approach. He saw the canteen in the middle of the trail. His gaze picked out Beth's basket beneath the pine.

Fear had a throat-choking taste all its own. He saw no evidence on a second searching sweep that there had been a struggle. But he couldn't call out.

He nudged Rebel closer to Mary's horse and leaned over to flip open her saddlebag. The gun was gone. The box of .44 shells lay where he had placed them.

Rafe slid from Rebel's back with rifle in hand. He walked to the place where Beth's basket lay. The thick carpet of dried pine needles showed no footprints, but it had been disturbed. Muffy was in the basket. Beth, going off without her doll?

He saw the kitten was missing. If she'd taken off the way she had this morning and Beth had chased after her, Mary would have quickly followed.

He was driven forward into the shadowed stand of trees by an inner voice. He had to find the path they had taken.

Or been forced to walk.

He had no doubt in his mind that he would find them together. Everything he had learned about Mary told him she would protect Beth with her life.

If she was alive. Chest-burning gall darkened the bitter taste in his mouth.

He was so intent on searching ahead that he stumbled. Rafe looked down and stared at the handgun he had given Mary. Here the brown carpet of needles had been churned until the earth lay exposed. He hunkered down to touch one spot.

The gouge in the earth was freshly made. Air, if not the weak sunlight filtering through the branches, would have dried the spot if it was more than an hour or two old.

Every instinct pushed him into a headlong rush to discover what lay ahead. What had happened to them? He had to fight down his own mind's demands, one by one.

If he had ever in his life needed to move with extreme caution, the time was now.

He couldn't slow the racing of his heart. A small boot had slid down and ripped the earth. He stepped to the side, his ears straining to catch the slightest sound as he continued up the gradual slope.

At the edge of the small clearing, Rafe was forced to stop.

Death carried a troubled smell of its own. He read the signs of what happened there. If Mary had done the shooting, where was she? Why had she abandoned her gun?

He searched the rocks above. Buzzards were already circling overhead. He prayed it was only the dead animals that drew them here. He started forward, then stopped.

Those buzzards hadn't come down yet. There was no sign of torn flesh. At his approach, one or two would have perched on the rocks to guard their carrion.

Something else kept them away. The same something that prevented Mary or his daughter from coming forth.

Don't let me be too late. This silent plea was buried under a landslide of towering rage that threatened his control.

At all costs, he dared not take any rash action or make any damning move.

And his wait ended.

"Step out in the open where I can see you, McCade!"

Balen! Rafe swept the area again, but found no sign of the man. He didn't move.

Balen, hidden behind boulders that skirted the canyon's rim, prodded Mary's prone form with his boot. "Get up. Tell him to show himself. Tell him why he'd better do it, too."

Mary shuddered. There was no choice. She poured every ounce of loathing she could into the gaze that targeted Balen's ice-blue eyes. It was the second time she had looked directly at him. The first had been when she begged him and his snorting laugh rang in her ears. From that moment, through the endless minutes he forced her to wait for Rafe to come, Beth's terrified eyes had been all she could stare at.

Mary wasn't bound. Balen had no need to tie her or to gag her to gain obedience and silence.

He held a knife at Beth's throat.

"Move! Tell him to do as I say!" he growled, then yanked Beth's head back by her braid.

Mary pushed herself to stand. The child's whimper made her forget the pain in her wrenched knee. When she jumped aside to avoid Balen, his blow had sent her slamming against a tree. And never had she felt so helpless as now.

She glanced at the rifle Balen had left propped against the boulder that hid them from Rafe's sight. It was too far for her to attempt a grab for the weapon. And she had no right to risk Beth's life by a move that had less chance to succeed than reasoning with this low-life killer.

But if she did what he wanted, Balen would kill Rafe.

Those piercing-cold eyes of his didn't offer a snipped thread's worth of hope that he would let Beth or her live to tell about it.

"You gonna let this kid die?"

Mary shook her head, daring now to try and buy an extra moment, just a minute or two. She was that desperate to gain Rafe and herself a measure of time. Something would come to her. She couldn't allow Balen to kill them.

"Then tell him!"

She motioned to her mouth, then tried to lick her lips. It was no lie. At this moment, her mouth and throat were as dry as desert sand. *Dear God, how far can I safely push him?*

"Ain't no cat that's got your tongue. I made sure of that."

His snorting laugh made Mary break out in a cold sweat.

The long, wide blade of his filthy knife was obscene against Beth's whitened skin. The child didn't cry. She hadn't cried from the second Mary saw her held captive and realized that the real danger had lain in wait behind them.

She wasn't a woman of violence, but murder was in her heart when Balen wrapped his free arm around Beth's chest.

"If you kill her, you'll never see Rafe McCade until he puts a bullet between your eyes."

"There's you."

"Me? I'm nothing but a hired woman to care for his daughter."

She could see that he didn't want to believe her.

Balen peered through the notch in the rocks. "I got your kid, McCade! Throw out your gun where I can see it. Then you come out."

His kid. But not his woman. Mary had somehow removed herself from being played against him. Or had Balen already killed her?

"One gun, Balen. Then you let Beth go. When I see her free, you'll get the second."

"We ain't making no deals, McCade. You do what I say or I'll kill the two of them now."

Then Mary was still alive. He had to keep her that way.

"Beth!" Rafe yelled. "Did he hurt you?"

"You'd better let her answer him, Balen," Mary warned in a voice that quivered. He stood holding Beth at an angle to her. His gaze was pinned on the notch that allowed him to see into the clearing.

Mary inched closer. Every breath she drew was laden with fear that she would see Beth die.

"Balen, you didn't hear him swear revenge on whoever paid those renegades to attack him and the army detail."

"Shut up!"

"If it's money you want, Rafe has plenty. He'd pay you more to let us go—"

"Shut the hell up, or you'll get a bullet now!"

He threw her a hasty glance that reinforced the snarled threat. Mary froze. But she saw that he was sweating. She barely swallowed past the lump in her throat. Her legs trembled. She didn't think they would support her for another minute.

But if she could keep him talking, distract him somehow, Rafe might have a chance to work his way around.

"I heard Rafe McCade promise death, Balen. I saw it in his eyes. If you don't let Beth talk to him, he'll kill you. She's only a little girl. For heaven's sake, let her go."

Mary sought Beth's gaze and attempted to put all the courage and strength she had left into a look that offered hope. She wiped her damp palms against her thighs and tried once more.

"People in Hillsboro know Rafe fought you. They

heard him warn you. Someone will hunt you down for murder, Balen.''

"I'm coming up there, Balen!" Rafe shouted. "You can't let me talk to Beth. You haven't got her. And you sure as hell can't disguise your voice. But I promised that next time I'd have a bullet marked with your name, Balen.''

"Throw out your guns, McCade. I'll show you what I got. I'll show you who's gonna die.''

Mary watched in horror as Balen's arm slipped from Beth's chest to reach between their bodies for his gun. But he still had the knife!

"Rafe! Don't trust him. He's got a knife—''

Balen swung his gun hand at her, and the staggering blow caught her shoulder. Her knee gave way.

"The gun, McCade!"

Metal clunked against stone.

"That's one, Balen.''

Balen backed away from the notch and took Beth with him. Mary couldn't move. Her hand closed over the rough edges of a rock. Her gaze didn't waver from Balen's barrel-chested body. For all that she watched, it came as a shock to see him fling Beth away from him.

Mary lunged forward and grabbed hold of Beth. The surge of relief that God had answered her prayers was so great that she couldn't utter a sound. She tightened her arms around the child's icy body.

She looked up in mute appeal toward Balen. He had clambered up the rocks.

Her prayers weren't answered. Mercy was unknown to the man motioning with his gun for them to move.

"Get out there," Balen ordered. "I told McCade he's gonna see who'll die.''

''When I move, Beth,'' she mouthed against the child's ear, ''crawl around the boulder.''

''Move!''

Mary lurched to her feet. She pushed Beth ahead of her. She felt as if lead weights dragged every step she forced herself to take. She prodded Beth in front of her. She staggered and threw one arm out, her hand grabbing for purchase against the heated rock. But she had managed to get between Balen and Beth.

''Now!'' she cried out to the child.

Balen fired. Rock fragments shattered above her head.

Rafe, with his heart pounding as if it would rip free of his chest, returned fire the moment he saw the battered edge of Balen's hat in the rocks above him.

Beth crouched in the shadow of the huge boulder.

Rafe could see her, eyes enormous in her pale face. It ripped him apart not to run to her. He had to believe that she was safe for the moment. But where the hell was Mary? Balen's first shot hadn't been aimed at him. Was she wounded?

A killing rage broke every civilized bond that had held him. He worked the repeating rifle's lever to pepper shots across the top edge of the rocks, where he'd seen Balen. Over the steady whine of his bullets, he yelled for Mary to answer him.

There was no response.

Balen had less than two feet of cover. He lay prone, counting off McCade's shots and saving his own. He replaced the bullet he had fired. And he suddenly realized he had left his rifle below.

The woman was crawling toward the rifle. He'd be pinned in a cross fire!

He whipped off two quick shots toward McCade. Another spray of bullets pinned him in place.

Then a strange, tense silence.

It was what Balen had been waiting for.

McCade had to reload. The woman's hand was inches from the rifle stock.

Balen rose to make a crouching run to the top of the boulder. He had all of them now.

Balen fired off three shots across the clearing into the trees to keep McCade away. Then he lowered his arm and brought the woman into his gunsight. He laughed. She struggled to raise the rifle to her shoulder.

His finger gently squeezed the trigger as he bent over.

Mary stared death in the face.

Two simultaneous shots split the silence.

Mary was too numb to understand. Balen's bullet kicked up dirt at her feet. She glanced helplessly at the rifle she held. She had not fired.

But Balen was falling. Toward her. His gun went off again. Harmlessly hitting rock. She saw it then, what her mind had refused to acknowledge. The small black hole centered between his eyes.

"Mary!"

Rafe, screaming her name. Rafe, somewhere behind the clearing. She shook her head. Balen faced her. He was going to kill her. Rafe couldn't have... It wasn't Rafe's shot that killed him!

Chapter Twenty-Two

Mary knew she couldn't hit the broad side of a barn. But it wasn't the barn that she spun around to fire at. On the rim above her was the tall, thin silhouette of a man. Rage shook her. His shot had killed Balen, but he had to be the second man. Rafe was still in danger.

"Call her off, McCade! I don't want to shoot her!"

Rafe had raced across the clearing when he saw Balen turn after firing at him. He had scooped up the gun he had thrown out and was flattened against the boulder where Beth crouched. Two simultaneous shots. He could not see Mary. He surmised that she had shot Balen. Shell Lundy's shout brought ice to chill his blood.

Rafe couldn't fire at him. Mary suddenly stood in the clear, a perfect target. But his repeated calls to her went unanswered.

Mary wasn't thinking. She was shooting at a dancing silhouette that dodged bullets with an ease that taunted her. She could not hold and sight the rifle against her bruised shoulder to aim high at his body, but she could and did hit the rocks.

A rolling roar of shouting came to her. She resisted

hearing the voices. All her concentration went to the enemy above. The burning weight of the barrel and the press of the stock were nearly impossible for her to hold any longer.

One more shot, she begged. *God, give me the strength for it.* She prayed for help to break a commandment. These two men and their violence had reduced her to a shaking mass of hatred.

She fired. The bullet ricocheted off rock, making a sound that reverberated through the air.

Above her, Shell dodged to his right and felt the burn of a bullet crease shoot up his leg.

When Mary started shooting, Rafe ran toward her. He realized Shell hadn't returned her fire. He ripped the rifle from Mary's hands and flung it away. He caught her against him, risking a bullet in his back, and carried her back to the shelter behind the boulder.

Holding her tight, he whispered over and over that she was safe.

Mary, shivering uncontrollably, clung to him. She couldn't respond to the sound of his husky voice, now hoarse with need, begging her to talk to him. The heat of his body slowly lessened the trembling cold of hers, but she couldn't look at him. She saw horror in her mind's eye.

Rafe's whispers penetrated her numbed state. He called her brave and daring, he begged forgiveness. She mouthed Beth's name. She had to know Beth had survived, or it was all for nothing.

"She's here and safe, thanks to you." The frantic look in her eyes shocked him. He lowered her down to the ground. He hated to leave her and Beth, but there was Shell to deal with.

"Hold tight to Mary, love." Rafe stepped around them, keeping close to the boulder. He still held his gun, and he wasn't about to give himself to Shell as a target.

"Just you and me, Shell," he called out. Rafe searched the uneven rim. Shell had disappeared at Mary's last shot. He wasn't sure if she had wounded him.

"You hear me, Shell? You let Mary and my daughter go, free and unharmed."

Again Rafe waited. Shell wasn't going to give up this easily. Not when he had the advantage.

"McCade!"

"I'm here. And waiting."

"Balen and me...weren't together."

Rafe thought he detected a note of pain in Shell's voice. He couldn't forget that the man had saved Mary's life. And perhaps Beth's, too.

"You hurt, Shell?"

"That's one hell of a woman, McCade. I saved her damn life and she shot me."

Rafe glanced down at Mary and Beth. He had seen eyes like theirs in the faces of young soldiers surviving their first battle. He had to get them away and fast.

"I'll owe you for that, Shell." Rafe waited until the echo of his shout died. "Spotted a small party of Apache in the next canyon. All that shooting is sure to bring them. You won't get away easily."

"Worry for yourself, McCade. From where I'm sitting, I can see your horses." There was a long pause, then Shell said, "I can't make a move against you now. But I'll be coming for you, McCade. An' it'll be just you and me."

"I'll be waiting." This time, when Rafe's echo died, there was only silence.

Rafe sagged back against the rock. He had to figure a way out. Only the intervening hand of the Lord was going to manage that. Any mercy or miracles due him had to be used to keep Mary and Beth alive.

Even in this moment's respite, Rafe's senses were alert. A faint sound had him dropping into a crouch, eyes narrowed and gun hand extended in a sweeping arc that covered their exposed side.

"McCade! Hold your fire. I'm coming in."

"Rafe? Is that him?" Mary roused herself to whisper. "You can't trust him?"

"Why not? If he wanted to kill us, he's had the time. And he saved your life." *When I couldn't. Didn't.*

Mary heard the bitterness in his last words. They made no sense to her. She saw that Rafe didn't lower his gun. She wondered if he was even aware of the contradiction. She held Beth tight, then turned to look for the man who had saved her life.

Shell showed himself at the edge of the trees across the clearing.

He was slim and dressed entirely in black. Mary swept her gaze from his boots to the bandanna tied around his middle thigh, up past the double holstered guns to the face half shadowed by the hat's brim.

He limped forward, leaning on his rifle and leading his horse, but he stopped within a few feet of the shelter of the trees.

"Why, he's little more than a boy."

"Don't be fooled by appearance, ma'am. I've got twenty years on me. Ain't no need to be scared, ma'am. I ain't the scum Balen was. My business is with McCade. I don't make war on women and children." He glanced at Rafe. "You tell her what I'm talking about."

Mary, bewildered, glanced from Shell to Rafe. This boy—no man—wanted to kill Rafe, and as much as she hated the thought of more killing, she didn't understand why Rafe was willing to talk to him.

"I figured whatever debt was between us got evened up, Shell. I didn't kill you that night in the saloon, and you stopped Balen from shooting the three of us at the widow's house."

"And there's now," Shell added.

"You want something. What is it?"

"Heard your woman's done some doctorin'. Can't reach the bullet crease she put in the back of my leg. I'll give you cover to get your pack animals and horses. Then we're quits till I come for you." His cool brown eyes swept over Rafe, Mary and Beth. His wry smile only touched his lips for a second. "Don't take long to decide, McCade. Those Apache parlayed long enough to be coming over the rim."

Mary didn't believe what she was hearing. But she had to believe that Shell Lundy—as impossible as it was—meant exactly what he said. He threw one of his handguns to land at her feet.

"Go on an' pick it up, ma'am. It's loaded. You'll feel a whole lot safer with it."

She stared at Rafe, wondering if her attempt to silently convey the confusion swirling in her mind could be read in a look. How could Rafe trust Shell? How could she?

"It's your decision I'll abide by, Mary. It's your help that Shell wants."

At her side, Beth whimpered. Mary reached for the gun. After all, she reasoned, she was the one who owed her life to Shell Lundy.

When she looked up, Rafe had disappeared down the slope to get the horses. Shell was mounted, walking his limping horse across the clearing.

"We make a sight, limping like a pair of greenhorns. My horse threw a shoe, or I'd have been here sooner.''

''You followed Balen?''

''Seemed the right thing to do, ma'am.''

Mary leaned back against the solid feel of the boulder and cradled Beth tight against her side. She started rocking herself and the child. She was more confused. What had just happened? She wasn't sure she wanted to know.

She whispered to Beth to close her eyes and think of only good things and forget. She wanted to do it herself. Forget the violence. Forget that death had stalked them. Forget this devil's bargain. For death still hovered as long as Shell Lundy lived.

They rode long past dark before they made camp that night.

Mary wrapped a shawl over her jacket, for the air was bracingly cool. A faint breeze carried the scent of pine and cedar.

An owl hooted from a nearby tree. Mary watched a pack rat cower at the sound and knew how the tiny animal felt. Within seconds, the pack rat scurried for cover in the cat's claw shrub growing at the base of the tree.

Above her, a bat poised, and wings fluttered in the air before it swooped off, pursuing insects. The night was quiet, but for the horses cropping grass. The stars hung like lanterns with their wicks turned down in the dark sky. All but one. It shone with brilliance.

She had banked the fire, but still sat up near its heat. Beth had finally fallen asleep cuddling her kitten. Rafe had found her mewling in a tree near their horses. They had both talked to Beth about her fear, and Mary could only marvel at the child's resilience.

She had whispered that she was happy the bad man couldn't hurt them again.

Mary's glance strayed across the fire to where Shell Lundy slept. She had tended his wound, but couldn't reconcile his polite manner with the idea that he was a hired killer.

Rafe had taken the first watch on top of the mesa, where a stunted cedar and jumble of rocks offered slight shelter.

Others had camped in this place through the years, which attested to its protected location.

The shallow depression on top of the mesa was almost an acre, scooped out from stone and tilted like a misshapen bowl. Scattered about were small basins, the natural stone *tinajas* that held rainwater. The grass grew thick and lush around them.

She needed to rest. It wasn't the first time she'd reminded herself. But she had gone past the point of exhaustion, to where tension held her awake.

She wanted to be with Rafe.

Mary poured out two cups of coffee, then hesitated. Would he welcome her or send her back?

When he returned with the pack animals and the horses, he'd told her there was no sign of the Apache. She hadn't believed him. There was his distant manner. And he wouldn't look at her directly.

The only explanation he offered—and Shell quickly agreed—was that the Apache were carrying news to their band. Some victory or defeat, or information about troop deployment, since the smaller forts were being closed.

Nothing else made sense. The Apache could easily learn how few they were. They were known to let fighting continue, then attack the survivors. As Rafe had pointed out, the Apache always wanted more weapons, but even more, they always needed ammunition.

The Indians remained a ghostly threat.

Mary was more concerned about the real threat, sleeping near their fire.

The coffee sloshed over the cup's rim as she climbed the short distance to where Rafe stood his watch.

Ominous and dark as the hour before a storm, danger lay in the shadows surrounding him. It made her pause.

"Couldn't sleep?"

"I thought you'd like some coffee."

"It's welcome. But your company more so." He didn't sound surprised to see her. "I know you've got questions about why I let Shell remain with us."

"You're doing it again, Rafe. Telling me what I'm thinking." She handed over one cup to him, and sat down.

They sat in silence on the folded blanket, shoulders touching, sipping the hot coffee.

Mary felt warmth seep into her body, chasing an inner chill. It came from more than his body heat, which was so much greater than her own. It was from the man himself. She felt safe with Rafe close to her. Comforted by his nearness. Eased of fear, until all she wanted was to rest her head against his shoulder and have him hold her.

"What you did today—"

"Don't, Rafe," she whispered. "I don't want to talk about it. Don't want to remember. Beth's safe. We're alive. That is all that matters."

"I can't forget, Mary. I won't. I was thinking I should take you back."

She stared at the cup she held, as if it offered a reason why. She shook her head in denial.

"Give me a chance to tell you my reasons before you say no."

"I can't. I don't want to hear them. You made a deal with me. You promised me six months."

"I didn't promise to get you killed during that time."

Harsh, impatient, his voice washed over and forced her to turn and look at him. Night caressed his features like a lover. Was that anger in the glitter of his gray eyes?

"And if I refuse?" she asked, fighting not to reach up and touch his face.

He looked away. "I almost got you killed today."

"Is that what you've been thinking about?"

"Partly."

"But I didn't get killed. And the threat of Balen is gone."

"Which brings us back to Shell." Rafe drained his cup and set it aside.

Mary no longer wanted coffee. She too, put her cup down. Then she waited, afraid to feel relieved that he'd dropped the matter of taking her back.

"I don't know if I can explain my reasons to you, Mary. It's more than needing his guns if the Apache come looking for us with a larger force."

"Earlier, you said it was my decision. I'm the one who owed Shell a debt—"

"There's that. I'm responsible for your being here. But I couldn't turn away a wounded man with a lame horse. If they found him, Shell wouldn't have had a chance. Doesn't make much sense, does it?" he asked with a shrug.

"I think you're a courageous man to act on your beliefs."

"But? There is a *but* in your voice."

"I don't know how you can trust him, Rafe."

"I know men like Shell Lundy. I've been friends with them. You may not believe that they have a code they live by, but it's true. I'm not talking about men like Balen, who'd kill anyone that got in the way. Shell was hired to do a job. There's—"

"How can you talk so calmly of his being sent to kill you as a job?"

"That's all it is, a job. Nothing personal."

"Nothing civilized, is what you mean."

"Am I civilized?"

"Yes," she answered without hesitation.

"But I once hired my gun to help a small rancher being squeezed by two larger ranchers who wanted his land and his water."

"What happened?"

"The man got careless and they killed him."

She looked at his strong profile and wavered. Did she want to know what followed? Before she thought about it, she asked.

"What did you do?"

"I finished the job I was hired for. That's why I trust Shell to keep his word. It's a twisted sort of honor that most women can't understand. Men abide by it or we'd all be dead. Like Balen."

Rafe looked at her. Her face was lifted toward him. Starlight was reflected in her eyes.

It was dangerous for him to lose his concentration on hearing the night's rustlings, but he had to kiss her. He needed to quell the doubts that telling her the truth could break the fragile bonds of trust between them. A primitive need welled inside him to taste her warmth, to celebrate in the most basic of ways exactly what she had said earlier—they were alive.

Her lips parted at the touch of his, smooth as a flower petal, potent as brandy. She gave herself to the passion of his kiss, as if his need were matched by her own.

Mary knew she could fight Rafe on any level but this one. To fight against desire's swift rise was to fight herself. She relished the feminine power that rose. Rafe never hid his feelings when he kissed her. From the quick intake of his breath to the way his mouth covered hers, greedy with hunger and yearning to forget.

He shifted her onto her back, partially covering her with his body. His masculine heat and strength bearing down on her brought a momentary panic that she quickly buried. His hands were gentle framing her face. She knew this was Rafe, and he would never hurt her.

Mary skimmed her hands over his back as his tongue swept her mouth, demand and seduction in one. She couldn't stop the sound of naked longing from escaping.

She gave in to the urges of her body. She was taken by his assault on her mouth into new, uncharted territory.

She moved as he moved, turning to her side. The shawl and jacket she wore were swept aside. Her shirt and the thin camisole were no barrier against the heat of his hand cupping her breast. Sensitive flesh swelled beneath his sensual caress.

And she wantonly ached for more.

One more taste, Rafe swore to himself. Her breast was small and soft, the skin hot under his hand, the nipple pebble hard and begging for his mouth. She caught fire so quickly that she seared him to the bone with her response to his every kiss, every touch.

He sucked in his breath. His stomach muscles clenched, then quivered, when he felt her hand slide to his hip. He nudged her onto her back, bringing his hand down between their bodies. He eased her fingers away, only to press the palm of her hand to the rigid flesh that strained the button placket of his pants. She froze. He coaxed her with dark murmurs and showed her what he wanted.

"Just once. Let me feel you touch me, Mary."

He groaned deep in his throat at her gentle stroking.

Rafe had to return the pleasure. He cupped his hand over womanly heat. Her quivering leg muscles tensed. She murmured a protest he wanted to deny.

Rafe buried his lips against her throat. He enjoyed the aching pleasure of holding her, of feeling the cloth dampen beneath his hand, but only for a few seconds more. Then he released her.

He rolled onto his back, one arm flung over his eyes. She was dangerous to him. One touch and she made him forget where they were and what waited out there for them.

And he had to admit that as badly and needy as he was to feel her moist body close around him, he didn't want their first time to be on a bed of rock.

Her stifled sound made him realize that he had been too abrupt. He reached for her hand. He didn't trust himself to touch any more of her.

"Rafe?"

"Are you as frustrated as I am? Hell, I wouldn't blame you for wishing me to the devil. I had no right to arouse you—"

"No, you didn't. But these feelings between us frighten me."

"I know a hundred men who'd be happy to hear that admission, Mary, but not me. I don't want you to be afraid of me. But since we're confessing, no other woman ever turned me inside out the way you do. Or as fast."

"The voice of experience speaking?" She managed a calm voice, but inside she delighted over his admission.

"Would it bother you if I said yes? I'm no saint, Mary. I've told you that. I haven't had any other woman in my home, but there have been a few I've seen during the years Val was gone."

"I've known one man, Rafe. I don't have—"

"You have everything I want."

He squeezed her hand. He could have Mary tonight, but he might forfeit tomorrow. It wasn't a risk he'd take. For the first time in a very long time, he wanted a tomorrow with a woman. This woman.

The thought didn't send him fleeing, as it would have even a year ago, but it made him cautious.

He heard her deep, ragged breath, and he turned to his side. He couldn't resist tracing the lush fullness of her bottom lip.

"I don't make too many promises, Mary, but someday soon, I'll have you where I won't need to stop."

"You take a great deal for granted."

"Do I?" he asked in a soft, velvet whisper. How could she doubt the outcome of the passion between them? Mary was not a woman who played coy. Could it be that she truly didn't know?

She fought the need to touch him. "The only thing I am certain of at this moment is that you've forgotten about taking me back."

"Not forgotten, Mary. If that's what you want—"

She pressed her fingertips over his lips. "No. That is not what I want."

A statement that begged him to ask what she did want. Need tremored in her fingertips against his mouth, and despite all his good intentions, he wanted to bring her beneath his body and show her the pleasure they could share. His body urged him to do just that, his blood demanded it, but he sat up. He drew her up beside him.

"You'd better get back to camp and get some sleep. I want to get an early start in the morning." Distance was the only way he could stop a hurried coupling that wouldn't satisfy either of them.

She reluctantly stood up and took the cups he handed to her. He was right to send her back. If she stayed, she would cast aside every moral tenet she lived by and throw herself into his arms and let the devil take tomorrow.

"What are you going to do about Shell?"

"I haven't decided yet. But I will by morning, Mary."

Without reason to linger she walked back to camp, fretting over what that decision would be.

Rafe was a man, tempered by time and circumstance.

Shell Lundy, despite his claim of a man's years, still had a youth's recklessness.

She could only hope that Rafe's decision was the right one. If he let Shell live, pray the young man had the wisdom to walk away.

Chapter Twenty-Three

They moved out before dawn. Squares cut from blankets muffled the animal's hooves. Mary had tended to both Beth's and Shell's wounds. She was thankful that neither showed signs of inflammation.

Rafe redistributed supplies from one of the mustangs to the other pack animals, and saddled the horse for Shell to ride. His own trailed behind them. If they were forced to make a run for cover, the animal couldn't keep up.

Rafe didn't share his decision with her. Unless she took the fact that Shell traveled with them as a decision. Somehow, she sensed there was more to it.

Fog rose from the land to cut visibility. They rode with tension that didn't lessen as the sky lightened but remained overcast. Mary kept her voice to a whisper whenever she spoke to Beth. But the child was aware of it, too. She rode quietly in front of Mary, wrapped in a blanket, clutching the handle of her basket, despite its being securely tied to the saddle horn.

Rafe led them off the back of the mesa, opposite the trail where they had ridden up. He skirted most of the canyons, and found trails where Mary swore there were none to be seen.

Twice he left them and rode off alone, only to return within the hour and change their direction.

Mary couldn't lie to herself. There was a level of pitched excitement mixed with the danger. It heightened her senses in a way she had only known in Rafe's arms. She could compare it to nothing else. Every detail impressed itself on her mind, every scent was savored.

They nooned in a dry wash, eating cold pan bread and bacon that Rafe had cooked in the morning. Mary longed for coffee, but Rafe said no fire, it wasn't safe.

A subtle darkening warned that nightfall was approaching when Rafe rode back and asked if Mary could ride another hour.

"We've a stretch of flat, open land to cross, then we'll be home." He leaned over to touch Beth. "That all right with you?"

Beth roused herself and nodded. She cuddled closer to Mary and promptly closed her eyes.

"Mary, can you stand Shell's presence one more night?"

"It's not for me—"

"Yes, it is. I promise you that's all the time he'll be with us."

"You don't make promises, Rafe."

He stripped the lead rope from her saddle. "Shell will take them across. You ride in front of him. When I move out, whip Owl after me. There's a twisted pine and a boulder against the canyon wall. It looks like a dead end, but go around the boulder."

She reached out and caught his arm. "Rafe, where will you be?"

"Covering you. Don't look back. I'm depending on you."

He rode back to hand over the rope to Shell. She wanted to tell him she couldn't do this. She was frightened. But to give in to the fear meant risking Beth's life and her own.

"Hold tight, Beth."

She urged Owl up past Shell. Her hands were wrapped around the reins, her heels poised in the stirrups to slam against her horse's sides the moment Rafe moved out.

Then Mary went very still. *"Where will you be?"* she had asked Rafe. *"Covering you,"* he'd replied.

The Apache were here!

Rafe raced out across the flat. She had no time to think. Mary loosened her grip on the reins, giving the horse her head. She slammed her bootheels into Owl's sides, and the startled horse moved in a sideways hop before she took off in a ground-eating stride after Rebel. She saw something move in the rocks, but her shout was lost in a volley of shots.

The roar of guns and the shrill cries of the Indians were all about her.

Ahead, she saw Rafe slide from his saddle, giving her and Beth covering fire as they swept past him. Rebel had started up the trail. Mary caught up his reins and swept him along. Shell was coming up behind her with the pack animals and needed the room.

But Rafe was down there, alone and on foot.

Rebel came to a sudden stop. Pawing the earth, tossing his head, the horse wouldn't move, despite her tugging the reins. Mary turned to ask Shell for help and found herself alone with Beth and the pack animals.

Then she heard the alternate methodical firing, so at odds with the pounding that filled her ears.

As quickly as the shooting had begun, it stopped.

Mary waged war with herself. Rafe depended on her to stay with Beth. But she was afraid that Shell had gone back to kill him.

Without warning, Shell limped into view on the trail.

"McCade's coming," he said. "The Apache won't follow. They believe this place is haunted."

Mary nodded. In her pocket, her hand remained on the gun Rafe had returned to her. She would believe him when she saw Rafe. She waited agonizing minutes.

He arrived as Shell had, without warning. "Let's go home."

All Mary remembered of the next hour was that they climbed higher. Once they had to get down and walk the horses through a tunnel formed by nature. The roof, Rafe said, was a slice of mountain. The muffled sound of the animals echoed from the walls.

The cooler air warned her they neared the end of the tunnel. The difference in darkness was too faint to matter. The fact that Rafe had carried Beth told her they were safe. Rebel's shrill cry was made in the open, and brought answering whinnies and the thunder of running horses.

Grass tips brushed Mary's knees, and the rich scent of pine and cedar filled every breath she drew. Rafe's voice pierced her exhausted state. He spoke in normal tones as he moved among the milling horses toward her.

He held Beth in one arm, his other arm was spread in invitation.

Mary stepped closer. His arm tightened around her. There was no need for words, beyond his whisper of her name. It only lasted a few moments, this silent need to touch, to hold and be held. Mary became aware of how deeply frightened she had been when the wash of relief left weariness in its wake.

Rafe pressed a kiss to her temple, nearly knocking

off her hat. "Can you ride a little farther? It's too long a walk to the house."

She mounted with his help. "Let me take Beth."

"She's asleep, Mary. A heavy burden."

"Not to me." She didn't imagine his hesitation, or the underlying message they had exchanged. She felt as if she had won a victory when he lifted Beth up to her, but it was too much to sort out tonight.

It seemed only minutes later, though she knew it was longer, that Rafe took Beth from her, then returned to lift her from the saddle. She wanted to protest that she could walk, but the words remained unspoken. She felt the give of the bed beneath her, the brush of Rafe's lips against her own, then the tug of her boots coming free. Her eyes felt too heavy to open. The thick warmth of a blanket covered her.

She murmured some protest, for she heard Rafe whisper in her ear. "No, you rest now, Mary. Let me be strong for you."

She tried to stay awake, needing to tell him that they could be strong together, but the soft pillow and the feel of Rafe's hand stroking her hair urged her to sleep. She wasn't fully aware that she turned onto her side and drew Beth's small body into the nestling curve of hers.

Rafe stood watching them. There was a rightness to the two of them lying there, the same rightness that urged him to lie down beside Mary and hold these two precious beings in his arms.

There was more love and courage in this fragile-looking woman than any man could hope to find. And he wanted to keep her safe for all of her days.

But Shell waited.

He leaned over to kiss his daughter's head, then couldn't resist brushing his lips against Mary's cheek.

He touched the shadow beneath Mary's eyes and knew he could wait a little longer to make his claim.

Mary woke to a furball's rumble. Yawning and stretching she blinked sleepy eyes at the kitten curled on her chest.

Gently moving her to Beth's side, Mary sat up in a stream of sunlight from the room's single window. She had vague impressions of their arrival last night.

A fire burned low in the stone fireplace across from the wide double bed. The mantel was a thick slab of stone, with a lone candlestick and a bluish-green pottery vase its only ornaments. The walls were lined with the pale red and cream streaks of split cedar.

Nowhere she looked, from the wall pegs holding her hat, jacket and shawl, to the straight chair where her carpetbag sat unopened, to the plainly made yellow pine chest next to the chair, did she see signs of Rafe's wealth. Even the water pitcher and washbowl on the pine stand were of the same dull glazed bluish-green pottery as the vase.

The room pleased her in its simplicity. She slipped from the bed and noticed the small rugs scattered on the wide planked floor. Bright colors were woven in designs she knew were from Navajo weavers.

The door was closed. Rising, she pushed back her tangled hair and realized she had slept in her clothes. Yesterday's toll was measured in muscle twinges as she stepped across to her bag.

A little while later, when Mary lifted the latch and opened the door, she found herself in a short stone hallway. The murmur of male voices and the aroma of freshly brewed coffee lured her past a closed door, toward the curtained arch at the end of the hall.

The large room's stone walls were spattered with

sunlight from a recessed window three times the size of the one in the bedroom.

Mary looked at where Rafe and Shell sat on curved-backed chairs at a trestle table in front of the window. She had a brief glance at the view offered, the lush length of the valley they had traversed in the dark last night.

But Rafe saw her and rose. She had eyes for nothing else.

There were faint shadows beneath his eyes—a match, she thought, for her own, seen in the mirror. He was clean-shaven, and his high cheekbones were prominent. His black hair was mussed, as if he had been running his hands through it. That truant lock drew her gaze down to his open-necked shirt and the dark curling hair on his chest. It was an enticing peek at the muscled hardness beneath the sage-green shirt that intensified the gray of his eyes.

Having made his own head-to-toe survey to assure himself that she was all right, Rafe smiled.

"Come and join us, Mary. I'll make the official welcome with coffee and breakfast."

"Just coffee, please." The male appreciation in his gaze and the slow smile creasing his lips were food enough for any woman. Despite having picked out the dark brown skirt and white shirtwaist as the least wrinkled of her clothing, she knew she didn't look her best. Rafe made her feel beautiful. Pinching her cheeks hadn't brought too much color to her face, but she could feel the heat of a blush spread now.

Shell, who sat with his back toward her, had not turned around. Mary knew she had interrupted them. She became aware of the tense air between them.

She approached the table and saw not the expected remains of breakfast, but coffee cups. In the center of the table were a folded piece of paper, with a deck of cards on top, and a gun. Rafe's gun.

"Beth's still sleeping," she volunteered, as if it mattered, as if anything mattered but that gun on the table. Her legs were trembling. She sat down opposite of Rafe. She sipped the coffee that Rafe poured for her. He resumed his seat. There was some sensible reason for that gun being on the table.

"I'm glad you're up, Mary. I wanted you to hear the deal I've offered Shell. This way, we'll both have a witness."

"A witness?" she repeated, unable to tear her gaze from those three items. There was nothing to fear, she told herself. Rafe is speaking so calmly, there can't be any reason for this stomach-tightening sensation.

"I've offered to play a hand of poker with Shell," Rafe explained. He saw her pale, and wanted to reassure her, but she didn't look up or question him.

"You know what Shell was hired to do, Mary," he continued. "I'm offering Shell an opportunity to take another path."

"Hell, spell it out plain for her, like you did to me, McCade." Shell tossed down the last of his coffee and pushed his cup aside. "He wants to play poker for your lives."

"Our...what?" Mary had to look at Rafe. She had seen his face through a range of emotions, but never so set with a hardness that chilled her. A denial went begging on her lips, but Rafe nodded.

"It's true, Mary. And simple enough. If Shell draws the high card, he wins the hand, and he walks away a rich man. I told him I'll sign over my shares to the Cañón del Agua mine to him. But he'll have to deal with the men who hired him. Vargas, Trent and Malhar are his problems."

"And if you win, Rafe?" she asked, unable to keep

a quiver from her voice. She wanted to scream that they were both crazy. She sat there.

"If I win, I'll have to kill him. Shell has his own code of honor, as I explained to you once before. He won't stop hunting me until he kills me. Remember, Mary, nothing personal. Just business."

"No. No, you can't—"

"I can and I will, Mary. I did mention to him that despite his reluctance to make war on women and children, he'll have to eliminate you and Beth. Then he needs to return to Hillsboro. Sarah and Catherine know about him. And I warned Shell not to be fooled by townsfolk calling them merry widows as if they were flighty bits of fluff. Those two are handy with their guns. But that's something Shell will find out for himself. He'll worry, too, who else they may have told.

"I've made no secret of the letter I sent to my lawyer naming Shell Lundy and Balen as hired killers. I also authorized him to take twenty-five thousand dollars from my estate as a reward for each man who brought them to justice."

"A damn high price you put on yourself, McCade."

Rafe looked at Shell. He smiled at the younger man with his lips, but there was nothing but a cold promise in his eyes.

"No, it's not that I place a high value on my life. I want to make sure that every bounty hunter, even worms like Balen, will crawl from their rocks to track you."

"Rafe! For the Lord's sake, stop this. You can't mean to—"

"Why not? It's civilized, Mary. A bloodless business deal."

His emotionless delivery infuriated her. She pushed

back the chair and rose, her hands gripping the table as she felt her control slip. She closed her eyes, then shook her head. She looked at Rafe again. No. She had not been mistaken. There was a plea for understanding in his eyes. A plea to trust him as she never had before.

As abruptly as she rose, Mary sat down. She held on to the cup with her hands wrapped around it. Suddenly she was cold.

"There, Shell, it's now your call. Cards or—"

"McCade, I've met some men in my time, men as crazy as sheepherders trying to settle on a cattle range, but you... Ain't never met a man like you."

Mary heard admiration in Shell's voice, and she thought of what he said. She wished she was dreaming. Then every breath wouldn't hurt so much. She tried glancing around the room, but couldn't take in one detail. And she found herself answering Shell.

"You're right. You never met a man like Rafe. And what's more, you never will."

The slight inclination of Rafe's head made her feel proud. Absurd, but true. Mary realized that Shell had tilted his head and was watching her.

"You'll do the honors and shuffle the cards." He passed the deck to her before she could protest. "To keep it all fair. McCade won't object."

"Rafe?"

"Go ahead, Mary. Like he said, to keep it fair."

This wasn't happening. She told herself that, even as she reached for the deck. The words strung together like a litany, but she couldn't keep her hands from trembling so badly that all she could do was divide the cards into small piles and restack them. She managed that much twice before Shell took pity on her and passed the deck to Rafe.

"Let's keep it honest and simple, McCade. One cut. High card wins."

Mary watched Rafe. He wasn't even looking at the cards. He split the deck evenly, fanned a pile in each hand, then smoothly fit the deck into a whole again. There was no hesitation in his long fingers as he spread the deck across the table in front of him. With the flip of one card, the row was faceup and once more formed into a piled deck.

"Enough?" he asked Shell.

"You put the stakes on the table, McCade. You draw first. And you've got more riding on that one card than I have."

Rafe sliced a small pile of cards from the deck. He set it facedown in front of him.

Mary wasn't sure if he knew the card he'd drawn. He didn't smile, nor did Rafe look worried. She tried to take heart from the firm set of his granite-cut features. All she saw was the tarnished silver of his eyes.

"Before I make my cut, McCade, I want you to know that I like you. I think we're two of a kind. Another time and place we'd have been friends. You're a man I'd ride the river with."

"We can be friends, Shell, if you draw the high card."

Shell nodded. He shifted his body in the chair and hoped no one saw his swift move to wipe his palm on his pants. He raised his hand to the deck. He'd done a share of gambling, and he was not easily bluffed, but McCade made him fight to keep his hand steady.

"Go on, Shell, cut."

"How do you know I'll keep my word, McCade? I could take that paper you signed and still hunt you."

"You could." Rafe sat back in his chair, one arm hooked over the curved edge. "But if a man gives his word, and can't abide by it, what kind of a man is he, Shell?''

"He can't be called a man at all."

The words were whispered. Shell cut the deck. He held the cards faceup toward him. His eyes narrowed, and he looked at Rafe.

"Set them down. Let's see what you've drawn."

Shell's pile was almost half the deck. The seven of diamonds lay on top.

"What are the odds—"

"About sixty-forty that I've drawn the higher card," Rafe answered before Shell finished his question.

"Mary? Are you praying?"

"What?" She looked up to see a smile on his lips.

"I asked if you were praying."

"Yes. Yes, I'm praying." The words were torn from her.

Rafe turned over his cards. The two of spades was on top.

Chapter Twenty-Four

She worked through the day as if a devil were riding her, when she should have felt relief. Rafe had packed supplies for Shell and led him out of the valley, where he'd cross the Plains of San Augustine then go north to Santa Fe.

There was little to do in the kitchen, which was no more than an alcove off the main room. Rafe and Shell had stocked the storeroom with the supplies. There was a well, and a stream that ran down the far side of the valley.

She checked on Beth, who was seated beneath the spreading branches of an ancient pine, where she served a lunch of pinecones and needles to her doll and the sleeping kitten.

Slabs of stone formed a path from the back door that led to a stone overhang. The small herd of horses, her mare among them, cropped the lush grass.

The scene was one of tranquillity, but Mary was filled with a vague restlessness that refused to leave her, and refused to be named.

She added a log to the fire and stirred the kettle of ham and beans simmering with squaw cabbage. There was no stove. The kettle hung from a thick iron hook

hinged from a rod that allowed her to move the kettle.
It was too early to make biscuits. She returned to the
main room.

Here, too, the fire required replenishing. She stood
for a moment watching the flames. Like the one in
the bedroom, the large mantel was of stone. An old
Spanish helmet sat next to an Indian pottery bowl
filled with musket balls.

Mounted above the mantel was a stone-pointed
spear tied with strips of rawhide, the remains of two
black feathers hanging from the shaft. On one side
was a cavalry saber, an inscription on the hilt that
was far too dusty to read.

No feminine touches softened the room. On the inside wall, filled with bookshelves, stood a desk and a
chair. She could picture Rafe sitting there, reading,
the lantern turned up, but the image bore the stamp
of loneliness.

The gray stone had the patina of years, and when
she looked closely, she saw that no mortar had been
used. Each stone was cut by a master's hand and wed-
ded to the one below.

A larger Navajo rug covered the floor. The massive
chairs of yellowed pine were covered with soft tanned
hides.

Mary had no sense of another woman's presence
here. If this *was* the house that Rafe had lived in with
his wife and child. It was more than five years since
she had left him. The reminder didn't chase the feeling that Rafe lived here alone.

"I hope that curled hand is for a woman itching to
attack this room with a feather duster."

"Rafe." She spun around. The vague restlessness
disappeared as she raced across the room to his wel-
coming arms. She couldn't stop saying his name. One

hand cupped her head, the other was tight around her shoulders.

"Does this mean you're glad to see me?"

There was laughter in his voice, and she jerked back to look up at him.

"He's gone?"

"With luck, Shell will be in Socorro tonight."

"Why did you do it, Rafe?"

"Why? You can ask me that? Was what I did so terrible, Mary? Haven't you ever been so sickened by something that you refuse to do it again?"

"Yes. I can understand that." Her hands slipped from his shoulders to grip his arms. She searched his face, looking deep into his eyes, unaware that doubts clouded her own gaze.

"But the risk, Rafe. You could—"

"The hell with trying to explain. I'll have to show you why." He barely controlled his anger. His hand closed over hers. He gave her no chance to pull away, but drew her along with him to the back door and brought her to stand in front of him.

"Look at her, Mary." He enforced his demand with the hold he took on her shoulders. "She's laughing. That is what I *wouldn't* risk. I've finally brought my daughter home, and I don't want more blood on my hands. I lied and I cheated this morning. The deck was fixed before I drew my card. There was no risk that I'd lose. And Shell got paid off."

Before she said a word, he spun her around to face him. His fingers clamped on her arms.

"I won't let you, or anyone, tell me that what I did was wrong. My daughter and I have known too little happiness. You understand that, Mary. I know you do. So what the hell good is knowledge and money if I can't buy peace any way I can?"

"Stop, please, Rafe. Oh, I can't tell you how sorry

I am for doubting you. I should have known." She rose on tiptoe, struggling for every inch she gained as she worked one hand up between their bodies so that she could touch his lips.

"I meant what I said to Shell. There will never be another man like you, Rafe McCade."

He gazed into her lovely green eyes and wanted all traces of sad shadows gone. The anger had dissolved as quickly as it had risen.

"Are you sure, Mary? Even if I lied and cheated? Aren't you afraid I might do the same to you?"

"Would you?"

"No. But all you have is my word on it. That and time."

She looked away. His gaze was too intense. And when her answer came there was no reason to hide it from him. Rafe's word...*trust*. She did trust him. Without any reservations?

"Mary, what is it that makes you hide from me?"

"I..." *Say it. Tell him.* But she couldn't. She pushed against his chest. He wouldn't release her. She was foolish to think of running. There no longer was a place she wanted to run to.

"Mary, what am I going to do with you? You won't tell me, and I can't plumb the depth of your female mind. Ask a man to climb the Divide unaided first. It'll be a far easier task."

His was a teasing plea, with real need beneath it.

"I will tell you. I suddenly realized how much I trust you."

He pressed a kiss to her fingertips. "Such a terribly hard admission?" There was no laughter in his voice.

"For me, it is."

Rafe gentled his touch. He whispered in her ear, "I'm glad to hear you say the words, Mary. I've wanted your trust almost as much as I've wanted you.''

He knew his words pleased her. Her hand fell to the open edge of his shirt, fingers curled around the cloth. Her head nestled against his chest as tension seeped from her. He warmed her with his body and regretfully enforced his control on the desire that ripped through him.

As much as I've wanted you... She repeated the words. The evidence was undeniable, not only in the velvet whisper that never failed to excite her, but in the hardness pressing against her belly. She clung to him when she felt her body mirror the tiny shudders of desire rippling from his powerful body.

''Mary.'' He kissed her eyelids, trailing his lips to her cheek. A wildness shook him at the way she clung to him. His lips wove a heated exploration over the soft shell of her ear.

''Rafe, don't. Beth will see.''

''Remind me to share Beth's secret with you, Mary. But later, not now.'' Nibbling at the fleshy lobe, he blew softly at the moisture he left behind. Drawing her lobe between his lips, he gently scraped his teeth over the sensitive flesh. She rewarded him with a small, needy sound.

Above her head he saw that Beth had ended her play. Carrying her basket, she skipped toward them.

''Must I wait longer than tonight, Mary? Will you give me the ultimate trust a woman can give to a man?''

His lips silenced her with a brief kiss. He held Mary at his side when Beth came running.

''You're kissing Mary.'' Her bright smile included both of them. She giggled when Rafe winked at her.

''She's in need of lots of kisses, don't you agree?''

''Oh, yes, Papa. Lots and lots. I had the nicest tea

party. Now will you show me the horses? You promised.''

''And what's a man if he can't keep his promises?'' Rafe answered Beth, but he looked at Mary. ''All of them,'' he added.

''All of them?'' Joy spread inside her when his eyes darkened and he nodded.

''Give me your basket, Beth. And you two go along.''

Rafe trailed his fingers along the curve of her jaw. Holding her chin, he once again pressed a light kiss to her lips. ''To keep me. And think about what I said, Mary.''

''I—''

''No.'' His warm gaze held hers, his lips creasing into a very male, very seductive smile as he shook his head. ''I'll wait to know your answer. The anticipation lends spice, Mary.''

''Papa.''

Beth's impatience made him move. He scooped up his giggling daughter into his arms. They both looked at Mary.

She was reminded of the first time she had seen them. Two pairs of matching gray eyes watching her. But there was a definite difference this time. One pair was filled with love. The other with a heated promise.

Spice. The word wouldn't leave her mind.

It went beyond her having heard Rafe's husky voice filled with promise the first time he said the word. Spice was sprinkled in his conversation, from his description of the two-year-old filly's coat that Beth had picked out for her own horse to his compliments about supper.

Surprises lent spice to everything in life, he had remarked as he carried Beth to bed in her own room.

The closed door had indeed held surprises. Beth's infant cradle became Muffy's and the kitten's bed. Beth slept in a single, sturdily built bed against the wall. A rocking horse large enough for an older child took up one corner. The mane and tail were horsehair gathered from the herd. There had been no doubt in Mary's mind as she trailed her fingers over the beautifully carved wood that Rafe had made this horse, too.

A child's table and chair, the china tea set, tops and books, the exquisitely dressed French bisque doll—each one was a gift for the years he had missed being with his daughter to celebrate a birthday. He had murmured the words to her, sharing his child's joy and his love. And he had caught her looking at his hands, those strong, long-fingered hands that could be so gentle. When she raised her eyes to meet his knowing look, warmth flooded through her.

It was a warmth that expanded beyond passion when Beth whispered the end to her prayers. "Let Papa and me have Mary to love us forever and ever."

Spice. The scent of carnations, sweet and spicy, surrounded her from the French milled soap as she washed.

She glanced at the closed bedroom door. Beyond that barrier, Rafe waited for her.

Come to me, Mary. We've both waited too long.

She started, as if he were there in the room with her, whispering the words. Her toes curled against the rug. She brushed her hair and thought her reflection wanton in the candle's light.

She had delayed as long as she could.

Mary wrapped her shawl over her nightgown. She was covered from neck to toe, from wrist to shoulder.

But she felt naked. Trepidation filled her. It was as if she had stepped back in time to her wedding night with Harry. Fear had been part of her dress that night. Fear of not knowing what to do, what would be expected of her.

But this is Rafe who waits for you.

You're not a girl. You are a woman who made a choice of the man you want for a lover. A man you love.

And the excitement rose to lessen fears that she would somehow disappoint him. Rafe. She had never known such passion.

Her hand poised above the door latch. Perhaps she had never known what she could share with a man, because she had never truly loved with every fiber of her being.

She thought of the secret she withheld and swiftly buried it. She opened the door.

Rafe stood bathed in candleglow and firelight. One arm rested against the mantel, one leg raised with his foot braced against the woodbox.

He stared into the flames, and saw only images of Mary. Her eyes. Her smile. He heard her laugh. Her voice, needy with desire. He felt her touch and thought of all he yet hungered to know. Her scent filled his every breath.

He thought of the claim he would make this night, and for all the nights to come.

He sensed her nearness. But he didn't turn.

Anticipation lends spice. His own words held him still. But there was more. He wanted the choice to be hers each step of the way.

It was agony to wait. He remembered how quietly she walked, but her scent was embedded inside him. He would know his Mary in the blackest of nights.

He looked at the half-empty glass of brandy he had sipped while he waited for her. Candlelight played within the liquor's amber depths...the color of Mary's hair, the potency of her kiss, the smooth glide of the liquor's richness heating his blood. He could have it all with the touch of her lips.

He had debated about wearing a shirt. Twice he had snatched it up, only to discard it. And how would she come to him? He could wait no longer.

Firelight gilded his body with gold and shadows in a soft caress she wished was her own. He straightened as he turned to face her. His feet bare, black cloth hugging the long length of his legs, the lean hips and waist. Soft-looking dark hair curled over his finely honed chest. Her hands curled at her sides with the need to touch him. She stood no more than an arm's width away from him. Her chin lifted and her gaze met his, while she wished she was young and beautiful for him.

He had told her once that she was a woman. She knew when a man wanted her. If she had ever a doubt about Rafe's desire, he dispelled it this moment.

And he whispered the very words she had heard in her mind.

"Come to me, Mary. We've both waited long enough."

He held out one hand to her. Her luminous eyes made the blood simmer wildly through his body. Even as he warned himself to go slowly with her, he felt the rush of his body changing to meet the honest femininity of Mary herself. He was filled with a need that was as basic and as necessary as breathing itself.

"I wish I was young and beautiful for you." Her fingertips touched his.

"You are beautiful, Mary. But I can't share your wish for youth. I wouldn't have known how to love a woman like you." His hand closed over hers and he slowly drew her to him.

Her bare feet sank into the thickness of the sheepskin that covered the rug. "You make me feel lovely and new. I wish I could bring that gift to you."

"Is that what you want, Mary?" he asked in a passion-laden voice as his arms closed around her. He slipped the shawl from her shoulders and tossed it aside. The silky weight of her hair covered his arms.

Her breath shortened as his did. The thin barrier of cloth couldn't hide the tightening of her nipples against his chest. He told himself she couldn't truly burn cloth and skin, but he felt scalded by her nearness. A faint tremble passed over her and sank into him. He warned himself to bide his time a while longer, no matter the cost. Her choice every step of the way.

"Tell me what pleasure I can bring to you." He stroked her spine with the tips of his fingers, resisting the need to trace the flare of her hips and bring her against him, hard and tight to ease his own aching flesh.

Pleasure. Yes, she could take all the pleasure she wanted, without consequence. And take and take, while giving him all the love she held in her heart.

He lost his breath when she tilted her head back to look up at him. He raised one hand to her cheek. Her warm breath fanned across his palm. Her gaze held his with questions. Then her lashes veiled them as his thumb touched the corner of her mouth.

She stirred against him, and the sweet scent of her body rose. His sigh was deep. With both hands he held her face and lowered his head. His kiss was as tender and cherishing as he could control himself to give her. It was an offering of himself, and it brought to life the need to hold her like this for always.

"So giving," he whispered, barely lifting his mouth from hers. "Marry me, Mary. Let me—"

She silenced him with her kiss. Marry him? Every

turbulent thought that ran through her mind poured
into the heated mating of her lips with his. Her hands
clung to his shoulders, savoring his strength, savoring,
too, the slightly rougher texture of his skin.

But he broke the kiss, and she saw the fire high-
lighting the bladelike cut of his face, the very masculine curve of his mouth and the powerful, lean
body.

As he gazed at her, Rafe knew he wanted this
woman for his wife. He needed the commitment from
her as badly as he needed to lose himself in her
warmth. She watched him with hunger in her eyes.

"Say yes, Mary."

He dropped to his knees before her, his hands sliding down to cradle her hips. He pressed his face
against the soft curve of her belly. "Mary, marry me.
I'll swear to love you as no other ever could. I'll fill
your life with whatever makes you happy and fill your
arms with babes. I spoke the truth to you before. But
there is more. I have never loved, Mary. Not till now,
not till you."

And with a wound that set her heart to bleeding,
she pressed his head against her, holding him tight
while she found the courage to speak.

The love she bore him helped steady her voice.

"But you promised me pleasure to share, Rafe. For
this night, I want that more."

"Do you think it's passion that—"

"No. I know you meant every word, Rafe. I can't.
Don't ask—"

"Mary, I've found gold where other men found
nothing. Remember that. And I'm a man who found
a woman for all his tomorrows. And I'll show you
that."

He reached up to open the ribboned ties, holding
her gaze with his. He wished Mary could see her eyes

as he did, see the eyes of a woman in love, no matter
what denial she spoke.

Barren woman. Worthless woman. Harry's taunting
voice shouting from the past.

Mary silenced it the only way she could. She sank
to her knees and whispered Rafe's name, bringing a
kiss as intimate as they had ever shared to his lips.

She came to him with all her woman's heat, all her
softness, all her need and generous giving. And she
gave. And gave. Before he could ask. Before he knew
he needed. Her pulse was a wild beat beneath his
hand. He drank the ragged sound she made. Her
tongue sought his for a hungry kiss. His arms closed
tighter around her, arching her into his body, bending
the supple flesh more deeply to his, satisfying her
instinctive need to match woman's heat with his hard
flesh.

The room spun around her, and she drifted along
with it, taking the hot, dark taste that was Rafe as
balm and arousal. He lowered her to the thick softness. He didn't break the kiss, and she felt his weight,
the ripple of his muscles, the blunt ridge of flesh, the
hardness of his thighs. She trembled even as she
pressed him closer.

"You're trembling, Mary."

"You are, too."

"I'm shaking from the hunger of wanting you."

"Show me, Rafe."

He pulled open the last two ties and brushed aside
the cloth and the fall of silky hair that hid her breast.
Hammer blows of desire thudded inside him. The firelight licked over her pale skin. He envied it until he
thought of how he would cover her flesh with a passion's flush nothing else could do as well. The smooth
rise of her breasts and the dusky rose nipples were a

rich, lovely sight to feast his eyes upon. Passion sent hunger prowling, and he needed to see all of her.

Between dark murmurs, heated kisses and caresses inspired by her generous giving, he stole the cloth from her body.

"More lovely than any words I know," he whispered. His gaze alone touched the taut swell of her hips, the slightly convex curve of her stomach, and lower still, to the rich amber-hued triangle that hid damp heat from his eyes.

He rose quickly then, to strip off his pants, for he sensed her vulnerability in lying naked before him. Her arms rose in welcome when he returned to her side.

Rafe angled his hand and head down to her breast. The small rise of flesh fit perfectly in his palm, and he drew her nipple into his mouth. Her soft moan of pleasure made him shudder.

Flickering his tongue over the swollen tip, he forced himself not to think of the deep, pulsing need of his own body, but only of showing Mary how much she was loved.

The spicy-sweet floral scent rose from her flushed skin. Her breath fanned over his shoulder, one hand gripped his arm, the other his head. She arched against him, burning and shivering. He risked the pleasure and the pain of his own building, savage arousal for more of her needy cries.

He lowered his mouth to her other breast and felt her heart thundering. He wanted to give her more, to give her everything, to know that she craved the way he did.

Beside her the fire shot hissing sparks, and inside her another fire burned, hotter and brighter. She could see him through the pleasure haze that blurred her vision. His dark, fierce need almost tangible, muscles

ippling as his lips raced over her skin and his hands
vooed her to fever.

She gripped him so hard that Rafe lifted his head.
His hands stilled on the flare of her hips. He fought
o control the violent shudder that tore through him.

As he levered back, she reared up, her arms tightening possessively, her lips, blind with need, search-
ng for his. He had once whispered of the magic
brought by a kiss, and she felt it now, for it was colored with love. Bright gold and shiny, spinning glim-
mering lights as everything inside her grew taut. She
ached so, and nothing she could do would ease the
throbbing. She began to writhe beneath him. Greedy
now, Rafe pushed her to the edge.

He drank her cry and absorbed her shudders, and
wanted more.

The restless movement of her sleek legs drew his
hand. He tugged rhythmically on her breast. He knew
Mary was too aroused to feel his gentle bite. With a
hungry look in his eyes, he lifted his head. Her rosy
nipples pouted and seemed to beg for his mouth
again, but her cry was a plea he couldn't deny.

The soft curls parted at the touch of his hand. He
stroked her with his thumb. She was hot and wet and
more ready than she knew.

"Mary. Mary, hold me," he whispered.

The cry he drew from her was wilder, a wanton's
call.

"Again."

She melted moments later against his hand, and he
took her mouth with the same gliding penetration with
which his caress took her body. He found himself still
greedy as once more her sleek softness yielded a hard
nub of desire.

His name was the only sound she could make.
Once more her body tightened, then racked her with

shivers from the hot, intimate touch of his hand. Sh
watched with dazed eyes as he rose over her, her leg
parting to make a place for him. There was only Raf
in her world, the taste of him, the scent, the touch o
this one man.

"You were made for a man to love, Mary. Thi
man, and this is with love."

And he sheathed himself in silken softness tha
shimmered with pleasure from his touch. He ha
asked her for the ultimate trust a woman could giv
to a man, and now that it was his, he trembled wit
emotions that went deeper than passion and wer
more powerful than need.

It began so gently, the stroking that rode with th
waves of passion's aftermath still shaking her, an
brought him deeper, then deeper still, into her body.

His mouth scattered kisses over her face, moving
to her neck, where he bit her with hot restraint.

Mary's hands clenched on his shoulders. He filled
her completely. She moved with him, her hips finding
a sinuous motion, measuring him again, and again,
wanting him to burn as she did.

He drove into her, the force of need rocking her,
and still she wanted more. She had learned her power
as a woman in Rafe's arms. Hot with hunger, her
mouth mated with his.

Her name hissed with a groan from his lips.

His hands gripped hers and drew them out to the
sides.

"Look at me. Open your eyes, Mary, and look at
me."

And in that timeless moment, they gazed into each
other's eyes, drawn to passion's pinnacle, trembling
and watching as love took them over the edge.

Chapter Twenty-Five

"Don't leave me," she murmured as the tremors faded.

"I won't. I can't." But he shifted his body, just enough to see her. "I don't want to ever leave you." The firelight bathed his face and was reflected in his eyes. "I never loved anyone like this, Rafe."

"New, then, for both of us. But let me take my weight off you. I'm too heavy—"

"And still—"

"Hard as if I never had you? Yes. I can't lie, can I? Not like a woman can hide."

Her intimate smile invited his. A subtle shift, and she showed him that she wasn't hiding from him.

"I'll leave you sore," he whispered, nuzzling her ear.

"A threat? Or a promise?"

"Where's my prim Mary?" He braced himself on his elbows and looked down at her. Mary's eyes were still dark with passion. Her hair spread like a burnished flame around her face.

"Where is she?" he asked again.

"Here, with you. Where she wants to be. And there's only one woman, Rafe. A woman who found

more pleasure than you promised, more magic th.
she ever dreamed of knowing.''

And he saw within her lovely green eyes that lo
of love she would not admit to. But he could and d

"I love you. I'll love you all night long, and f
all the nights to come. All you have to do is say yes.

Mary longed to say the words to him, to free wh
she held in her heart. But she would first have to te
him— No! She would not taint what they shared wi
her sorrow.

"Yes," she whispered against his lips, showir
him what she could not say.

She learned that his love could take her to drin
deeper from desire's well, and later, yet again, on
slower path that climbed to tumultuous heights.

She watched the embers in the fireplace darke
with ash, even as dawn lightened the sky outside.

Rafe asked her again to marry him.

Mary was thankful that she faced the dying fi
while his body curled spoon-fashion behind her. Sh
didn't want to look at him when she refused.

The touch of his warm lips kissing her bare shoul
der distracted her. What could she say? *I'll swear t
love you as no other ever could. I'll fill your life wit
whatever makes you happy and fill your arms wit
babes.* She had to remember Rafe's words. And re
member, too, that the last was impossible. She ha
only to think of what she had endured during he
marriage with the arrival of her irregular cycle.

"Mary? What's wrong? Why can't you answe
me?"

She simply couldn't tell him. His admiration, hi
trust, and the very love he professed to have for her
would all be gone. He was a man who deserved to
have sons and more daughters. He needed a woman
who could give them to him.

But it wasn't words of refusal that she said.

"Give me time, Rafe. Give both of us more time."

"Don't you believe that I love you? Can you tell me that love isn't returned?"

She turned within the circle of his arms, and her lips silenced his questions with a plea for him to love her again.

And with that Rafe had to be content.

Or so Mary thought. In the following days, she began to suspect that Rafe had hidden a sly side. She knew he enlisted Beth's help to draw her away from household tasks.

The very next afternoon, she had asked Rafe about the old Spanish helmet. He told the story of finding a few flakes of gold in the stream bed that had led him into the valley. He hadn't discovered the stone house at first. And as he pointed out when she and Beth followed him outside, the valley itself was shaped like a loop in a rope. Where the stone house stood was the loop itself, but the stream almost ran in a straight line up the neck of the valley, where the sheer stone walls narrowed like the tunnel they had entered to get there.

They had seen where he first found gold.

He carried Beth through first, for the only way to get there was through the stream. Then he came back for Mary, although she insisted she could walk. Mary's suspicions started then. To the accompaniment of his teasing and kisses, they finally joined Beth.

A few cattle grazed in the cul-de-sac. At the back wall of straight rock was the cabin he had built. It had fallen into disrepair. On the other side, he showed them the mine.

Mary thought her heart would stop when she viewed the deep notch cut at the base of a pinnacle

of rock. It was seamed with cracks and crevices tha
appeared ready to shatter at any moment.

"There's always talk of lost mines in these moun
tains, and of the Spanish who lived here and worke
them. There are the cliff dwellings of what most ca
the ancient ones. Those dwellings, like the house, stil
stand, but it seems as if those who lived in then
meant to return.

"I never found the bones of the men who worke
this mine, but I understood why they hesitated going
in there to take all of the gold out. I had to sto
working it. And the seam is still rich, but not worth
my life."

"Is this the reason the Indians believe this place is
haunted?" Mary asked, finding herself full of dire
imaginings as she stared at the notch.

"I never had one follow me here. Behind that brush
is a cave filled with shards of pottery, animal bones,
and the remains of fires. It's where I found the spear.
It's another place that appears to have been suddenly
abandoned."

"Let's go see it, Papa!"

Beth ran off. When Mary suggested that she go
back, Rafe wouldn't hear of it.

"Oh, no. I'm not letting you go that easily."

Later that night, Rafe cleared one of the bookshelves so that Beth and Mary could display their
finds. He held Beth on his lap and read to her while
Mary sewed. She was filled with such peace and con-
tentment, and she knew it was hers for the taking for
all her tomorrows. The crackling fire was soothing.
She looked up to find that Beth had fallen asleep and
Rafe was watching her. She couldn't say it with
words, but hoped her look conveyed that she was as
eager as any bride for the night to come.

Her eagerness was noted and appreciated. How

much appreciated, Rafe showed her with lovemaking that was more tender and cherishing than the night before.

He and Beth woke her in the morning with breakfast. She wasn't given a moment to herself for the rest of the day.

Rafe admitted there were a great many things lacking—a cow for Beth, chickens, for all three of them missed having fresh eggs. By nightfall he had added a stove for Mary to his list. She burned the bread. A first for her, and she blamed Rafe for his insistence that she joined a game of hide-and-seek.

Beth named her father the seeker because he was the oldest. Mary teased and disagreed, but their two votes overrode hers. Rafe found her each time, kissing her senseless before they would run off and find Beth.

Mary hadn't fully understood that Rafe's wealth meant he didn't have to work. He chopped wood to see them through the winter, and that took a good part of his day. She often stopped some chore to watch him. His muscles rippling with each swing of the ax, sunlight gleaming on his hair. A sensual excitement filled her the moment he stopped and saw her watching him.

He came stalking her then, demanding a reward for his hard efforts to keep her fireplaces fueled. Beth would giggle, then whisper to her doll or kitten, while Mary allowed herself to be caught. But Rafe was sly, as she had come to know. He'd sometimes settle for a slice of herb bread, or a taste of what she had cooking. At other times it was a hug, or a chaste kiss. And there were rare times he'd swing her into his arms and carry her back to the woodpile. He insisted she sit where he could watch her, despite her halfhearted protests that she'd burn supper or left chores undone.

But he conspired with his daughter, too. He'd catch

hold of Beth and she'd shriek for Mary to rescue her—the price, a kiss.

Beth's wound healed with small scars that Mary hoped would fade with time. Just as the child's nightmares faded away. She no longer had her haunting dream, for she knew her wounded spirit was healing. How could it not? She was in love and was loved in return.

Rafe taught them to pan for gold in the stream. Beth insisted on weighing the small but growing pile of flakes they found each night. Rafe turned it into a lesson in arithmetic, as he did counting the herd of horses, then mares, fillies and colts.

Mary used the books and the growing number of arrowheads to do the same.

On the days Rafe hunted, Mary taught Beth to sew. The kitten often wore the results, much to Beth's delight and Mary's surprise.

They all called her Kitty, but Beth would shake her head with a secretive smile and say that wasn't her name. She wouldn't tell what it was. Her secret. Hers and Muffy's.

Mary helped Rafe break a few of the horses to the saddle again. None were truly wild, but he had been away for a long time. Beth had her daily riding lessons, but dressed warmly as the weather turned colder.

There were picnics on idle days when Rafe and Mary told childhood stories, with Beth an avid audience. It was on such an afternoon that Mary was struck by the bonds of love and laughter the three of them shared. Rafe had just finished a tale of a bear that had raided the mining camp repeatedly to steal sides of bacon. The bear had outwitted them at every turn, finding bacon wherever the miners thought to hide it.

"I swear it's true," he declared. "Those miners, me included, took to strapping those sides of bacon to our backs just so we wouldn't have to eat plain beans. No one would leave his claim to get supplies."

"And did the bear go away, Papa?"

"Not on his own. We each cut strips from our bacon and planted a trail one night that led across the creek to another camp. Those men howled the next night. But that bear didn't come around to bother us again. Days later, Three-Fingered Jack, who'd been hunting gold for almost forty years, chased that bear up the mountain into a cave. He come running right out swinging his pick, and tore a chunk of rock off the cave's entrance. He hit a pocket of gold that took him all the way to San Francisco in high style."

"Oh, Papa, you did a bad thing but made it good. Just like you promised me."

"I'm trying, Beth. Trying real hard to keep that promise."

The engaging smiles on father's and daughter's faces led Mary to believe she figured prominently in that promise.

Later that night, after they made love, Mary asked Rafe if it was true.

He was braced on his arm above her, the blanket draped over his hips. With the fire behind him, Mary couldn't see his face clearly.

"I promised to marry you," he answered. He brushed her hair back from her cheek. "Beth loves you. She wants you to be with us forever. Her words. My desire. Mary, I want you for my wife, my love. To have and to hold, to cherish and to protect."

His hands drifted from her cheek to her neck, where his thumb measured the wild beat of her pulse, before he cupped her breast. "I know you're happy. It's rare to see the sadness in your eyes anymore.

And,'' he teased, "despite all you do, you've put
weight.'' He lowered his head to taste her. "Ri
here. I can tell.''

He rolled onto his back and lifted her as thou
she weighed nothing. She took him deep, so deep
hands reached to grip his. She rocked, matching
rhythm, matching the savage tempo of her own pul:
And Rafe was with her, sweat-sheened skin bronz
by fire, holding her, cherishing her with so much lo
that she nearly fainted from the ecstasy they creat
together.

Mary knew she had to tell him.

But in the morning, Rafe announced his intenti
to go hunting for a Thanksgiving turkey. Mary w
surprised. Almost two months had slipped by witho
her noticing. She thought of the merry month-lo
holiday she and Sarah had shared with Catherine la
year. From Thanksgiving to the first day of the Ne
Year. She vowed she would help make these first ho
idays that Rafe shared with Beth very special ones.

Her mind was busy with the cookies she could be
gin baking. When Rafe asked for a kiss for good luc
she absently pecked his cheek.

"Ah, Mary, that's a wifely kiss you give a man
send him off. What's taken your thoughts?''

"Spices,'' she murmured. "I'm thinking abo
what I'll bake to celebrate.''

"Spices, is it? Then give me a kiss,'' he demande
in a mock growl that sent Beth into giggles. "A ki
worthy of your thoughts, to keep me while I'
gone.''

She was too happy to scold him for behaving lik
this in front of Beth. Or, as she told herself later i
the day, she was coming to believe that Rafe woul
not stop loving her even if she couldn't give him
child.

That day marked a flurry of activity. There were spices to grate, sugarloaves to be crushed and rolled, dried fruits to soak. Planning Beth's gift for her father took two days to reach a decision, required hours of secrecy and no end to Rafe's grumbling when Mary and Beth shut themselves up in the child's room.

Rafe brought home several turkeys. Beth, in the spirit of the day, was whooping through the house in a headdress of rawhide and turkey feathers. She wore Rafe's fringed buckskin shirt as a dress. Mary and Rafe were declared Pilgrims.

Mary had tied a white linen square for a shawl collar over her new wine-colored gown. Rafe told her with words and with his frequent looks how beautiful she looked. She watched as he carried corn bread and steaming biscuits to the table, then returned for beans baked with molasses and bacon, the bowl of stewed tomatoes and herbs, hominy and maple syrup. Mary turned the turkey on the spit and gave a stir to the gravy. The dried apples had been made into a pie, and there were sugared doughnuts—bear claws, Rafe called them, and swore men would travel one hundred miles to have a taste of one—sugared nuts and spice cookies for dessert.

The turkey was golden-brown, the aromas tantalizing enough for each one to declare they were starved for their feast.

Mary bent over to stir the gravy, then taste it. "A pinch more of salt," she murmured, straightening and turning. She dropped the spoon as a wave of dizziness and an attack of nausea left her weak. She clutched the mantel with one hand as the room swirled around her.

"Rafe!" she called out, and felt herself falling.

When she opened her eyes, she discovered she was lying on the double bed, a wet cloth on her forehead and two anxious faces hovering over her. Her quilt covered her to her chin, and her shoes were gone.

"Mary, don't worry. Papa said I could be your nurse."

"What happened?" Mary asked. Rafe curtailed her attempt to sit up.

"Just lie still," he ordered. "You fainted."

"Fainted? I've never in my life—"

"They say there's a first time for everything. This is one of those times."

A frown creased Mary's brow, and he quickly smoothed it with a gentle touch. "Don't you know?"

"Know what?"

"Beth, be Papa's angel and let me talk with Mary alone for a few minutes. Go make sure your kitten hasn't eaten our supper."

"But Mary might need me, Papa."

"She will. I promise you that. But not right now. Go on."

His look brooked no argument. Beth left them, and Rafe closed the door after her. He returned to sit on the bed and took hold of Mary's hand.

"Don't look so bewildered, love."

"But I am. You're being deliberately—"

"No. It's not deliberate, Mary. I always figured it was a woman's place to do the telling."

Rafe slowly drew the quilt down until the edge rested across her thighs. He lifted the cloth from her head and set it aside.

"Rafe?" Mary was almost paralyzed with fear. She wanted to close her eyes against the blaze of tenderness in his. Tears welled in her eyes, tears she couldn't explain. But he didn't seem to find them exceptional. He simply brushed them away as they slipped down her cheeks, and waited.

And Mary knew she had run out of time.

"Rafe?"

She had to close her eyes. Somehow that would make the telling easier.

"I'm here. I'll always be here for you, Mary."

She reached up to take his hand and hold it tight with hers.

"Do you remember Beth's tale of the ghoulies coming because she wished for too much?"

"I'd slay dragons for you."

"But sometimes you can't see them. They live inside the mind. I've wished too much. Wanted too long." She squeezed his hand, finding the words so hard to say. "I thought I knew what love was. I thought I loved Harry when I married him. But I didn't know. Love is you. And I'm afraid to believe, afraid to trust."

"Ah, love," he whispered softly, and leaned down to kiss her lips. "Don't torture yourself like this. The past doesn't matter, Mary. I won't let it."

"But it does matter. When I couldn't conceive, Harry became bitter. I wanted to give him a child more than anything else. But that was a blessing withheld. He said—"

"Don't. I won't let you do this to yourself."

"But I need to tell you. I need to," she repeated in an agonizing whisper. "He called me worthless as a woman, as a wife because I couldn't give him a child."

"But all I want is you. A man twice blessed to have you and Beth. It's enough. I told you that. The love I have for you, Mary, has no conditions, no boundaries. Except for one—that you marry me. I want the world to know you are mine."

"And if I could give you more?"

He wished she would open her eyes. He wanted to see love shining within their green depths. But his lovely lady required every ounce of patience he coul command. Where they touched he felt her body's ten sion.

"Hold me. Please hold me."

He drew her up into his lap, holding her close an aching for the way she clung to him. Her hot tear fell on his shirt. He rocked her, as if she were Beth giving silent comfort and willing her pain to pass. H asked nothing from her.

"I was afraid to tell you. Afraid you wouldn't lov me." She was too distraught to be embarrassed by her noisy sobs, and the flood of tears that followed a she held on to him, trying to climb inside him fo safety, as if she were a child and not a woman grown

He ran a hand up and down her back, circling i slowly so that she gradually relaxed against him.

"It's frightening to need someone so much, Rafe I thought all I wanted was to have some small finan cial independence. I thought I was contented with my life."

Mary lifted her head from his shoulder and gazed into his eyes. All the barriers were gone, all her de fenses were shredded.

"I want to have your child, Rafe. I want so much to give you the most beautiful gift in the world. A gift that lives in endless beauty and endless promise. A child born of love."

Rafe raised her hand to his lips and pressed a kiss to her palm. "Don't you know yet that you are the gift of love to me?"

"I feel I am being given a second chance, Rafe. A chance to love you and Beth. But if I am wrong and there is no child—"

"Hush, love, hush. I'll fill our home with all the children you want, if that's what it takes to make you happy." He kissed her softly and gazed into her eyes, which brimmed in wonder with all the love a man could ever want. And he smiled to see that there were no shadows of sadness.

"I'll take you to New York, Mary. There are orphanages filled with needy children. We'll adopt a dozen. Two dozen, if you like. We'll live wherever you want. I'll give you everything—"

"Rafe. Oh, Rafe, I want only you. And Beth. I've been—"

"Loved," he finished for her. There was a brightness in her face that confirmed her words, despite the sheen of tears. He held all that was bright and beautiful within his arms.

"I love you, Rafe. I've wanted to say those words to you a hundred times. You once said that I made magic for you. It isn't quite true. You are the one who makes magic."

He watched her eyes grow luminous. He wanted to capture this moment and savor it for all of his days. He lowered his head and kissed her. Sweetly, cherishing her with tenderness. A kiss of love and of promise.

He gently ended the kiss. "I'm glad we came here," he whispered, "to discover what we could have together. Tell me again. I need to hear you say the words."

"I love you, Rafe."

"That, too. But say you'll marry me. For all the right reasons."

She laughed and tightened her arms around his neck. "I will marry you for all the right reasons."

There came a soft tapping on the door, and Beth's hesitant voice calling them.

"Come in, Beth." Rafe spread one arm to hold her close when she climbed on the bed. Mary's arm came to rest above his around Beth's waist.

"Is Mary better?" Beth asked. "She's got tears."

"Happy ones, Beth. Very happy ones," Mary repeated, and hugged her closer.

"Beth, Mary is going to marry us."

"Truly? Oh, Papa, you kept your promise." She lifted her hand to Mary's cheek. "I told Papa you'd be the best mama ever. I told him I'll show you how."

"Yes, Beth, yes." Mary drew the child's head to her shoulder. "I am the happiest and luckiest woman alive."

Rafe's hand stole between them and curved over Mary's belly. He shook his head, then mouthed, "Not yet. Ours for a little while."

Beth suddenly jerked her head up. "Oh! I must go and tell Wishes." She squirmed free and ran to the door, then spun around. "I forgot something else, too! The turkey's burning."

"Beth, wait," Mary called out. "Who is Wishes?"

"That's my kitten's name. I couldn't tell till my wish came true, Mary. You said I could wish and wish and wish as much as I wanted. You gave me all the magic words so I could. I have to tell her."

"Wise beyond her years, Mary. Magic. She's right. You make that with me, for me. And the hell with the turkey. I've a fire of my own that needs quenching."

Epilogue

"That man of yours was mighty sure of himself. Told him you were a lady and it weren't right for him to be buying you fancy underpinnings. 'Course, Mary, I got to admit those silk nightgowns are just about the prettiest things I ever did see. He'll likely scold me for telling you, but Sarah said as how you were worried 'bout not having time to make one."

"Yes, I was. Nita, would you mind terribly if I had a few minutes alone?"

"Shucks, honey. I'm running on, when I should be getting downstairs an' get me a good seat. Shame the church wasn't finished. But Sarah sure fixed the parlor pretty for your wedding."

Mary closed the door and turned to lean against it. She remembered so clearly that morning she had awakened to the dream. It seemed ages ago. She thought of the question she had asked herself. How would she cope with the days that stretched before her? Who would she be?

The mirror beckoned her. She glanced at the bed,

but her quilt was no longer there. It waited for her at home.

Home. She loved the sound of the word. The thought of all it meant to her. And she looked at Mary, the woman she was now. Faint laugh lines at the corners of her eyes. She smiled, for their home was filled with laughter. The eyes that looked back at her were bright and filled with dreams.

She had thought, that long-ago morning, that she had so much to be thankful for. Then she had opened the door to a man and child who changed her life.

She touched the cornet of braids that Rafe had asked her to wear, for he, too, had remembered. She draped a length of wide lace in place of a veil over her braids and pinned it in place. She had made her own bouquet. Pine that Beth helped her pick, for hope. Dried sprigs of rosemary for remembrance, a corn husk for riches, and chervil for sincerity. Dolly had sent over a cutting from her ivy plant that made the bouquet complete. Ivy for friendship, fidelity and marriage. Pale green ribbons trailed down from the greens.

Mary smiled. Rafe had wanted roses, but she had told him she didn't need that special flower. She kept his love in her heart.

A soft tap at the door interrupted her thoughts. She opened it.

"We have come to escort the bride," Catherine announced. She made a quick turn. "What do you think? I couldn't believe this still fit me."

"You look beautiful enough to be the bride." Mary meant it, too. A blue ribbon banded her throat where she had pinned on a cameo. The color almost matched the pale blue gown that fell from her bare shoulders in a wide ruffle.

Sarah, dressed in a gown of deep pink, came to stand beside her cousin.

"Your groom grows impatient," she said, slipping an arm around Mary's waist. "Happiness suits you. You glow like a candle, Mary."

"It's love. I never knew a body could have so much. And I'm glad we're private for a few minutes. I want to tell—" Her voice broke, and she closed her eyes briefly.

"Don't you dare cry, Mary," Catherine warned, and she, too, came to stand beside her.

"I am expecting a child."

"Oh, Sarah, we'll be aunts. Bring on the knitting needles."

"Joy, cousin. All the joy you richly deserve."

There were hugs and kisses, with nary a thought to crushing gowns. Catherine said nothing more about tears, for she shed a few of her own.

But a breathless Beth arrived, her cheeks flushed, her blue satin sash undone. Mary knelt to retie it and smoothed the lace edge of her collar.

"Oh, Mary, you'd better hurry. Papa said Mrs. Hudspeth put too much starch in his collar. And Mr. Jobe built up the fire, so everyone's hot. And—" she pressed a finger to her lips "—the marry man is here."

The parlor was crammed full of neighbors. The mantel held a bank of candles amid boughs of pine tied with pale ribbons. Beth skipped ahead to take her place by her father's side. Mary heard the whispers but not the words of those who had gathered to celebrate. She had eyes only for Rafe.

He looked so tall and handsome in his black suit. She walked toward him with all the eagerness of a blushing young bride. The gray silk vest and white linen shirt held her gaze for a moment, but then she looked up into his eyes.

There were no doubts, no last-minute jitters. The whispers came to an end as they turned to face the minister. She didn't hear the words of the service any more than she had the first time. But for a different reason. In her heart she was already wed to the man beside her. Her love for him glowed through her, and she longed to turn and face everyone as his wife.

She watched Rafe's hand as it clasped hers. Strong, long fingers that showed her there was strength and gentleness. She listened to his husky voice, not quite hearing what he said, or her own replies. She watched as Rafe slipped the plain gold band she had asked for on her finger. It was so shiny and new.

Once again she looked up into his eyes. Gray eyes intent on hers.

"I now pronounce you man and wife."

She lifted her face for his kiss, her first kiss as his wife.

"Papa, I take Mary, too. Can't I, Papa? You said she'd marry both of us."

"And so she did. All right, little one," Rafe said as he lifted Beth into his arms. "Now you may take Mary, too."

And in a very solemn little voice, Beth said, "Mary, I take you to be my new mama."

"Oh, Beth, yes. I want that, too."

"Didn't I say it right, Papa?"

"You did just fine."

"Then why is Mary crying?"

"She's happy, Beth. Just like we are."

They were surrounded by well-wishers. Sniffles and laughter, then someone struck up the fiddle and merriment prevailed. With most of the furniture pushed back against the walls, there was space for dancing.

In the kitchen, the table and counters groaned beneath the weight of food, for each woman had brought a dish to share.

Mary learned from Dolly that J.P. had made another larger contribution to the church building fund once her brother agreed to the idea of a plaque.

There were new people to meet, the Walkers, who had opened a lumber mill, and Peter Austin, editor of the new *Hillsboro Bulletin*. Julian Krausse and his wife, Adeline, now had a butcher shop.

Rafe lost track of Mary and went looking for her. He found her in the midst of a group of women and heard all the well-meaning advice from matrons on the best ways to keep him happy. When Mary caught his eye, he rushed in, to a great deal of teasing, to rescue her.

The hallway was empty, and Rafe held her. He had no need to ask if she was happy.

"You can still change your mind, Mary. We can take a wedding trip to wherever you'd like. Sarah told me again Beth can stay with them until we get back."

She nestled her head against his chest. "I want to go home, Rafe. But there is one thing I'd ask. Can Sarah come in the spring?"

"If she'll agree. But we can stay here until the baby is born."

"No, I want to go home."

His hands framed her face. "I can't refuse you anything."

"Nor I refuse you."

"What more can a man ask?"

"That we were alone?"

His eyes crinkled with laughter that spread to his lips. "Ah, Mary, love, I knew you didn't need all that advice. You once accused me of reading your thoughts. I turn the tables on you. That is exactly what I was thinking."

"And I should be angry with you for being so sure of yourself, Mr. McCade."

Mary saw the effort he made to appear contrite. He couldn't carry it off.

"Took a great deal for granted, didn't you, ordering—"

"But, Mary, love, you know I'm a gambler who only bets on a sure thing."

He loved her smile, and her sweet scent that made him think he held spring within his arms. He leaned into her touch, brushing his hair from his forehead, and caught her hand to his lips.

"Do you know, Mrs. McCade," he whispered in a rich, husky voice, "that in your arms I'm all the things I wish to be. Brave and strong and true."

"And loved. Loved so much, Rafe."

He saw the need within her eyes, a need that heated his blood. He swept her up into his arms and headed for the stairway.

"Rafe, we can't just leave."

"Oh, yes, we can. That party is getting rowdy. For sure they'll be talking about the merry widows for a long time to come. But you and I, Mary, are going to taste magic."

She wrapped her arms around his neck. "Like the first time we kissed."

"Like forever," he whispered.

* * * * *

Author Note

Dear Reader,

I hope you enjoy the "Merry Widows" trilogy.

Despite the problems that bring two cousins and their friend to live together in one house, each confesses to finding more joy in her widowed state than grief, for each woman carries a secret sorrow as a legacy of her marriage. Mary, as you have seen, was desperate to disprove a taunting curse, Catherine seeks the one thing denied her, then sacrifices it, and Sarah—she hides the blackest secret of them all.

As a year of mourning passes, the music and the laughter from their home brings the townspeople of Hillsboro, New Mexico Territory, to dub them the merry widows.

I hope you will come to care as deeply as I do about the widows and their courage in risking all for happiness.

Theresa Michaels

If you enjoyed this book by

THERESA MICHAELS

Here's your chance to order more stories
by one of Harlequin's favorite authors:

Harlequin Historical®

#28843	FIRE AND SWORD	$3.99 U.S. ☐
		$4.50 CAN.☐
#28876	ONCE A MAVERICK	$4.50 U.S. ☐
		$4.99 CAN.☐
#28916	ONCE A LAWMAN	$4.99 U.S. ☐
		$5.50 CAN.☐

(limited quantities available on certain titles)

TOTAL AMOUNT	$
POSTAGE & HANDLING	$
($1.00 for one book, 50¢ for each additional)	
APPLICABLE TAXES*	$ _____
TOTAL PAYABLE	$ _____

(check or money order—please do not send cash)

To order, complete this form and send it, along with a check or money order
for the total above, payable to Harlequin Books, to: **In the U.S.:** 3010 Walden
Avenue, P.O. Box 9047, Buffalo, NY 14269-9047; **In Canada:** P.O. Box 613,
Fort Erie, Ontario, L2A 5X3.

Name: _____

Address: _____ City: _____

State/Prov.: _____ Zip/Postal Code: _____

*New York residents remit applicable sales taxes.
Canadian residents remit applicable GST and provincial taxes.   HTMBACK2

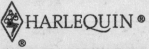

HARLEQUIN ®

Look us up on-line at: http://www.romance.net

Take 4 bestselling love stories FREE

Plus get a FREE surprise gift!

Special Limited-time Offer

Mail to Harlequin Reader Service®

P.O. Box 609
Fort Erie, Ontario
L2A 5X3

YES! Please send me 4 free Harlequin Historicals™ novels and my free surprise gift. Then send me 4 brand-new novels every month, which I will receive before they appear in bookstores. Bill me at the low price of $3.94 each plus 25¢ delivery and GST*. That's the complete price and a savings of over 10% off the cover prices—quite a bargain! I understand that accepting the books and gift places me under no obligation ever to buy any books. I can always return a shipment and cancel at any time. Even if I never buy another book from Harlequin, the 4 free books and the surprise gift are mine to keep forever.

347 BPA A3U.

Name	(PLEASE PRINT)	
Address	Apt. No.	
City	Province	Postal Code

This offer is limited to one order per household and not valid to present Harlequin Historical™ subscribers. *Terms and prices are subject to change without notice. Canadian residents will be charged applicable provincial taxes and GST.

CHIS-696

©1990 Harlequin Enterprises Limited

Let's Celebrate!

LOVE & LAUGHTER™

invites you to
the party of the season!

Grab your popcorn and be prepared to laugh
as we celebrate with **LOVE & LAUGHTER**.

Harlequin's newest series is going Hollywood!

Let us make you laugh with three months of terrific
books, authors and romance, plus a chance to win a
FREE 15-copy video collection of the best romantic
comedies ever made.

For more details look in the back pages of any
Love & Laughter title, from July to September,
at your favorite retail outlet.

Don't forget the popcorn!

Available wherever
Harlequin books are sold.

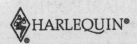 HARLEQUIN®

HE SAID

♥

SHE SAID

Explore the mystery of male/female communication in
this extraordinary new book from two of your favorite
Harlequin authors.

Jasmine Cresswell and Margaret St. George bring you the
exciting story of two romantic adversaries—each from
their own point of view!

DEV'S STORY. CATHY'S STORY.
As he sees it. As she sees it.
Both sides of the story!

The heat is definitely on, and these two can't stay out of
the kitchen!

Don't miss HE SAID, SHE SAID.
Available in July wherever Harlequin books are sold.

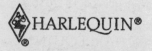

◆ HARLEQUIN®

Look us up on-line at: http://www.romance.net   HESAID

Breathtaking romance is predicted in your future with Harlequin's newest collection: Fortune Cookie.

Three of your favorite Harlequin authors, Janice Kaiser, Margaret St. George and M.J. Rodgers will regale you with the romantic adventures of three heroines who are promised fame, fortune, danger and intrigue when they crack open their fortune cookies on a fateful night at a Chinese restaurant.

Join in the adventure with your own personalized fortune, inserted in every book!

Don't miss this exciting new collection!

Available in September
wherever Harlequin books are sold.

HARLEQUIN®

And the Winner Is...
You!

...when you pick up these great titles
from our new promotion at your
favorite retail outlet this June!

Diana Palmer
The Case of the Mesmerizing Boss

Betty Neels
The Convenient Wife

Annette Broadrick
Irresistible

Emma Darcy
A Wedding to Remember

Rachel Lee
Lost Warriors

Marie Ferrarella
Father Goose

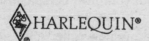 

Look us up on-line at: http://www.romance.net

ATWI397-R

HARLEQUIN WOMEN KNOW ROMANCE WHEN THEY SEE IT.

And they'll see it on **ROMANCE CLASSICS**, the new 24-hour TV channel devoted to romantic movies and original programs like the special **Harlequin® Showcase of Authors & Stories.**

The **Harlequin® Showcase of Authors & Stories** introduces you to many of your favorite romance authors in a program developed exclusively for Harlequin® readers.

Watch for the **Harlequin® Showcase of Authors & Stories** series beginning in the summer of 1997.

ROMANCE CLASSICS

If you're not receiving ROMANCE CLASSICS, call your local cable operator or satellite provider and ask for it today!

Escape to the network of your dreams.

Free Gift Offer

With a Free Gift proof-of-purchase
from any Harlequin® book, you can receive
a beautiful cubic zirconia pendant.

This stunning marquise-shaped stone is a genuine cubic
zirconia—accented by an 18" gold tone necklace.
(Approximate retail value $19.95)

Send for yours today...
compliments of ⬥HARLEQUIN®

To receive your free gift, a cubic zirconia pendant, send us one original proof-of-
purchase, photocopies not accepted, from the back of any Harlequin Romance®,
Harlequin Presents®, Harlequin Temptation®, Harlequin Superromance®, Harlequin
Intrigue®, Harlequin American Romance®, or Harlequin Historicals® title available at
your favorite retail outlet, together with the Free Gift Certificate, plus a check or money
order for $1.65 U.S./$2.15 CAN. (do not send cash) to cover postage and handling,
payable to Harlequin Free Gift Offer. We will send you the specified gift. Allow 6 to 8
weeks for delivery. Offer good until December 31, 1997, or while quantities last. Offer
valid in the U.S. and Canada only.

Free Gift Certificate

Name: _____

Address: _____

City: _____ State/Province: _____ Zip/Postal Code: _____

Mail this certificate, one proof-of-purchase and a check or money order for postage
and handling to: HARLEQUIN FREE GIFT OFFER 1997. In the U.S.: 3010 Walden
Avenue, P.O. Box 9071, Buffalo NY 14269-9057. In Canada: P.O. Box 604, Fort Erie,
Ontario L2Z 5X3.

FREE GIFT OFFER   084-KEZ

ONE PROOF-OF-PURCHASE

To collect your fabulous FREE GIFT, a cubic zirconia pendant, you must include this
original proof-of-purchase for each gift with the properly completed Free Gift Certificate.

084-KEZR